"Save your warnings, Mr. Grimshaw." She stood toe-to-toe with him and fixed him with a blistering glare.

Did she not realize the danger in which she'd placed herself? He had only to raise his arms and bend forward a few perilous inches and she would be captive in his embrace again, his lips on hers, taking what they wanted.

Or did she know exactly what she was doing? Was she trying to provoke his lust to test how much power she could exercise over him? Every muscle in Simon's body tensed with the effort to keep his hands from her.

"I am not the kind of woman you think," Bethan insisted. "I would never have come to your bed last night if I'd known that was all you wanted from me. I suppose you reckoned that once you'd ruined me I'd have to take what I could get from you, but you're wrong. I may have been a green little fool for trusting you, but I'll be no man's whore!"

* * *

Wanted: Mail-Order Mistress
Harlequin® Historical #1037—April 2011

Author Note

Welcome to the third book of my series, *Gentlemen of Fortune,* about the self-made men of Vindicara Trading Company! While I love reading and writing about dashing aristocrats, I've always had a fascination with the man who makes his own fortune and charts his own destiny. Such men make great romance heroes because they have large, definite objectives and an intense motivation to succeed. They will fight for what they want and refuse to let anything or anyone get in the way of achieving their goals—even when it comes to love.

Ford Barrett, Hadrian Northmore and Simon Grimshaw all left Britain for various reasons, going halfway around the world to make their fortunes. Now, though they have money, power and success, they discover those things mean nothing without a special person to share them. As destiny throws three unique women into their paths, these driven men discover that achieving material success is easy compared to the challenge of forging a close, passionate relationship that will last a lifetime.

Wanted: Mail-Order Mistress is the story of Simon Grimshaw, the partner left behind in Singapore to carry on the business after Ford and Hadrian return to England. Betrayed by every woman he has ever trusted, Simon is determined never to wed again. When he enlists Hadrian to find him a mistress, Simon gets far more than he bargained for in Bethan Conway. The spirited Welsh beauty mistakenly believes Simon wants a bride, while she has her own secret reason for coming to Singapore— a reason she dares not confide in him!

I hope you will enjoy *Wanted: Mail-Order Mistress* and the stories of those other *Gentlemen of Fortune!*

Wanted: Mail-Order Mistress

DEBORAH HALE

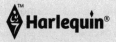

TORONTO NEW YORK LONDON
AMSTERDAM PARIS SYDNEY HAMBURG
STOCKHOLM ATHENS TOKYO MILAN MADRID
PRAGUE WARSAW BUDAPEST AUCKLAND

Recycling programs
for this product may
not exist in your area.

ISBN-13: 978-0-373-29637-8

WANTED: MAIL-ORDER MISTRESS

Copyright © 2010 by Deborah M. Hale

First North American Publication 2011

This book is dedicated to my faithful readers,
who waited so patiently for the release of this series,
and to editors Suzanne Clarke and Jenny Hutton,
who were committed to making it the best it could be.

Chapter One

"So this is it, then?" Brushing a stray auburn curl out of her eyes, Bethan Conway leaned forward in the boat that was ferrying her and her travelling companions into the harbour. "Not a very big town, is it?"

While part of her was thrilled to reach her destination after five months aboard ship, another part wanted to plead with the man at the tiller to turn the boat around and head back out to sea!

"This place would fit into Newcastle's pocket, right enough." Bethan's young friend Ralph gazed around at the mix of buildings that lined both banks of the river. Some were made of timber with huge, shaggy thatched roofs while others had white-plastered walls topped with orderly rows of neat red tiles. "Hasn't been around long, though, has it? I heard Mr Northmore say there was nowt much here at all when him and his partners landed six year ago."

"I wouldn't care if it was nothing but jungle," croaked

Wilson Hall. "As long as I can get solid dry ground under my feet again, I'll be happy."

Poor Wilson! Bethan recalled how seasick he and the other three lads from Durham had been at the start of their voyage. They'd envied her ability to keep her food down even in the roughest weather, but they'd been grateful, too. If she hadn't tended them so capably when they retched and moaned in their hammocks, some might not have recovered.

For the past several days they had talked of little else but how happy they'd be to reach their destination and start work at the Vindicara Trading Company for Mr Simon Grimshaw. Every time she heard that name, a bilious wave had roiled through Bethan like a belated attack of seasickness. While the lads had been hired from the coalmines of northern England to work for Mr Grimshaw, she'd been recruited to *marry* him.

If she hadn't been so desperate to reach these distant shores, she never would have pledged her life to a stranger. But she'd been anxious to get there soon, while there was still a faint hope someone might recall what had become of her brother or his ship. At the time, her marriage had seemed too far in the future to be quite real. The closer it came, the more it worried her.

As the boat eased up to the jetty, Bethan inhaled a deep draught of warm air that mingled the tang of the sea with an exotic whiff of coffee and spices. She had made her bargain. Now she must honour it by doing her best to be a good wife to Mr Grimshaw. She only prayed her new husband would not be too old, ugly or ill tempered.

The mooring lines were barely secured when the Durham lads swarmed ashore. Only Wilson had the manners to turn and offer Bethan a hand to disembark, while the others asked anyone within earshot the way to the Vindicara warehouse.

There was no shortage of people on the quay to question. There were a great many men with bare chests the colour of mahogany wood, who wore white turbans and bright-hued skirts wrapped around their legs. Other men, with lighter skin and slanted eyes, carried sacks slung from poles draped over their shoulders. They wore baggy trousers and black-sashed tunics. The front parts of their heads were shaved bald while the jet-black hair further back was braided in long tight plaits. Tall bearded men, wearing white turbans and long robes, looked as if they'd just stepped out of a Bible story. The only thing all these strange people had in common was trouble understanding the broad north-country English of Bethan's companions.

After a good deal of shouting, waving and pointing, Ralph turned to her. "I think they're trying to tell us Mr Grimshaw's warehouse is on the other side of the river."

"There's a bridge." Wilson pointed up the sweeping curve of the quay to a spot where the river narrowed and a slender wooden span connected the two sides of the harbour. "We can walk around."

The rest agreed and they set off at once. Though Bethan forced one foot in front of the other, her shoes felt strangely heavy. It did not take long for her to fall behind her companions.

The men working on the quay turned to stare at her as she passed. Could it be because they noticed her resemblance to a young man they remembered? Reason told her it wasn't likely. Their curious interest was probably on account of her skin colour, or because she was a woman.

But it wouldn't hurt to ask, would it? She'd come all this way and bartered her freedom in hope of finding the last bit of family she had left in the world. She needed to start somewhere.

"Pardon me." She turned toward a young man wearing white leggings and a turban who smiled at her. "I'm looking for news of a crewman from the barque *Dauntless*. His ship came to Singapore three years ago. Do you remember it?"

The man's smile broadened further and he answered in a language she didn't understand.

"I'm sorry. I don't know what that means." Bethan shook her head and gave an exaggerated shrug. "I didn't even understand English very well until the past year. And I don't suppose you know any Welsh."

Another voice spoke up, heavily accented but in English. "Say again who you look for, lady?"

Bethan turned eagerly towards the speaker, a man with dark, almond-shaped eyes, who wore a large, round straw hat. "I'd be grateful for any help you could give me. His name is Hugh Conway. He'd be taller than you." She raised her hand to indicate her brother's height, then pulled back her bonnet and pointed to her head. "His hair is almost the colour of mine."

She could do better than try to describe him with gestures and words the man might not understand. Reaching back to her nape, Bethan unfastened the silver locket that was her most precious possession. Then she opened it to show the miniature portrait inside. "He looks like this. At least he did the last time I saw him."

The tiny painting wasn't of Hugh himself, but it was the nearest likeness she had.

A flicker of interest kindled in the man's eyes as he stared at the locket. Did he recognise the handsome young face? If Europeans were as scarce in Singapore as they appeared to be, those few must stand out, easily noticed. Perhaps easily remembered.

"Have you seen him?" she asked. "Please, I'm very anxious to get word of him."

The man nodded slowly. "Maybe I saw this one. Not sure."

Bethan's heart leapt. Even in her most hopeful dreams, she'd never imagined getting a lead on her missing brother so soon. "He was in Singapore three years ago. I got a letter posted from here. Do you know what happened to him or his ship?"

The man's high forehead furrowed as if trying hard to remember where and when he'd seen that face. "I look closer?"

"Yes, of course." Bethan pushed the locket into his hands. "I wish I had a bigger picture to show you."

A small crowd had gathered around them as they talked. Suddenly someone tapped Bethan on the shoulder from behind. Did another person recognise Hugh from a distant glimpse of the miniature? Or did they recall his name?

She spun around only to find a bank of expressionless faces staring back at her.

"Did one of you have something to tell me?" she asked. "Have you seen Hugh Conway? Do you remember his ship?"

None of them replied except with sheepish grins.

"Think it's great fun hoaxing a stranger, do you?" Bethan snapped. "I see some things are the same wherever you go."

With an indignant huff, she turned back to her informant. By now he'd had plenty of time to study the likeness. But when she looked around, all she glimpsed of the fellow was the back of his faded blue tunic disappearing into the crowd.

"Come back!" she cried, tearing after him. "Thief! He has my locket. Someone please stop him!"

But no one on the quay seemed willing to help her. Quite the opposite, in fact. Men who moved aside to let the thief escape quickly stepped back into Bethan's path, hindering her pursuit.

"Wilson! Ralph!" she called, though she knew her travelling companions must be far out of earshot by now. She didn't dare stop to look around for them or she might lose sight of the man who'd stolen her locket.

"Please," she cried, "you can have the necklace! Just leave me the picture!"

Catching sight of the bridge out of the corner of her eye, she hoped the thief might run that way and perhaps overtake her friends. Instead he darted down a crowded street in the other direction with Bethan in breathless pursuit. After five months aboard ship, she was not used to running, especially in such oppressive heat. Sheer desperation pushed her forwards.

The thief dodged into a side street. Bethan reached it just in time to glimpse him entering the mouth of an alley. By the time she staggered to the spot where she'd seen him disappear, she was gasping for air while a hot flush smarted in her cheeks. No doubt he would have slipped away, leaving her with no idea which way he'd gone.

But, no. When she peered into the alley, there he was, strolling towards her as brazen as could be—the same clothes, dark eyes and shaved head.

Planting herself in front of him, she signalled him to stop. "I want my picture back. Come now, it can't be worth anything to you."

The man scowled at her as if she was the one who'd done *him* wrong. He muttered an answer in his language.

"You could speak English well enough a few minutes ago!" cried Bethan. "Or did you forget it all while you were making away with my property?"

The man's scowl turned into an outright sneer as he pushed past her.

"Oh, no, you don't." She caught his sleeve and hung on. "I'm not about to chase you through the streets again in this heat. Just give me back my picture!"

Tugging his sleeve roughly out of her grasp, the man unleashed a flood of words Bethan could not understand. But she recognised violent anger when she heard it, no matter what the language. This *was* the man who'd stolen her locket, wasn't it? Were his cheekbones perhaps a little higher? His face a trifle thinner?

"I—I beg your pardon if I mistook you for someone else." She pointed down the alley. "Another man ran that way. He had something he stole from me. Did you see which way he went?"

The man she'd accosted heaped more abuse upon her. Suddenly Bethan realised he was not alone. She was surrounded by a score of men all dressed the same, all glaring at her in a way that sent a shiver down her spine.

Was she in danger of disappearing in this lawless, foreign outpost the way her brother had? And if she did, would anyone care enough to come looking for her?

"The mace and nutmegs sell for seventy-five Spanish dollars a picul," Simon Grimshaw informed the Swedish captain from whom he'd just bought a cargo of iron. "You won't get them cheaper from any of the other merchants in town. The situation in Java has driven prices up for everyone."

The craggy Swede scowled. "Maybe I take my iron to Batavia and trade direct with the Dutch for their spices."

"Be my guest," Simon bluffed. He'd hate to lose that cargo of Swedish iron. "Pay the outrageous tariffs they charge in Batavia. You'll have less money in your pocket at the end of your voyage. That is, if you're lucky and the pirates don't get you between here and Sumatra. Perhaps I could come down a dollar or two on the mace, but not the nutmegs. My partner is due back from England soon and he'll have my hide if he catches me giving our goods away at such prices."

Part of him eagerly awaited Hadrian Northmore's return. It would be a relief to have someone else shoulder half the workload. Since both his partners had gone back to England—Hadrian for a brief visit and Ford to stay—Simon had taken on the responsibility of three men.

In spite of that, he was reluctant to surrender control of the company to his senior partner. Hadrian was an ambitious, astute man of business, but he had a reckless streak of which Simon had never approved. He preferred the steady, cautious course and seldom acted on impulse. The few times he had, he'd later regretted it.

Might he regret asking his partner to fetch back a young Englishwoman to be his mistress? While the Swedish captain considered his terms, Simon mulled over that question.

When the south-west monsoons had signalled the arrival of ships from the West, he'd begun to have second thoughts about his plan. It would be good to have a safe outlet for the desires he had not entirely managed to stifle with long hours of work. But what kind of woman would willingly journey halfway around the world to serve as a hired bedmate? Only one with an unsavoury past, he feared. How could he risk taking a woman like that into his home?

The Swedish captain gave a deep rasping cough that jolted Simon out of his troubled thoughts. "What is it you English say—'a bird in the hand…'?"

"'…is better than all your birds in the hands of pirates.' That's what we say here in Singapore." Simon extended his hand to seal their bargain.

Few things gave him as much pleasure as making an advantageous deal. Unlike affairs of the heart, he knew where he stood in a clear-cut matter of business. That was the sort of relationship he'd had in mind when he asked Hadrian to find him a mistress—a straightforward exchange of things they wanted from one another, without dangerous sentiment to complicate matters. Now he wondered if such a thing would be possible.

As he and the captain shook hands, one of Simon's Malay workers appeared, leading four European lads who looked quite distressed. "Master, these boys say they came from England to work for you."

"This is the first I've heard of it." Simon eyed the four suspiciously. "Captain Svenson, if you'll excuse me, I must see to this. Ibrahim, send some boats to begin unloading the iron."

As Ibrahim and the captain headed away, Simon rounded on the boys, who were growing more agitated by the minute. "What is all this about? I didn't hire any of you."

"Please, sir," said a sturdy, handsome lad who looked to be their leader, "Mr Northmore sent us. He said there'd be work for us with his company."

Before Simon could reply, a gangly lad with a shock

of red hair cried, "The boat let us off on the wrong side of the harbour!"

"And we've lost Bethan!" added a third fellow. "She was right behind us…and then…she wasn't."

They all started jabbering at once, so that Simon could not make out what they were trying to say.

"Quiet!" he ordered at last, silencing them with a fierce scowl. "You say Mr Northmore *sent* you. Why didn't he come with you?"

"I don't know, sir," admitted the leader. "Perhaps he explained it in the letter he gave Bethan."

One of them had mentioned that name earlier. Could she be the mistress Hadrian had engaged for him?

"But she's lost!" The rusty-haired lad pointed back toward the quay. "We've got to find her!"

"So we do." Simon marched towards the quay, his heart hammering against his ribs. "This part of town is no fit place for a woman alone."

Especially not a European woman, of whom there were only a handful in the whole settlement. "Where did you last see her?"

"I thought she was right behind us when we crossed the bridge," said a lumpy lad with overgrown teeth. "But now I'm not sure."

They'd reached the quay by this time, heading for the bridge with as much speed as Simon could muster. "You left her on her own in Chinatown? If any harm comes to her, none of you will be working for me, I don't care what Northmore promised you!"

Work? Simon fumed. They'd be lucky if he didn't have them all flogged. Though Singapore was a place of great opportunity, violence always lurked beneath the surface. Piracy had been a w.y of life in these waters for centuries and it wasn't much safer on land. Since coming here, he'd witnessed riots and outlaw raids. Murderous rampages were common enough that there was a term for them in the Malay language—such attackers were said to run *amok*.

As Simon marched across the bridge and on to the south bank of the harbour, crowds of labourers parted to let him pass like waves cloven by the sharp-angled prow of a ship. The four English lads scrambled along in his wake.

"Where is the white woman?" he demanded in Malay, then again in mangled Cantonese. "Did anyone see which way she went? If any harm comes to her, there will be bad trouble!"

Answers came hurling back at him.

"She was accosting strange men on the quay."

"She ran after Jin-Lee, shouting at him like a savage with no manners."

"She chased him into the Chinese kampong," a Malay speaker informed Simon, "up Oxcart Road."

What sort of brazen harlot had Hadrian procured for him? Simon was half-tempted to let the hussy face the consequences of her scandalous behavior. But he could not bear to have another woman's death on his conscience.

One of the English lads tugged at his sleeve. "Please, sir, what did they say? What's happened to Bethan?"

Simon could not deny the genuine note of concern in the young fellow's voice. He and his friends obviously cared about this woman. That did not tally with what he'd just heard of her actions.

"This way." He charged up the wide dirt path, which lead away from the south end of the bridge, pausing only to seek further information.

People were eager to talk, venting their outrage over

the woman's forwardness. Simon sensed a gloating satisfaction at their being free to criticize a member of the small but powerful European community.

He and the boys followed her trail down a side street rife with gambling houses and opium dens. Simon had supported the efforts of Sir Stamford Raffles to ban such places, but Raffles's more pragmatic successor had insisted on licensing them as a source of revenue. Simon shuddered to think what could happen to an unprotected woman in this part of town.

Then he glimpsed a billow of ruddy hair amid a sea of straw-sedge hats. Curls of that colour did not belong to any true native of Asia. Simon waded into the crowd, shouldering the gawkers aside, issuing all manner of dire threats about troops being summoned. At last he reached the woman.

There she stood, backed against the timber wall of a gambling house, surrounded by a crowd of angry Chinese. Her bright hair had come undone, tumbling over her slender shoulders. She held a wide-brimmed bonnet in front of herself, like a flimsy shield. Her face was flushed bright red and misted with sweat. Her eyes were wide with fear. She was the perfect picture of a damsel in distress.

Distress she had brought upon herself with her brazen behaviour. And yet…

As he got a closer look at her, Simon found she was not at all what the onlookers' reports had led him to expect. There was nothing coarse or common about her features—indeed, they were *uncommonly* delicate. Her nose was dappled with freckles that lent her an air of wholesome innocence. Her lips, full and pink as hibiscus petals, looked as if they had never been properly kissed.

That thought sent a bolt of heat surging through him to settle in his loins, where it smouldered. An ominous silence jolted him out of his dangerous distraction. He needed to get this woman and her four young friends back across the river before this unfortunate incident turned even uglier.

"There you are." He seized her by the arm and began to scold her loudly in Cantonese, for the benefit of their large, hostile audience. "Have you gone mad to act so shamefully? Come with me now or you will be sorry!"

He must make the onlookers believe she would be harshly dealt with. Then they might leave her punishment to him rather than taking matters into their own hands. If he made sufficient fuss, it might distract the crowd long enough to get her and the boys to safety. Simon's left leg was beginning to throb with familiar pain, but he ignored it, hoping it would not slow down their retreat.

In this situation, any delay could be very dangerous indeed.

Chapter Two

When the broad-shouldered man with brown hair and a stern, handsome face waded through the angry crowd to her rescue, Bethan had never been so happy to see anyone in her life. For as long as she could recall, she'd secretly hankered for a chivalrous protector like Tristan or Sir Gawain from the old Welsh hero tales. Her knees grew weak as she pictured the stranger sweeping her into his arms and carrying her off to safety.

Those soaring fancies crashed to earth when instead her *gallant rescuer* grabbed her by the arm and began ranting at her in a language she could not understand. The harshness of his tone and the severity of his stark blue gaze did not frighten her the way the sullen hostility of the crowd had. Instead it ignited a blaze inside her, part indignant anger, part a strange fevered yearning she'd never felt before.

Compared to the native Asians, he appeared tall and imposing. He was smartly dressed in buff-coloured trousers and a tan coat. A wide-brimmed straw hat cast a shadow over his straight, jutting nose and chiselled cheekbones. His lips were neither too full nor too thin, but set in such a rigid line that Bethan fancied they might shatter if he tried to smile.

"Let me go!" She struggled to throw off his iron grip, but couldn't quite manage to. "It's no use jabbering on at me that way, for I don't understand a word you're saying. You've got no call to be vexed with me and neither do any of these people!"

Her bold words did a better job of loosening his grasp than her squirming had.

Leaning towards her, he muttered, "Save your protests and come with me, *now*, while there's a chance we might get away in one piece! If you give me any more backtalk, I swear I'll leave you to your fate."

The insistent pressure of his hand and the urgency of his tone convinced Bethan to abandon her defensive position against the wall. She sensed he was a man of strong will, whom others crossed at their peril.

From the moment she'd first glimpsed him striding towards her, she'd had eyes for no one else. Now, as her forbidding rescuer marched her down the street, Bethan suddenly realised he'd brought Ralph and the other lads with him. Whatever happened, she did not want her young companions to suffer for her folly. If that meant she had to obey the stern orders of this overbearing man, she would. But she didn't have to like it.

As they moved down the side street and out on to the main road, he continued to berate her in that other language, now and then slipping in a few words of English. "Keep a steady pace. If we look like we're on the run, some of them may pounce. Keep your eyes downcast. Pretend you're ashamed of yourself, as you should be."

"I've got no call to be ashamed," Bethan protested, but she did bend her head as if burdened by the weight of his reproaches. "One of those men stole something from me. I went after him to try to get it back."

"I don't care if he stole every penny you own." The man pitched his reply for her ears alone. "You should have stayed with your friends and not gone chasing into Chinatown. You could have lost a good deal more than whatever that thief took. And you still might, so stop arguing and keep walking."

He switched easily back into the other language, scolding her more fiercely than ever. Was it only a show he was putting on for the benefit of the angry crowd? A grudging flicker of admiration stirred inside her for the man's cleverness. If he'd rushed to her rescue brandishing a weapon, he might have made the situation worse.

As if to signal that he did not mean the insults he was heaping upon her, the man rubbed the pad of his thumb against the sensitive flesh of her inner arm. It felt almost like an encouraging caress. That trifling sensation made Bethan's knees grow weak. She almost stumbled, but her escort tightened his hold again to keep her from falling.

At the end of the road, the bridge beckoned with a promise of greater safety on the other side. If nothing else, its narrow width would prevent them being followed by the crowd that had dogged them this far with dark scowls and darker mutterings.

Her rescuer seemed to sense Bethan's thoughts. "We aren't out of danger yet. If we're attacked, run across the bridge and keep going until you reach the *sepoy* lines. Tell the soldiers they're needed here."

"What about you?" Bethan whispered back. "And the lads?"

"We'll slow down anyone who tries to go after you."

Slow them down, how? Bethan wondered, more anxious for their safety than hers.

Fortunately her rescuer's feigned bluster continued to divert the crowd and no attack came. When they reached the bridge, he called out something to the people behind them. No one followed as their small party crossed over the river.

"What did you say to them?" asked Bethan. "It seemed to do the trick."

"So it did, thank God." The man exhaled a sigh of relief. "I offered the entire community an apology for your disgraceful behaviour and assured them you would be severely dealt with."

"Apology?" Bethan sputtered. "Punished? For being robbed and threatened? What sort of mad place is this?"

"Not *mad*—just different. These people have different ways than ours. We may not understand or approve, but if we hope to live among them in peace, we must try to respect local custom. We transgress upon them at our peril."

What did he mean? Bethan hated to look a fool by asking. Since leaving Wales she'd worked hard to learn English, but this man used some words she didn't yet know.

"Besides," he continued, "I have no real intention of punishing you further for your folly. I trust you've learned your lesson."

The nerve of the man, to talk as if she were a naughty child!

Before she could summon her voice to protest, Wilson

spoke up. "Are you all right, Bethan? Nobody hurt you, did they?"

"I'm only a bit shaken." A shiver went through her as she glanced across the river to see the crowd breaking up. "I'm safe and sound now, thanks to all of you and Mister...Mister...?"

Much as she resented his high-handed manner and gruff rebuke, Bethan could not deny she owed the man her gratitude. Wilson and the others could never have got her out of such a dangerous scrape on their own.

Abruptly letting go of her arm, the stranger bobbed a curt bow. "Simon Grimshaw, of course. What other man in Singapore would have reason to storm into Chinatown and pluck you from the mercy of an angry mob?"

Bethan's mouth fell open. Why had she never thought her rescuer might be her intended husband? Perhaps because she'd never pictured him so young and fine looking. That was two of her three worries well scotched. She wished she could say the same of his temper.

"Why are you staring like that?" Simon snapped at Bethan as he ushered the five young people into his warehouse. Her expression reminded him of a freshly gutted jackfish in the wet market—eyes wide and mouth hanging open. "I suppose I am not what you expected."

She shook her head slowly. "Nothing like it."

Had she been daft enough to imagine her keeper would be a handsome young buck? Perhaps. After all, she'd been daft enough to pursue a thief into the back alleys of Chinatown.

"Well, you are not what I expected either," he snapped, vexed with himself for giving a damn what she thought of him. "But there's no help for it. I reckon that's what comes of making such arrangements by proxy."

Her dazed stare changed to a look of bewilderment, as if he'd slipped back into Cantonese. "Speaking of my proxy, where the devil *is* Hadrian Northmore? I'm told you have a letter from him. I hope it will explain what's going on."

"Er…yes." Bethan rummaged through a reticule that hung from her elbow. "Mr Northmore told me to give it to you."

Simon eyed her reticule with suspicion. "I thought you said one of the coolies stole that from you."

"Not *this*." She fished out a sealed packet of paper and offered it to him gingerly, as if she did not want her hand to brush his. "A silver locket I've had for a long time that means a great deal to me."

Seizing the letter from her, Simon broke the seal and unfolded the paper. He wondered why a thief would have taken the locket but ignored her reticule. And how had the fellow managed to get her locket? The easiest way would be to yank it off her neck, breaking the chain. But that would have left marks and her lovely neck did not bear the smallest nick or bruise.

While a brief inspection of that fair flesh made Simon's breath quicken, it also made the hairs on the back of his neck bristle. Was she lying to him already, over something so trivial? His earlier misgivings about taking her as his mistress redoubled, even though the prospect stirred all his senses to a keen pitch.

An awkward silence followed while he read Hadrian's letter and digested the news. It seemed he would remain in sole charge of the company's Singapore branch for the foreseeable future. Though he welcomed the challenge, Simon didn't like being ambushed by this abrupt change of plans. That included taking on four new workers, none of whom impressed him a great deal at the moment. Not to mention a prospective mistress who provoked as much doubt as desire.

While he scanned the last few sentences of Hadrian's letter, one of the boys addressed Bethan. "I'm sorry we didn't take better care to keep you an eye on you, lass."

"As well you should be." Simon stuffed the letter into his pocket. "My partner confirms that he has promised you all employment. Considering how poorly you looked after Miss Conway, I shall be reluctant to trust you with much responsibility."

He'd learned Bethan's full name from the letter, which also confirmed she was the woman Hadrian had hired to be his mistress. But it was already too late for Simon to think of her except by her given name.

"Don't be angry with them." She stepped between him and the boys, as if to shield them from his anger. "What happened was *my* fault. I was so taken with all the strange new sights that I dawdled behind the others. I've lived most of my life in the Welsh countryside and they come from a little mining village in Durham. None of us had any idea how dangerous a place this could be."

Simon's opinion of her rose, for being willing to accept responsibility and defend her companions. "Now that you have discovered how easy it is to land in trouble around here, I trust you will all tread more carefully."

None of them answered with words. The boys hung their heads, duly chastened. But Bethan tilted her chin a little higher and fixed Simon with a direct, challenging stare. He was not convinced she'd learned her lesson.

"Let us consider the matter closed." He forced himself to look away from her bewitching grey-green eyes. "While I arrange quarters for my new workers, Miss Conway, I will send you on to my house to get settled."

Simon beckoned them to follow him, but when he took a step, shards of pain slashed through his leg, making him stagger and bite back a groan.

"What's the matter?" Moving too fast for Simon to evade, Bethan grabbed his arm to steady him, as he'd done for her on the bridge. "I thought you were walking with a bit of limp. Did someone in the crowd strike you?"

He was not prepared for the warmth of her touch or the soft note of concern in her lilting voice. It had been a very long while since anyone had cared what happened to him. At the same time his pride chafed at being reminded of his slight infirmity by a beautiful young woman. Concern was too close to pity for his liking.

"It's of no consequence, I assure you." He pulled away from her, with some difficulty. "An old injury I forget half the time—unless I've had a long day on my feet or I am obliged to move quickly on short notice."

"A battle wound?" Bright glints of silver and green sparkled in her eyes. "Were you a soldier before you became a merchant?"

She sounded intrigued, admiring. The truth was far less heroic, but Simon had no intention of revealing it to her. He'd never told anyone about his ordeal and he was not about to start with a woman who'd thrown his well-ordered world into turmoil within minutes of her arrival.

"Nothing of the kind." Steeling himself against the pain and the tormenting memories it stirred, Simon moved forwards again, trying not to be too obvious about sparing his injured leg.

Bethan scurried along beside him. "What *did* happen to you, then?"

This was the first time his curt tone and stony scowl had failed to discourage intrusive questions about his past. No wonder the woman had landed in trouble the moment she'd stepped off the boat.

It alarmed Simon to find himself tempted to confide in her. With ruthless force, he quelled the mutinous urge. "I prefer not to dwell on the past. I will thank you not to raise the subject again."

Bethan's lush lower lip thrust out in a rebellious expression. Her changeable eyes flashed with sparks of emerald vexation and something even more dangerous to his peace of mind.

Burning curiosity.

What had happened to the man that he was so grimly determined not to speak of? Bethan fairly sizzled with curiosity as he bundled her into a two-wheeled gig driven by one his workers.

"Mahmud, fetch Miss Conway back to the house and tell Ah-Ming to make her comfortable." Simon Grimshaw took leave of Bethan with a stiff bow. "I will see you at dinner this evening. We can talk then."

As the gig pulled away, she wondered what they would talk *about*. How would they ever become acquainted if he refused to tell her about his past? It was bad enough having to wed a stranger. But how much worse would it be, married to a man who seemed resolved to remain one?

She didn't know what to make of Simon Grimshaw. As she had freely admitted, he was nothing like what she'd expected. In many ways he was a great deal better. He could not be much above thirty and he was quite attractive in spite of his grave severity. He'd shown great courage, facing down that hostile crowd to rescue her from danger. And he'd used his wits to do it, rather than brute force. Set against all those fine qualities was his forbidding manner and secretive, solitary air.

Besides, he was clearly disappointed in her. No doubt he'd wanted a meek, mousy wife who would never question him about anything and always behave with perfect propriety. What would he think if he suspected she'd come to Singapore in search of a mutineer? He might toss her back on the streets, among those angry people whose language and ways were a dangerous mystery to her.

Bethan was still so shaken by what had happened that she did not dare speak to the driver, a brown-skinned man who wore a white turban. It felt rude to ignore him, but she feared he might take offence at her innocent overture. To cover her confusion, she stared around her as if spellbound…which was not far from the truth.

The gig moved quickly through a tight-packed, bustling area of shops and warehouses along the banks of the river. Then it passed through a large open square with only a few large white buildings around the edge and lines of tents off in one corner. A hill topped by a cluster of low buildings and a tall flagstaff towered behind it. After crossing the square, the gig headed down a wide road lined with large properties, each occupied by a big white house nestled in spacious grounds.

"My word!" Bethan's eyes widened as they drove through a gate and stopped in front of a sprawling villa with spotless white walls and a vast red roof. A deep, pillared veranda wrapped around the whole house.

She'd known Simon Grimshaw was a successful merchant, but only now did she realise how great a fortune he must have. Why had such a man been obliged to send all the way to England for a wife? And why on earth had Mr Northmore thought an inexperienced Welsh nurse-maid would be a fitting mistress for this grand house?

Her driver turned Bethan over to the care of an Asian servant woman, whose high-necked tunic and baggy trousers looked three times too large for her tiny frame. With the most perfect courtesy and no hint of surprise at her master's unexpected guest, she introduced herself as Ah-Ming, the housekeeper. She wasted no time seeing to Bethan's comfort, offering all manner of food and drink. When those failed to tempt the guest, Ah-Ming made another offer of hospitality that Bethan could not refuse—a bath.

After her long voyage it felt blissful to bathe and wash her hair. The luxurious soak relaxed Bethan, restoring a measure of her usual hopeful spirits. By the time she finished, her trunk had arrived and she was able to change into clean clothes.

With her hair combed out and left hanging long to dry, she thanked Ah-Ming and accepted her offer of tea. While the housekeeper went to fetch it, she wandered into the spacious sitting room.

In some ways it looked like the house where she'd worked back in Newcastle. But the ceiling was much higher and the walls were not papered but clean, stark white. There were many more windows, too, all tall and narrow, with rolled-up blinds made of thin wooden slats instead of curtains. And there was no sign of an imposing mantelpiece the likes of which dominated most rooms back home. The whole place had an air of light and openness that appealed to her free spirit.

A warm breeze blew in through the windows, carrying the fresh tang of the sea mingled with aromas of tropical flowers and spices. After the bustle of the harbour, Simon Grimshaw's house was a haven of tranquillity. The only sounds Bethan could hear were the familiar, calming rhythm of the sea and a shrill clicking sound she'd never heard before.

Then she picked up another sound, faint but growing louder as it drew nearer—a pair of high-pitched voices talking back and forth in hushed tones, speaking a language Bethan could not understand.

A moment later, another Asian woman appeared. She wore the same sort of loose tunic and trousers as Ah-Ming, but she looked older and even tinier. She was accompanied by a little European girl. The child wore a white muslin frock with a pale green sash. Her dark hair was plaited in two long braids, tied with green ribbons to match her sash. She had delicate features and enormous brown eyes that fixed on Bethan with a look of uneasy curiosity.

"Pardon me." The child made a graceful curtsy, then began to back away. "I didn't know we had company."

She spoke with a charming accent, a bit like the French governess at the house in Newcastle where Bethan had worked.

"Please don't go on my account." Bethan dropped to one knee and smiled warmly. "Shall we introduce ourselves? My name is Bethan Conway. I've come from England. Do you live here?"

Perhaps Simon Grimshaw had another partner besides Mr Northmore.

Before the child could reply, her companion spoke in a sharp tone, as if offended by the question. "Missy lives here, of course. She is Rosalia Eva da Silva Grimshaw. Her father is master of this house."

Father? The word rocked Bethan. She was quite

certain Mr Northmore hadn't said anything about Simon
Grimshaw having a child. But perhaps this explained
why he'd chosen a nurserymaid as a wife for his
partner.

She could not decide how she felt about coming into
a ready-made family like this. The childlike part of her
longed for a little playmate to romp about with, and
this dainty little creature was vastly appealing. But marriage would be a difficult enough adjustment without the
added responsibility of a young daughter right away.

"You came from England?" Rosalia gave Bethan
no time to sort through her confused feelings. "That is
where Uncle Hadrian went. Ah-sam says it is very far
away. Did he come back to Singapore with you?"

It was clear from her tone that Rosalia was eager
to see Mr Northmore again. Bethan hated to dash her
hopes. She remembered the bitter disappointment of
waiting in vain for the return of a loved one.

"I met your Uncle Hadrian in England." She tried to
break the news as gently as possible. "I think he means
to stay there for a while. I don't think his wife would
want to make such a long journey with a wee one on the
way."

Rosalia's dark brows bunched. "A wee *what* on the
way? Where was it coming from?"

"Er…" Bethan chided herself for speaking so freely
to a young child about such matters. She was certain
Rosalia's father would not approve.

Fortunately the servant woman rescued her from awkward explanations by crying out, "Wah! Mr Hadrian has
found a wife and started a family? This is good news!
First Mr Ford, now him. Only one left now."

All trace of her earlier annoyance with Bethan disappeared, replaced with a beaming smile reserved for the

bearer of welcome news. "What brings you to Singapore, my lady?"

A shrewd twinkle in the woman's dark eyes suggested that she guessed the reason. Bethan made a special effort to mind her tongue, for the child's sake. If Mr Grimshaw had not told his little daughter of his marriage plans, she did not want to blurt out the news that Rosalia would soon be getting a stepmother. She would rather make friends with the child first.

"I've come for a...*visit*." With a beseeching gaze she silently urged the servant not to betray her suspicions. "And I might stay longer if things work out." Quickly she changed the subject. "Rosalia isn't a name I've heard before, but it's very pretty. It sounds a bit like Rhosyn. That's a Welsh name I always liked."

"Yours is very nice too." One corner of the child's rosebud lips arched upward in a bashful half-smile. "I hope you will stay. So many ships come here, but we never get any company."

Rosalia's wistful tone went straight to Bethan's heart. "When I was your age, I lived in a quiet little village. We never got much company, either. At least you have your father here with you. My daddy had to go away to work."

His visits home had been the best times of her young life. The *worst* had been the day her mother told her he would never be coming home again.

The servant woman said something to her young charge in another language.

Rosalia replied with an eager nod, then held out her hand to Bethan. "Would you like to see our garden?"

Rising from her crouch, Bethan took the child's outstretched hand. "Yes, I would, thank you. Tell me, what's that clicking sound? It seems to be getting louder."

"The cicadas, you mean? They're bugs who chirp—the hotter it gets the louder the noise they make. Do they not have cicadas in England?"

As Rosalia led her away, the servant called after them.

"What did she say?" asked Bethan, marvelling at such a young child being fluent in two languages.

"Ah-sam told me to be a good girl so you will want to stay with us."

The offhand remark troubled Bethan. She knew how easily a sensitive child could take such well-meant warnings to heart.

"I'm sure you are a very good girl." She gave Rosalia's hand a squeeze. "Whether or not I stay in Singapore will have nothing to do with how you behave."

More likely it would depend on *her* behaviour, Bethan reflected. After the trouble she'd caused at the harbour and the way she'd questioned him about his injury, Mr Grimshaw might decide she was not the proper sort of wife for him.

Provided he let her stay long enough to look for her brother that might be for the best. Despite Simon Grimshaw's fortune and his fine looks, Bethan was not at all certain she wanted to surrender her newfound freedom to such a cold, disapproving man.

Chapter Three

"What is that noise?" Simon Grimshaw demanded as he strode out on to the deep veranda of his new villa.

Though his housekeeper hovered nearby, attentive as always, Simon's question was not addressed to her or anyone else. He scarcely realised he'd spoken aloud as he scanned the back garden for the source of the unfamiliar sound. Was it the call of an exotic bird he'd never before encountered? Or perhaps the music of some traditional Malay instrument wafting down from the Sultan's *istana*?

The sound rose again from among the brightly flowering shrubberies below, this time accompanied by a similar one, deeper and warmer in timbre. Together they created a beguiling harmony. With a start, Simon realised he was hearing the clear, merry laughter of a woman and child. Had he not heard that sound for so long he'd forgotten it?

An instant later Bethan Conway burst into view, her vibrant auburn hair streaming behind her as she ran. The fluid grace of her movement reminded him of a wild antelope he'd seen in India. Her winsome peal of laughter seemed to reach into his chest and strike a reluctant trill over the cords of his heart.

As he fought to subdue that foolish reaction, Rosalia appeared from behind the rhododendron bush and called out to Bethan. Her accent, which mingled Portuguese and a trace of Cantonese, sounded very much like her late mother's. Had the child grown taller since the last time he'd seen her?

That thought dealt Simon a faint stab of guilt. Ever since he'd taken sole charge of Vindicara, he'd had little time to spare for Rosalia. After they'd moved to this spacious new house from the old one beside the *godown*, he'd seen less of her than ever.

His attention was so tightly fixed on the garden below that he did not notice Ah-Ming standing beside him until she spoke. "Mr Hadrian chose well for you. The lady is polite and cheerful. She will make you a good wife."

"She is *not* here to be my wife," Simon replied firmly in Cantonese. "I mean to take her as my…*concubine*."

He knew that was not precisely the right word, but it was the closest he could come in her language.

"Aiyah!" Ah-Ming shook her head. "You will take a concubine before a wife?"

"*Instead* of a wife," Simon growled. He was sick to death of the constant, subtle pressure to remarry from his housekeeper and Rosalia's *amah*. "One marriage was more than enough for me. I will not wed again."

The housekeeper responded with a smug chuckle. "Mr Hadrian and Mr Ford said they would never marry, but something changed their minds."

"My partners and I are very different men." Simon turned and strode away.

Perhaps Hadrian's remarriage should not have surprised him so much. After all, his partner had been happily wed once, but lost his wife and child in an epidemic. It made sense that one day his grief would ease and he would risk trying to recapture what he'd lost. As for Ford, he'd inherited an estate and title that would require an heir. His marriage might have been a matter of necessity.

Simon had better reason than either of them to be wary of marriage and he was by nature far more cautious. He'd already begun to wonder if taking a mistress might be too great a risk. Meeting Bethan Conway had done nothing to ease his misgivings.

But her beauty had roused long-stifled desires that ached for relief. What else could he do with her now that she was here? It was not as if he could pop her on another ship tomorrow and send her back to England. Sea traffic could not sail west again for several months, when the winds shifted. He was not about to subject her to an eastward voyage across the vast Pacific and around the treacherous tip of South America, simply because he had second thoughts about their arrangement.

Having brought her all the way from England, he had an obligation to take care of her. If he did that, everyone in Singapore would assume she was his mistress. And if it got out that she was *not* sharing his bed, he would be the laughing-stock of the European community, not to mention what the she might think of him.

He was in too deep to back out now. He must go forwards with assurance and make it clear to his imprudent young mistress that he would not tolerate any nonsense.

What had Simon Grimshaw been thinking as he stood on the veranda, glowering down at her and his daughter?

Bethan mulled over that question as she dressed for dinner. She'd spied him out of the corner of her eye as she chased about the garden with Rosalia, but pretended not to notice.

Had he been looking her over, trying to decide whether he should call off their wedding? Was he pleased to find her getting on so well with his daughter or did he disapprove of their noisy laughter? The latter, most likely, by the look of him.

She hoped he wouldn't spend the whole evening finding fault with her. She'd never been able to accept correction in the proper meek spirit, even when she deserved it. Unfair criticism made her bristle like a cornered cat.

Once she'd fixed the final pin in her hair, Bethan hesitated at her bedroom door. She was half-inclined to avoid this encounter with Simon Grimshaw by snuffing out the lamp and crawling under the insect netting into bed. But the mouthwatering smells wafting up from the kitchen tempted her out. After months of shipboard rations, it would take worse than her forbidding host to keep her from a good meal!

She found Mr Grimshaw in the sitting room, planted in front of the open windows with his hands clasped behind him. He looked the very picture of severity.

Refusing to be cowed, she breezed in as if she had not a care in the world. "Am I late? You should have sent someone to fetch me."

He hesitated a moment before answering, his icy blue eyes fixed upon her. Was there a stain on her dress? Something wrong with the way she'd done her hair?

"You are not late." The words burst out of him, followed by others, stiff as starch. "Ah-Ming will inform us when dinner is served. I hope she took good care of you this afternoon and that you found everything to your satisfaction?"

"She couldn't have been kinder. She drew me a bath and washed my hair. She and Ah-sam were so pleased to hear about Mr Northmore getting married."

Bethan knew at once she'd said something wrong by the way the line between Simon Grimshaw's brows deepened. "I suggest in future you refrain from gossiping with the servants. The European community is very small and private matters can too easily become public tattle."

There! Just as she'd expected. Almost the first words out of her mouth and already he was finding fault.

"I wasn't *gossiping.*" Two spots on her cheeks blazed with heat. "Ah-Ming asked me about Mr Northmore and I told her. I don't know why his marriage should be a secret. It's nothing to be ashamed of."

What about her speculating that Mrs Northmore might be breeding, her conscience demanded, not only to the servants but in front of his young daughter?

"Perhaps I don't know my place as well as I should," she admitted. "I was in service myself, back in Newcastle, so I'm more at ease with servants than masters."

What would Simon Grimshaw make of that?

"Were you?" The news did not seem to surprise him as much as she'd expected. "In what capacity?"

"I was a nurserymaid." She threw the words down like a challenge, daring him to sneer at the honest work she'd done.

"That might explain what you were doing out in the garden with Rosalia." From his tone it was clear he objected to that as well.

"I like the company of children," she retorted. "They

don't mind about position and fortune and they don't look to find fault with everything you do."

Mr Grimshaw's firm jaw clenched tighter and his deep-set eyes narrowed.

Bethan wished his severity made him look sour and ugly, then she might not have a single regret over what he was about to do. More the pity, he still looked far too attractive for her liking. "Go ahead and say what's really on your mind, Mr Grimshaw."

Her words seemed to catch him off guard, but he soon rallied. "Do you presume to know my mind, Miss Conway? Perhaps *you* should tell me what I am thinking."

"Very well. You're thinking Mr Northmore made a bad choice and I don't suit you at all. You want to send me back to England. Well, let me tell you, after the way you've treated me today, I'll be glad to go!"

Her feelings all churned up, Bethan spun away from Simon Grimshaw, only to find his housekeeper standing in the wide, arched entry. Ah-Ming looked calm and composed, as if she hadn't heard a word of the bristling exchange between them.

"Dinner is ready." The housekeeper bowed. "Cook has prepared a fine feast in my lady's honour."

"Thank you, Ah-Ming," Mr Grimshaw replied. "We will be along shortly."

The servant bowed again, then padded away.

"You must stay and eat." Mr Grimshaw didn't sound the way Bethan had expected—outraged or disapproving.

"Is that an order?" Keeping her back to him, she flung the words over her shoulder.

"More a sort of…plea." He sounded almost amiable. "There will be no living with Cook if he went to all that trouble for nothing. One of the other merchants might finally succeed in hiring him away from me and that would be a domestic disaster."

While Bethan was deciding how to reply, he added, "You see, servants are not without power in my house."

She steeled herself against the hint of wry humour in his tone. "All right, then. But only because the food smells so good and because I don't want to hurt your cook's feelings. And I have one condition."

"What might that be?"

"I don't want a nice meal spoiled by carping and quarrelling. If you can't say something pleasant to me over dinner, don't say anything at all."

"Agreed," Mr Grimshaw replied after a moment's hesitation. "You could have driven a much harder bargain than that, you know."

He walked around to stand in front of her. "I admit I had doubts about your suitability. But you are wrong to assume I intend to send you back. I fear we got off on the wrong foot today. Is it too late to put that behind us and start again?"

His firm, determined lips spread into a smile that came and went as swiftly as a flash of summer lightning. Like a bolt from the blue, its potent force jolted Bethan's heart and made her breath catch.

Simon Grimshaw wanted to give her another chance? Didn't she owe him the same after the way he'd come to her rescue? Besides, while she chafed at criticism, she had never been very good at holding a grudge.

"It can't be too late already, can it?" She returned his sudden, fleeting smile with one of her own that blossomed more slowly but lasted longer. "We should give it at least a week before we decide we can't stand each other."

Her quip coaxed a bark of rusty-sounding laughter from him. "I agree. We should not become sworn enemies on the strength of anything less than a week's acquaintance."

"Can we start over properly, then," she proposed, "and pretend like I just arrived in Singapore this minute?"

He nodded. "An admirable suggestion."

"I'm pleased to meet you at last, Mr Grimshaw." She thrust out her hand. "My name is Bethan Conway."

"Allow me to welcome you to Singapore, Miss Conway." Instead of shaking her hand, as she'd expected, Simon Grimshaw bowed over it. Lifting her fingers, he grazed them with his lips as if she were some elegant lady. "Or may I call you Bethan? I think I might be allowed that familiarity under the circumstances. Don't you?"

The velvet brush of his lips sent a strange warmth tingling up her arm. When she tried to speak, her voice came out husky. "You may call me whatever you please."

He straightened up. "And you are welcome to call me by my given name, if you would care to."

The turnabout between them, in the few minutes since she'd entered the room, was enough to make Bethan quite dizzy. "Thank you…Simon. I think I would."

His name sounded so appealing, spoken in Bethan's clear, lilting voice—almost like an endearment.

She was a most unusual woman in Simon's experience, so forthright in her manner. She didn't say one thing while meaning another, then expect him to guess what was on her mind. And when he'd made an effort to put things right between them, she'd accepted without sulking, wiping the slate clean to begin afresh. Perhaps Hadrian had made a better choice for him than he'd first thought.

"We have a lot of getting acquainted to do." He offered Bethan his arm. "Tell me, how was your voyage from England? Not too great an ordeal, I hope."

"Not at all." She tucked her hand into the crook of his arm, a sensation he had not experienced in a very long time. "It was a great adventure! The seas were rough at first and the lads from Durham were sick as dogs, poor fellows. But as we sailed further south and the seas grew calm, they got better. They all complained it wasn't fair, me not being ill a minute. But who would have looked after them if I'd been seasick too?

"I loved the smell of the ocean and the rocking of the waves," she continued as they entered the dining room and Simon held out her chair. "I'm glad your house is near the sea so that I'll still be able to hear it. Though I never expected the place to be so big and grand!"

"This villa is a far cry from our first quarters in Singapore." Simon rounded the table and took a seat across from her. "Hadrian and I, and our third partner, Ford, built our first house out of timber with a palm-thatched roof."

That was one part of his past he didn't mind revealing. "Until recently, no one was allowed to own land or erect permanent buildings, because it was feared the Dutch would invade or the government would order us to leave. Once we got word that a treaty had been signed to make Singapore a British possession, there was a great scramble for land and a building boom. Hadrian was a canny fellow to have invested some of our profits in a brick kiln."

Simon caught himself. "Forgive me. I meant to find

out more about you. Instead I am boring you with all this talk of business and politics."

Carlotta had often chided him and his partners for continually turning dinner conversation towards their two favourite subjects.

"Don't stop on my account. I want to learn all I can about Singapore." Bethan's rapt expression assured him her interest was genuine. "It sounds like such an exciting place with so much going on. How many ships stop here in the course of a year?"

Before he could answer, Ah-Ming padded in and set shallow bowls of steaming soup before them.

Bethan seemed to forget her question as she inhaled deeply. "This smells very good. What kind is it?"

"My favourite—turtle." Simon sipped a spoonful of the broth, relishing its hearty flavour.

"I've never had that before." Bethan seized her spoon and began to consume the soup with the sort of gusto some English ladies might have considered unmannerly.

But Ah-Ming beamed with approval.

"Mmm." Bethan set down her spoon at last with a sigh of satisfaction. "That tasted even better than it smelled. I feel sorry for people who don't like to try new things. They don't know what they're missing."

"You should have been here a few months ago," said Simon. "One of the Chinese merchants hosted a banquet of all their rarest delicacies. Shark fin and bird's nest soups. Rashers of elephant tail in a sauce of lizard eggs. Stewed porcupine in green turtle fat."

Bethan's eyes grew wider with every dish he mentioned. He kept expecting her make a sour face at the thought of eating such outlandish foods. But her expression conveyed fascination rather than distaste.

"The highlight of the banquet," he concluded, "was a dish of snipes' eyes, garnished with a border of peacocks' combs. I was told it cost two hundred Spanish dollars. That's almost fifty pounds."

"I could feed myself for years on fifty pounds!" cried Bethan. "Here now, you aren't hoaxing me to see if I'm daft enough to believe you? When I first got to Newcastle from Wales, the other servants used to have great fun doing that."

The miserable rascals, having a jest at the expense of an inexperienced girl! The rush of indignation he felt on her behalf surprised Simon.

"You should take some unlikely stories with a grain of salt," he advised her as Ah-Ming removed their bowls and served a dish of Bengal mutton. "But I wouldn't hoax you, I promise. You can ask anyone who attended the banquet. There was even a report of it in the newspaper. The snipes' eyes weren't bad, as a matter of fact. A bit like caviar without the fishy taste."

Bethan cast him a puzzled look and it occurred to Simon that she'd probably never tasted caviar…perhaps never even heard of it.

"Mutton should be familiar to you if you lived in Wales." He steered the conversation back to her again. "What part of the country do you hale from?"

Bethan took a bite of meat, rolling her eyes appreciatively. "I've eaten plenty of mutton in my life, but none as tender as this. I come from a little village up north on the River Aled. It's as different from Singapore as can be—nothing but hills and sheep and lots of snow in the winter. What about you? Have you always lived in the Indies or did you come here from England?"

The silvery sparkle of interest in her eyes made Simon

answer, in spite of his resolve to guard his privacy. "I grew up north of Manchester, in the Ribble Valley."

It was a harmless enough scrap of information, yet it stirred up more memories that he preferred to forget. Bethan Conway had an unfortunate knack for doing that.

"Your village does sound very different from Singapore," he continued before she could ask him another question. "What made you leave it to come halfway around the world?"

Bethan almost choked on the bit of meat she was trying to swallow. But a cough and a sip of ale got it down.

When she was able to speak again, she replied, "I was looking for a change, I suppose. Some place new and exciting, in the middle of things."

Ah-Ming set another dish before them.

"This isn't like anything I've seen before." Bethan inhaled the mouth-watering aroma rising from the savoury jumble of food.

"Something else new that I think you'll enjoy," said Simon. The prospect of introducing her to all the novelties of Singapore appealed to him. "It's one of Cook's specialties—rice with duck, yams and shrimp."

"Oh, my," breathed Bethan after she'd savoured her first mouthful of the spicy-sweet-salty dish. "This must be what they eat in heaven!"

Simon nodded. Had Cook added some new, secret ingredient to his duck rice tonight? It tasted even better than usual. Or was it Bethan's contagious enjoyment that made him feel as if he, too, were tasting it for the first time?

"When my mother died," she continued between bites. "I had my own way to make and there was nothing more to keep me in Llanaled. I decided it was time to see the world and really *live* my life rather than letting it pass me by."

Surely she didn't expect him to believe she'd made such a long, perilous journey and sacrificed any hope of a respectable future in a naïve quest for adventure? Simon sensed Bethan was concealing something from him. The way she avoided his gaze and the note of false brightness in her voice gave her away.

The truth was not difficult to guess. Some man in Newcastle must have taken advantage of the green country lass eager to experience new things. Things like love, perhaps? Once her reputation was compromised, she must have decided she had nothing to lose by sailing to the Indies to become the mistress of a rich merchant.

A rush of hot anger swept through Simon at the thought of her innocence exploited.

In response to his outraged silence, she added, "That all sounds like a daft dream to you, I suppose."

Simon marshalled his composure before replying with more gentleness than he'd thought himself capable, "Not daft. A *big* dream, I would say, carrying greater risks than you might have realised. Your little Welsh village may not have been the most exciting place, but at least you were safe there."

Now that she had come to distant, dangerous Singapore, he felt an obligation to be her protector in every sense of the word. He suspected her greatest peril lay in her own impetuous, trusting nature.

Despite whatever trouble had befallen her in Newcastle, Bethan did not seem convinced that she'd have been better off staying in rural Wales. "No harm has come to me yet. And even if you were to send me home tomorrow, I'd still have seen and done more than my mother did in her whole life."

Was she ashamed to admit what he knew must have happened to her? Simon wondered. Or did she truly not consider the betrayal of her trust and the loss of her virtue as harmful? He wanted to ask her, but he was enjoying this pleasant meal with her too much to risk spoiling it with such probing, judgemental questions.

"Let us have no more talk of sending you home," he insisted. Though he still had doubts about Bethan Conway, the prospect of giving her up no longer appealed to him. "Besides, I couldn't do it tomorrow, even if I wanted to."

He explained about the fluctuating monsoons and how they prevented ships sailing westwards for part of the year.

"Fancy that!" Bethan appeared as delighted with this scrap of information as she'd been with the toothsome new foods he'd offered her. "So I shall *have* to stay in Singapore until November at least?"

He directed a warm gaze across the table at her. "I hope I can persuade you to remain here longer than that."

She did not avoid his gaze this time, but met it squarely. Simon caught a glimmer of uncertainty in her changeable eyes, as well as a glow of wondrous possibility. A deep hum of awareness vibrated between them.

"Perhaps you can." Her lilting murmur fell on Simon's ears like a favourite melody.

It took only those words and that gaze to stir up the ashes of his long-suppressed desire and make the embers smoulder once again. Simon tried to blame it on the turtle soup, which the local folk credited as an aphrodisiac. But he knew better.

Chapter Four

She had five whole months in Singapore to find out what had become of her missing brother. Bethan could have kissed Simon for providing that precious assurance! But would she *wed* him for it? Her feelings on that question were sharply divided.

On one hand, he *had* paid her passage and she'd made an agreement with Mr Northmore on his behalf. If he still wanted to marry her, how could she refuse? But what if she discovered her brother had gone somewhere else? Marriage to Simon would leave her trapped in Singapore, unable to follow Hugh's trail.

Aside from those practical matters there were other things to consider—such as her intense but confused response to Simon Grimshaw. His nearness, his touch and even his gaze stirred her senses in ways no other man's ever had. Finally there was his young daughter. The child seemed starved for lively company and the affection of someone other than her father's servants.

"Your daughter's a dear wee thing," said Bethan, as

Ah-Ming brought the pudding. "A bit quiet at first, but I think she enjoyed our romp in the garden."

"It sounded that way. I can't recall the last time I heard her laugh like that." Simon did not seem as pleased as she'd hoped.

For the first time since they'd agreed to begin their acquaintance afresh, Bethan sensed that stern Mr Grimshaw was still lurking beneath Simon's amiable surface. "I suppose she misses her mother, poor thing. How long is it since your wife died?"

Simon's fingers clenched tightly around his spoon and he stared down at his pudding as if it might be poisoned. His answer came out stiff and halting. "I've been widowed for more than three years. I doubt Rosalia has any recollection of her mother."

"I'm so sorry for you both." Bethan longed to reach across the table and give his hand a squeeze. She pitied his young daughter more than ever. "Rosalia must take after her mother, does she? She doesn't look like you at all."

Simon raised his eyes to hers and spoke with quiet but ominous insistence. "Rosalia is the very image of her mother. Now, if you please, I would rather talk about something else. As I mentioned earlier, I prefer not to dwell on the past."

"Of course," Bethan murmured, though she was fairly bursting with questions about his late wife.

How had she died? Did it have anything to do with how Simon had injured his leg? Perhaps that was why he hadn't wanted to talk about it earlier.

But there were other things she was curious about that should not stir up any painful memories for him. "You never did tell me how many ships come to Singapore in a year. I'm sure it must be a great many."

"It is, indeed, and more come every season." He sounded grateful for her change of subject. "The Bugis arrive in their *prahus* on the north-west monsoon. They bring spices from the South Seas. Then there's the junk fleet from China. They bring silks and tea. Ships from India and Europe come on the south-east monsoon, like yours did. They trade cotton, iron, glassware and such for goods from China and the South Seas."

As they ate delectable mango pudding and drank rich Java coffee, Bethan plied Simon with many more questions about Singapore and his business, gleaning pieces of information that she hoped might help her track down Hugh. Simon answered readily, impressing her with his masterful grasp of everything that affected his business.

It was clear he enjoyed telling her about it, too. She sensed he was becoming less tense and guarded. The beguiling hint of a smile seemed to hover on his lips, ready to blaze forth in full potency at any second. Bethan drank in the sound of his voice, noting every confident gesture and subtle change in his features.

A faint stab of disappointment struck her when Simon laid down his napkin at last and rose from his chair, for it meant their pleasant evening was coming to an end. "Before we burst at the seams, shall we step out on to the veranda to enjoy the night air?"

"That sounds lovely."

A few moments later they stood on the deep, roofed veranda that looked out over the garden where she had played with Rosalia. Beyond the garden lay a road and on the other side of the road stretched the beach. A tangy ocean breeze rustled through the leaves of several tall trees near the house. From the sea came the constant, soothing pulse of the breaking waves.

Bethan inhaled deeply. "What's that smell?"

"What smell?" Simon's hand covered hers as it rested upon the veranda railing. "I've become so used to it all, I don't notice any more."

It took a moment to muster her reply. Simon's touch seemed to reach beyond her fingers, sending an inviting sensation to whisper under her skin. But where was it inviting her? She was too inexperienced to know.

She sniffed again. "It's very sweet, but I don't think it's flowers. Something cooking, maybe?"

While she tried to describe the strange, appetising aroma, she drank in *his* scent too. It had a briny tang with a faintly bitter edge that was strangely appealing—like strong, dark coffee or rich chocolate.

"It might be coconut oil." Simon edged nearer until his arm rested against hers. "We use it in lanterns to light the streets at night."

"Singapore is full of nice new things." Bethan gave a sigh of pleasure, intensely aware of Simon's nearness. "I can hardly wait to see, hear and smell them all."

"Don't forget *touch*," he reminded her in a deep rustling whisper as he turned towards her and raised his hand to skim her cheek with the backs of his fingers.

It was such a different sensation from the way he'd clutched her arm on the quay. It intrigued her that a man who could command such protective force could also be so gentle.

"You're not at all what I expected, Bethan." When he'd said that during their disastrous first meeting, she'd been certain he was expressing displeasure. Now he seemed to be telling her something quite different. "How on earth did Hadrian ever find you?"

Uncertain of the proper response to Simon's touch,

she made none, though she was powerless to stifle the blush that flared in her cheek beneath his fingers.

"He put a notice in the newspaper," she replied in a breathless voice, "and I answered it."

"He did *what*?" Simon drew back abruptly, as if her innocent blush scorched his hand. "What in blazes was he thinking?"

"Does it matter *how* he found me?" Bethan shrank from the harshness of his indignation. Was he worried people would laugh at him for getting a bride out of the newspaper? "I'm here. That's what matters, isn't it?"

To her relief, Simon's voice softened. "I suppose so." He reached for her hand, twining his fingers through hers. "I'm surprised, that's all, by Hadrian's unconventional methods. And more surprised that a woman like you would answer that kind of notice in a newspaper. There must have been plenty of men in Newcastle who wanted you."

Bethan sensed a different question lurking beneath his words, but could not think what it might be. Anyway, she wasn't comfortable with this whole subject. What if her tongue ran away with her, as it so often did, and she told him her true reason for coming to Singapore? She wanted to be certain she could trust him before she mentioned her brother.

"I didn't meet many men working in the Bainbridges' nursery. And I didn't care much for Newcastle. So when I heard about Mr Northmore's notice, I thought it wouldn't hurt to try. I never expected him to pick me, but when he did, I felt as if I'd been offered a lucky chance. I couldn't refuse it."

The pale moonlight cast deep shadows over Simon's features, making it impossible to tell if he believed her. But his thumb rubbed over her palm in a way that roused her whole body and made her breath quicken. "I'm glad you didn't."

Lifting their entwined hands, he bent forwards and pressed his lips to her wrist…then her forearm, then the inner crook of her elbow. Each kiss brought Bethan a different, delightful sensation, even better than the smell of coconut oil or the taste of mango pudding. They woke a strange slumbering hunger in her—a craving that could not be satisfied with food, no matter how delicious. As Simon kissed his way up her arm, shoulder and neck, her mouth fell open, the better to inhale breath after urgent breath.

Simon must have taken it for an invitation. Leaning towards her, he tilted his head slightly and took possession of her lips with firm, certain purpose—not rough and demanding, but not tentative or awkward either. His tongue slid between her parted lips, exploring and tasting as if she were some new delicacy he was eager to relish.

Bethan had been kissed once before by Hugh's friend Evan. While stealing a hasty, awkward peck in a dark corner, he'd bumped her nose. That kiss had been as different from Simon's as a bowl of cold tripe from a dish of duck and rice. It had made her feel all sheepish and shameful, anxious not to let it happen again. Simon's amorous attentions had quite the opposite effect.

It sent ripples of heat pulsing through her body to pool in her breasts and loins. It whetted a ravenous craving that shocked her with its intensity. She could not seem to inhale enough air through her nose to feed the blaze he had kindled.

His breath hastened too, gusting from his nostrils like a hot wind against her cheek. His hands began to rove over her body, spreading a sultry yearning wherever he touched. Overwhelmed by the potent, bewildering sensations that possessed her, Bethan pulled back abruptly from Simon's embrace.

"Please! We only met…for the first time…this morning. I need a chance…to get to know you…and see more of this place…before I…" *marry you*—that was what she meant to say, but somehow the words stuck in her throat "…take such a big step."

How would Simon react to her request? Bethan searched his shadowed features. For an instant he looked shocked. Then his mouth tightened into a grim line and his icy blue eyes glittered with outrage.

Jagged shards of frustration slashed through Simon's body as Bethan jerked away from him.

An instant before, he'd been relishing the flavour of her kiss—a fresh, delicate sweetness that rivalled the prized mangosteen fruit. Together with the soft ripeness of her body beneath his hands, it had whipped up a tempest of long-stifled desires. His flesh throbbed with anticipation of the delights he would find in her arms. Any doubts he'd had about the wisdom of taking a mistress were drowned out by the swift crash of his heart and the wild gust of his breath. He could scarcely wait to whisk her off to his bed.

Then, without warning, she tensed and tore herself away from his embrace. It was as if a plaster had suddenly been ripped from his body, taking a great patch of skin with it. Instinct urged him to retaliate.

But one glimpse of her wide, anxious eyes doused the blaze of his desire with ice-cold shame. She looked far more frightened now than she had that morning, backed against the wall of an opium den by an angry mob.

"I need a chance…to get to know you…and see more

of this place…before I… She'd hesitated as if ashamed to speak aloud the scandalous reason she had come to Singapore "…take such a big step."

The obvious truth slapped Simon in the face. He'd guessed some man must have taken advantage of her trusting innocence. But Bethan's terrified reaction to his advances convinced him there'd been more to it. A girl like her would not have willingly surrendered her virginity. It must have been taken from her by force!

The realisation made Simon's belly seethe with violent outrage, like a volcano preparing to erupt. From tightly locked chambers of his memory, anguished screams escaped to ring in his ears.

He regretted his earlier suspicions about Bethan. No wonder she had tried to evade his questions about why she'd come to Singapore, with flimsy excuses about seeking adventure. What she really must have craved was safety and a complete change of scene to help her forget what had happened to her. The truth of her situation should have been obvious to him of all men. But he had let the urgency of his need blind him to it.

"Of course." With a supreme effort of will, Simon strove to bring his turbulent emotions back under control. It had been a long time since anything had come so close to shattering his composure. "Forgive me! I did not mean to alarm you. It is a great while since I have been close to a woman. I fear your beauty overcame my discretion."

Damn! That was the wrong thing to say. He should never have implied that what happened was in any way her fault—that her attractions somehow justified his loss of control.

Simon burned to know exactly what had been done to her. He wanted to learn the name of the blackguard who'd ruined her, so he could curse it. And if by some unlikely chance they ever met, he would thrash the vile dog within an inch of his life!

But how could he ask Bethan to dredge up such shameful memories when he'd refused to discuss parts of his own past that he longed to forget? He must respect her privacy and her efforts to put those troubles behind her.

To Simon's surprise, his ill-chosen words seemed to ease her alarm.

"You think I'm beautiful?" she mused as if she found it hard to believe.

"Oh, yes," he murmured, half against his will. "Far more beautiful than I ever expected."

A shimmer of starlight reflected in her eyes. "Well, I never thought you'd turn out to be so young and handsome."

Though the bashful sincerity of her admiration made Simon's chest swell, it also threatened his tenuous self-control. "You really shouldn't say things like that if you want me to keep my distance."

He spoke gently, almost jesting, but perhaps she sensed the dangerous undercurrent of desire lurking beneath his words.

Her lovely features tensed and she caught her lush lower lip between her teeth. "It isn't that I don't like you or don't ever want to...to—"

"I understand!" Simon cried, anxious to spare her from speaking the words that might have unpleasant associations for her. "You need time to become accustomed to...your new situation."

Time to learn she could trust him to treat her as she deserved. Time to conquer her fears of intimacy with a man. Time to come to terms with giving up any hope of respectability in exchange for his protection.

"How long do you think it will take?" The words slipped out before he could stop them, betraying the urgency of his need.

That might have been what made Bethan retreat a step further, clinging to the veranda railing. "I hadn't thought, really. I suppose a month should give us time to get to know one another better. Would that be all right?"

A whole month? Simon bit back a groan. Thirty evenings like this, struggling to ignore the old gnawing hunger she'd whetted with a fleeting taste of her favours. How could he stand it?

But how could he resist her lilting entreaty and her whole air of vulnerable innocence?

"If it's a month you need, then a month you shall have," he assured her. "You are quite right to call it a *big step*. I want to make certain it is one you won't regret."

That did not mean he would have to go a whole month without a single kiss or touch. Simon sought to pacify his thwarted desires. He must help her become accustomed to his attentions a little at a time, with the reassurance that he would not go too far or too fast. He must show her that he could be relied upon to protect and to provide for her, to treat her gently, and to bring her pleasure. He needed to kindle her desires while keeping a tight rein on his own, so that by month's end she would be as eager to take her promised place in his bed as he would be to have her there.

Simon bid Bethan goodnight with a restrained, mannerly bow as if their passionate embrace on the veranda had never happened. Though she knew he was only trying to oblige her request, Bethan could not subdue a perverse wish for something more. Another gallant kiss on the hand, or a lingering brush of his lips on her cheek.

As she undressed for bed, she found herself listening for sounds of him moving around in the room next door. The bewildering thrill of his kiss seemed to have awakened something in her. She was conscious of her body in a way she had not been in years, since it began the mysterious change to womanhood. When she stripped down to her shift, she could not ignore the sweet, subtle ache in her breasts. Her nipples jutted out against the fine linen like a pair of firm pink pebbles.

When she caught a glimpse of herself in the glass above her dressing table, she wondered if Simon was listening to her movements, picturing her undressing. That thought sent a sultry blush sweeping from her bare toes all the way to the roots of her hair. And when she pictured him removing his crisp white shirt then sliding his trousers down over his thighs, all the air seemed to go out of the room, leaving her gasping for breath. Ater her sheltered early years, Bethan had never expected to have this sort of response to the man she'd arranged to marry. She was not certain what to make of it and whether it was a good or bad thing under the circumstances.

Dousing the lamp, she dived under the tent of insect netting on to her bed. All was quiet in Simon's room, now. A warm breeze wafted through the slats of the window shutter, bearing a mixture of exotic fragrances, the call of a night bird and the swish of waves breaking upon the nearby shore.

As she thought back over the day's events, she could scarcely believe she had been in Singapore less than twenty-four hours. So much had happened in that short time and her feelings had shifted back and forth to such opposite extremes, she wondered if she would *ever* sort them out. Hopefully the one month's grace that Simon had granted her would be long enough to make a start. So much depended on what she was able to find out about her brother in that time.

Bethan prayed she would have better luck in her search over the next month than she'd had that day.

Chapter Five

"How do you like it here, so far?" Simon asked Bethan a few days after she'd arrived in Singapore.

Between a surge in shipping traffic from the West and four new workers to train, he'd been run off his feet since then. Last night he hadn't even been able to get home to dine with Bethan, much to his disappointment. With business running smoother today, he'd come home early to join her on the veranda.

"Very well, thank you." Bethan smiled at him, but quickly looked away as if she still wasn't quite comfortable around him. "Your servants have gone out of their way to make me welcome."

"But…?" Simon prompted her, sensing an undercurrent of discontent in her tone.

"It's nothing really." She fluttered her fan more rapidly. "I'm just not used to being idle. I wish there was more I could do, but I suppose it's not proper for the mistress to be doing maid's work. Ah-Sam did let me take Rosalia for a walk on the beach. I think she enjoyed it."

Simon's spirits rose at hearing Bethan refer to herself as his mistress in such an offhand way. Still, he wasn't certain he approved of Rosalia spending too much time in the company of his mistress. Not that he feared Bethan would corrupt the child's morals, as might have been the case if Hadrian had sent the sort of experienced lady-bird he'd expected. But it did put Bethan on a different footing in his household—too much like a wife for his comfort.

"I hope you don't feel obliged to earn your keep for the next month by looking after Rosalia. She has an excellent *amah*."

"I know that." Bethan bristled slightly. "I'm not trying to take Ah-Sam's place. It's just that I enjoy your daughter's company and we have a jolly time together."

"I'm pleased to hear it." That wasn't altogether true, but Simon was relieved she didn't *dislike* Rosalia and want the child sent away. "Though I was hoping you would enjoy *my* company. That is why I brought you to Singapore, after all."

"I do!" she cried, then immediately appeared flustered by her outburst. "I mean…I know that. But you're a busy man. You don't have much time to spend with me."

"I'm sorry I wasn't able to get home for dinner last night." Though he meant it sincerely, it irked Simon to apologise for his absence. He hadn't bargained on answering to his mistress for his comings and goings, as he would a wife. Then again, so many things about Bethan were not as he'd expected. "That's why I came home early today. I thought we might take a drive before dinner to see a little more of the town. Would you like that?"

He knew her answer almost before the question was

out of his mouth. Her whole face lit up with a winsome glow that took his breath away. "I'd love it!

She started towards him was if she meant to throw her arms around his neck. But before she could complete the impulsive gesture, she caught herself and jerked back.

Simon stifled a pang of disappointment. Perhaps an unguarded overture of that sort had led to the loss of her virtue. He must help her overcome such troubling memories and show her she had nothing to fear from him.

"Can Rosalia come with us?" she asked. "I'm sure she would enjoy a drive."

Simon bit back an impatient reply. "Another time, perhaps. I don't like to upset her nursery routine."

For a moment Bethan looked as though she might argue his decision, but when she spoke it was only to ask, "Should I change clothes first?"

Simon swept a glance over her as she rose from her chair. Her high-waisted muslin gown had an air of elegant simplicity that he liked very much. The colour reminded him of the unripe apples he and his brother had once hurled at each other in the orchard of his boyhood home.

"You look fine." He rose and offered her his arm. "Better than fine. All you'll need is a hat and a parasol."

What Simon neglected to mention was that there would be no need for her to dress up. He didn't expect to meet anyone on their little jaunt. Most of his acquaintances would be dining at this hour, then going for a stroll or a drive afterwards. He wanted to spare Bethan the necessity of introductions that might prove awkward, especially since their arrangement was still not fully settled.

* * *

His plan worked perfectly. When they drove up North Bridge Road a short time later, the street was quite deserted.

Bethan did not appear to notice. Perched beside him on the seat of the gharry, she peered about, trying to looking in every direction at once, firing questions at him. "What is this great empty space doing in the middle of town? Is it the market square?"

Simon shook his head. "At present its only function is to provide the *sepoys* with a parade ground." He pointed towards the military encampment at the base of the hill. "Our founder designated this part of town for public buildings. Originally he wanted them on the north bank of the river. But since that was the best commercial land, we merchants built our *godowns* there and Raffles was obliged to alter his plans."

"So trade is more important than government in Singapore?" Bethan flashed him an impudent grin that Simon could not resist returning.

"Without trade, how would those fine public buildings be paid for?"

She chuckled. "I think that makes sense. What about all those fine white houses overlooking the shore—do they all belong to important merchants like you?"

There could be no mistaking the sincere admiration in her tone when she referred to him as *important*. Simon's chest swelled.

"Most of my neighbours are merchants. The lot on my right belongs to Carlos Quintéra, the local agent for a large Calcutta firm. Others are officials, like the Surgeon, Dr Moncrieff." He nodded toward one of four houses facing into the square on the shore side.

They drove past the soldiers' encampment, taking a carriage road that wound around Government Hill.

"Where are we going?" asked Bethan.

Simon cast her a sidelong glance. "I want to show you the best view in Singapore. Several of the best, in fact."

"I'm certain they'll be very fine indeed. I can't get over the size of some of the trees here." Plucking Simon's arm to gain his attention, Bethan pointed toward a lofty jelawi. "That one looks as tall as the Lantern Tower of old St. Nicholas church back in Newcastle!"

Her unexpected touch sent a bolt of heat searing through Simon's veins. It took him a moment to master his voice. "Majestic, isn't it? The younger trees beyond it are all spice-bearing varieties. They are part of an experimental garden, a pet project of Sir Stamford Raffles. He had a number of trees and shrubs of commercial value planted here to see if they would thrive. The place has been rather neglected since he left. Our current Resident is more interested in politics than botany."

He'd barely finished speaking when Bethan grasped his arm once again, holding on a little longer this time. "Oh my gracious, look at those birds! Did you ever see such colours?"

Simon forced his gaze toward a pair of parrots with vivid dark-red plumage and bright blue markings on their faces and wings. Spectacular a sight as they were, he would rather have feasted his eyes on Bethan's face, aglow with the wonder of discovery.

"You'll see plenty of those around Singapore," he assured her. "There's another kind even more amazing—feathers every colour of the rainbow, only more vivid. You'd swear they were cast out of emeralds and rubies."

In truth, he'd never paid much heed to the bright colours of the birds or the soaring height of the trees. When he'd first arrived on the island, he had been too preoccupied with helping Ford and Hadrian establish their business, and trying to forget the humiliating situation he'd left behind in Penang. Now he found himself taking in his surroundings with fresh appreciation.

As the gharry rounded the far side of the hill, Bethan let out a soft gasp. Spread before them was mile after mile of wild, verdant jungle.

"I never thought there could be so many different shades of green," she whispered.

Simon hadn't either, though, in his opinion, none of them could match the elusive, mutable grey-green of her eyes. Until now, he'd thought of the surrounding jungle as nothing but a source of danger, harbouring tigers and bands of outlaws. Bethan made him see something more.

They drove on in silence for a while, privately contemplating the lush, untamed grandeur. Only when the road wound higher, bringing the town and the sea back into view did Simon venture to speak again. "The Malays call this Forbidden Hill. They say their kings of long ago are buried here."

"Does that other hill have a name too?" Bethan pointed towards a slightly lower rise to the north.

Simon nodded. "Selegi Hill, which I'm told means something to do with spears. Captain Flynn and his family live there. He is the harbour-master."

"Harbour-master?" Bethan sounded more intrigued by that than tales of ancient Malay kings. "Does he have any children Rosalia's age? Do you ever go there to visit?"

Her questions struck Simon as a trifle odd, but then again Bethan had proven herself an unusual young woman. "The captain does have children—a stepdaughter who's almost grown and an infant daughter. He has a son Rosalia's age. Ah-Sam used to take her to visit until the boy was sent to live with relatives in England."

"A child that age sent so far away from his family?" Bethan fairly trembled with outrage. "How could his parents do such a terrible thing?"

"They didn't have much choice, I'm afraid," Simon replied. "His elder brother died and the climate did not agree with him. Surely the child is better off in England than lying in the cemetery."

Bethan did not seem convinced.

In an effort to distract her, Simon began to point out other sights of interest. "Over there is the *dhobi* village. They are the Indian laundry folk who wash clothes on the banks of the Kallang River and down there in Bras Basah stream. They have raised the task almost to a science. It amazes me how they get all the laundry back to its proper owners without ever losing a single scrap of linen. I wish I could keep as good an account of Vindicara's inventory."

His distraction seemed to work.

Bethan's frown eased and she surveyed the view from the top of the hill with interest. "I can see your house and your *godown* by the river. My, what a lot of ships there are at anchor."

By now they had reached the hilltop. Simon stopped the gharry some distance away from the tall signal flagpole and hurried around to help Bethan out. He did not release her hand when she had alighted, but tucked it into the crook of his elbow and led her towards the best lookout spot. He was gratified when she betrayed no hesitation in taking his arm. He hoped it meant she was growing more comfortable around him and not simply that she was too fascinated by the vast number of ships to notice.

"Do many of the crews come ashore?" she asked.

Simon shook his head. "Only the odd few. There isn't a great deal for them to do. Very little of our food is grown here, so Singapore is not the best port for provisioning." He sensed her dissatisfaction with his answer. "Why do you ask?"

"No reason." The bright, carefree tone she affected struck a false note. "I'm interested in everything about the place, that's all. Tell me, what's that cluster of buildings over there near the shore?"

Simon recognised an evasion when he heard one, though he could not fathom why she felt it necessary. "That's the Sultan's *istana*. A palace of sorts."

A melodious trill of her laughter made him forget his niggling suspicions. "Living just up the road from a sultan's palace, am I? What would the folks back in Llanaled make of that, I wonder?"

He turned towards her, gazing down into her eyes. They reminded him of a Lancashire meadow swathed in springtime mist. "If those people have any sense, they'll say you belong in a palace, showered with the best of everything."

"If any of them could see your house, they'd think *it* was a palace." She lowered her gaze briefly, only to look up at him again through the delicate fringe of her eyelashes.

Was that an invitation to kiss her? It made Simon incapable of resisting his inclination. The best he could manage was to proceed slowly so as not to alarm her. That took every scrap of will-power he possessed.

Closer and closer he leaned, watching for any sign of reluctance, which he hoped would not come. Bethan had ample time to evade his kiss or fend him off with some remark about the view. But she did not speak or move, except the slightest quiver of her lips as his whispered over them.

Ever since their first evening together, the memory of her kiss, her scent and the feel of her in his arms had clung to Simon. By day they distracted him from his work and by night they invaded his dreams. Though they made a pleasant change from the nightmares that some-times plagued him, they were a sweet torment, whetting his hunger for her to an even sharper pitch.

Now the glancing brush against her warm, pliant lips unleashed a tempest of urgent desire within him. Simon clung tight to Bethan's hands in case the temptation to take further liberties overwhelmed him.

He was fighting so hard to control his hands that he had no will-power to spare for his lips. Bethan's kiss tasted like sweet cider to a man parched with thirst. How could he imbibe it by slow, cautious sips when he longed to quaff it in great, lusty draughts?

His lips ranged over hers and she responded with natural, innocent desire that only made him want her more. When her lips parted, he slid his tongue between them, immersing himself in the delights of her soft, sweet mouth even as he strove to ignore the hungry ache of arousal they inflamed.

Then suddenly Bethan tensed and jerked away from him.

Silently cursing himself, Simon struggled to regain his composure. He'd intended to maintain tight control of his desires, to tempt Bethan without frightening her. It vexed him to realise how relentlessly she tested his self-restraint. His flash of frustrated anger sought an outlet.

* * *

The low murmur of voices jolted Bethan out of the dark, lucious depths of Simon's kiss.

On their drive up Government Hill, they'd seen no one but a few soldiers off in the distance. As Simon introduced her to the many exotic wonders of Singapore, it had felt as if they were off in a world of their own.

She'd tried to concentrate on gaining information that might help her track down her brother, yet it troubled her to be keeping the truth from Simon. What would he think if he knew she had only used him to reach Singapore in search of Hugh? Could she risk confiding in him when he seemed so grimly determined to tell her as little as possible about his past?

Those conflicting thoughts slipped into the background whenever some new sight caught her fancy. Every fresh wonder Simon showed her felt like a precious gift. In truth, they meant more to her than his fine house, his fortune or his position in the community.

An even greater distraction was her deepening awareness of Simon as a man. It was difficult to concentrate on the things he was telling her when the mellow timbre of his voice caressed her ears. It was hard to take in the layout of the town when her gaze so often strayed to the strong lines of his profile. When he took her hand and stood close beside her, every particle of her flesh tingled in response to his nearness, and she could think of nothing else.

She hadn't been angling for a compliment when she said how strange it felt to be living so near a sultan's palace. But when Simon had declared that she belonged in a palace, something inside her rose up and took wing. When he turned towards her and stared into her eyes, Bethan lost herself in his bracing blue gaze. The next thing she knew, he was leaning towards her, his lips slowly approaching.

She quivered with anticipation.

The passionate intensity of his advances their first evening together had bewildered and alarmed her. Or rather, it was her fierce response to him that had made her pull back as she would from a dangerous, fascinating flame. But she had not been able to forget the delicious heat of his mouth. The sultry smoothness of his lips and tongue. The lush sweet taste of mango pudding mingled with the smoky richness of Java coffee, both laced with a faint bitter tang all his own. Often since then, her lips had tingled with the memory of his kiss and her mouth had watered with a hunger for more.

As she was about to get her wish, Bethan wondered if it would feel and taste as good the second time. When at last his lips grazed hers—inviting, promising, enticing—she was delighted to discover it thrilled her even more.

Then, out of nowhere, the muttering of voices, the shuffling of feet and the muted rattle of chains shattered the intimacy of the moment.

Who was coming? Who might have seen them? Much as she hated to break from Simon's kiss, Bethan stiffened and pulled back, her gaze searching for the source of the sounds. It did not take long to discover.

A dozen men, all wearing dun-coloured trousers, tunics and turbans, marched past them in a line. Each one was chained at the ankle to the man ahead of him and the one behind. As they filed past, with a pair of soldiers guarding them, the men stared at Simon and Bethan. Some of them grinned. Others sniggered.

Bethan's face felt as if she'd been bending over a roaring fire for several hours!

"Who are they?" she asked when the line of men had shuffled on down the road and disappeared around the bend. "What were they doing up here?"

"Convict labourers." Simon scowled after them. "They must have been doing some work around the Resident's bungalow."

"What sort of labourers?" Bethan wondered if she'd heard correctly.

"Convicts from India." Simon adjusted his neck linen. "A shipment of two hundred arrived a few months ago. The authorities there are relieved to save the cost of keeping them and it provides Singapore with cheap labour for public works."

"What did they do," Bethan wondered aloud, "to deserve such a cruel sentence? I wonder how many of them will ever get back to their families?"

She'd wanted to come to Singapore and had landed in the lap of luxury. Still she yearned to be reunited with her brother.

"Perhaps they should have thought of that before they broke the law," Simon growled. "There is too much crime in this part of the world…pirates…outlaws. What about that thief who stole your necklace? Don't you want him caught and punished?"

"I…suppose so," Bethan muttered. Though Simon's sudden severity troubled her, she wasn't about to back down. "But I care more about getting my locket back than taking revenge against the man who took it. Come to that, I'd let him keep the locket if only he'd let me have the picture from inside it."

"That is very lenient of you." Simon seemed taken aback by her response. "But if the thief escapes punishment, it will only encourage him to rob again or perhaps do worse. If there is to be any order in society, criminals *must* be punished."

His words made Bethan shudder.

Simon took her arm again and turned toward the gharry.

"We should be getting back to the house." He spoke as if nothing had happened. "Cook will be in a temper if we're late for dinner."

As they walked back to the gharry, then drove down the hill, Bethan struggled to concentrate on what Simon was saying. It was information about Singapore that she would have found fascinating half an hour ago. Now her thoughts were only half with him. Instead she pondered his comment about the punishment of criminals, relieved that she had not told him anything about her brother.

Clearly, she needed to keep her guard up around Simon Grimshaw.

Cursing himself in a colourful mixture of languages, Simon returned home from work three days later.

So much for his plan to win Bethan's trust and engage her desire. Ever since he'd lost control of their kiss on Government Hill, she had seemed subdued, even skittish, around him. Her reaction convinced him more firmly than ever that her virginity must have been taken by force.

Much as he hated to raise the distressing subject, Simon feared he had no choice. It took him a while to work his way around to it, though. He made several attempts during dinner to turn their safe small talk in a more serious direction, but all without success.

Finally, when Ah-Ming withdrew after serving the sweet course of pandan cake, he swept aside his misgivings and tried again. "Er...I wanted to talk to you about…the other day…on Government Hill…and what happened. I fear I may have upset you."

"Not at all," Bethan insisted. But the way she avoided his gaze and fumbled her cutlery contradicted her words. "I had a nice time."

Simon understood her reluctance to talk about what had happened, but now that he had broached the subject he could not drop it again without having his say. "I'm certain that is true for most of it. But there was one incident I know affected you. What is more, I believe I know why."

"You do?" All the colour drained from Bethan's face.

Simon nodded. "I guessed the very first night you arrived."

"You did?" Her voice sounded breathless.

"It was quite obvious there must have been…difficulties in your past that led you to come here. I was reluctant to raise the subject at first, but in light of recent events I want to assure you that I do not hold you responsible in the least for what happened."

"You don't?" She sounded bewildered..

Did she not believe him capable of taking her part against one of his own sex? Had she assumed he would blame her for the mistreatment she'd suffered?

"Of course not." Simon willed her to him. "Perhaps you thought me too severe in condemning those convicts, but that does not mean I am without sympathy for the innocent. On the contrary, it is *because* of my concern for them that I wish to see those who would harm or exploit them brought to justice."

"But it isn't always easy to know who's at fault." Bethan took a sip of wine, perhaps to fortify herself. "Who is the villain and who is the victim."

"For some people, perhaps," Simon agreed. "But I try not to jump to the conclusions others might. Is it too much to hope that you could put the unfortunate events of the past behind you and make a fresh start in Singapore…with me?"

The tip of Bethan's tongue peeped out to run over her lips. The memory of their satin smoothness and delicate flavour sent a surge of heat through Simon.

"It's not easy to forget the past altogether," she murmured in what sounded like a plea for understanding. "It's our past that has made us the people we are today."

Simon mulled over her words. "Few men have better reason to know that than I, my dear. I am only asking that you not let the present always be tainted by the events of your past. For my part, I will make every effort to conduct myself in a way that will not evoke unpleasant memories for you."

Bethan still looked somewhat bewildered. Or perhaps her expression was one of disbelief. He could not blame her for being wary. Yet it galled him to be viewed in the same way as the rogue who'd stolen her innocence, when he would rather die than commit such an outrage!

Before Bethan could hazard a reply, Rosalia's *amah* entered the dining room and bowed. "Master, but there is an important matter I wish to speak of, if I may?"

"Of course." The servant's sudden arrival troubled Simon. He could not recall the last time Ah-Sam had sought him out like this. "There's nothing wrong with Rosalia, I hope?"

"No, master. She is very well. Rosalia is a good child—clever and respectful. She will never bring dishonour upon her family."

"You've done an excellent job raising her." Simon

humoured Ah-Sam's preoccupation with Rosalia's behaviour. Having also raised the child's mother, perhaps she blamed herself for Carlotta's transgressions. "Now, what was it you wanted to tell me?"

Ah-Sam bowed again. "I have received word that my sister is very ill and wishes to see me. There is a ship sailing for Macau in two days. I ask that you find someone to care for Rosalia until I return."

"Of…course…" After all Ah-Sam's years of faithful service, how could he deny her request? Perhaps she also wanted to visit the graves of her ancestors, something her people set great store by when they reached a certain age. "But…two days? How will I ever find anyone suitable by then?"

Women were scarce enough in Singapore that most had no difficulty finding husbands. That left very few available to work as servants.

"I'd be happy to look after Rosalia," Bethan offered. "At least until you can find someone else."

"I'm not sure that's a good idea," Simon replied.

"Why not? I have plenty of experience minding children. Rosalia and I get on well together and I don't have enough to do while you're at work. By the time you get home, she'll be ready for bed."

"Wah! It is a fine idea," declared Ah-Sam. "Rosalia will be very happy."

Simon was not convinced, but his years in business had taught him when to cut his losses. "It appears I am outnumbered. Very well, then. Bethan may take charge of Rosalia. But only until I can hire a proper replacement."

The broad smile with which Ah-Sam greeted his decision made Simon uneasy.

Chapter Six

What had Simon been trying to tell her before Ah-sam interrupted them? Bethan had an uneasy feeling about their conversation.

In bed that night, she tried to sort it all out, with little success. Simon had used so many hard words, she wasn't always certain what he meant. Even when she thought she understood him, the things he'd said did not quite make sense.

Her heart had leapt into her throat when he claimed to know what was troubling her and said he had guessed all along. Strangely, he didn't sound angry about what he called the *difficulties in her past* nor did he blame her. Though he seemed to understand why she'd come to Singapore looking for her brother, now he wanted her to forget about Hugh and make a new life with him.

It was a tempting prospect, she could not deny that. Simon had the means to give her a better life than anything she could have hoped for back in Britain. As his wife, she'd be mistress of a fine house with servants at her beck and call. She would get to live in a colourful, exotic land where luxuries like tea, coffee, silk, sugar and spices of the finest quality were plentiful. Besides all those material comforts, she would have a precious little stepdaughter and a husband whose kisses made her heart flutter and her bones melt. But even for all that, how could she abandon her brother—especially if he might be in trouble and need her help?

Gradually Bethan fell into a restless sleep. Unable to escape her struggle, she spent the whole night dreaming about Hugh and Simon. In one dream her brother was drowning, calling out for her to throw him a rope. In another he was caught in a maze of high walls, crying for her to show him the way out. Each time, when she tried to help her brother, Simon appeared to distract her with the touch of his hand or the brush of his lips. Hugh's cries grew weaker and weaker until at last they fell silent.

She woke the next morning with her heart throbbing against her ribs and her stomach churning. Desperate for some distraction from the tug of war within her, she ate a hurried breakfast, then went to the nursery. There she found Rosalia watching with a woebegone expression as Ah-Sam packed her trunk. The child looked badly in need of a distraction, too.

"Good morning, Rosalia." Bethan held out her hand to the little girl. "Would you like to come for a walk with me?"

The child jumped up from her seat beside the window. With quick but dainty steps, she flew towards Bethan. "A walk—where?"

"I thought we might go down to the shore. I like being so near the sea."

Rosalia glanced back at her amah. "May I please, Ah-Sam?"

"She can go." Ah-Sam raised her forefinger. "One hour, then come home."

As they strolled away hand in hand, she called out in her language and Rosalia answered.

"What did she say?" Bethan whispered.

Rosalia broke into a grin. "Ah-Sam says I mustn't forget to wear my hat or my nose will get freckles like yours."

Bethan chuckled. The other maids in Newcastle had twitted her about the dusting of freckles on her nose, but she didn't see anything wrong with them. "When I was a wee girl, my daddy told me freckles came from fairies kissing me while I was asleep."

Rosalia's forehead creased in a puzzled look. "What's a *daddy*?"

"It comes from the Welsh word *tad*," Bethan explained. "It means father or papa."

Rosalia said nothing more while she and Bethan fetched their wide-brimmed hats and let themselves out the back door into the garden.

"Is your daddy in England like Uncle Hadrian?" she asked at last. "Do you miss him being so far away?"

The child's innocent question hit Bethan like an unexpected blow. It took a moment to gather her composure. "I do miss him sometimes. He's not back in England, though. He's gone away to Heaven. But when I remember things he used to say, like the bit about fairy kisses, I feel as if part of him is still with me."

"Is your mama in Heaven too?" Rosalia's small hand clung tighter to Bethan's as she opened a wrought-iron gate at the bottom of the garden.

They slipped out on to the road that ran along the

shore. The only traffic on it was a cart pulled by a black bullock.

Bethan nodded in response to Rosalia's question. "She's been gone two years now. Sometimes that doesn't seem like so long ago. But other times…"

"My mama went to Heaven a long time ago. I can't remember anything about her." Though the child spoke in a matter-of-fact tone, her words brought a lump into Bethan's throat.

She was about to suggest Rosalia ask her father to share some of *his* memories about her mother, then she recalled his abrupt refusal to speak of his late wife.

Lifting Rosalia down the embankment on to the sandy beach, she inhaled a bracing draught of sea air. "I love the sound of the waves, don't you? Look at all the ships anchored out there. I wonder where they've all come from and what sort of goods they've brought to trade."

"They're too far away to see very well," said Rosalia. "Our old house was on the river beside Papa's *godown*. I used to watch all the *tongkangs* loading and unloading. Sometimes the lightermen would wave and call out to me. I wish we still lived there. It wasn't big and quiet like the new house, but there was always something exciting to watch. Uncle Hadrian lived with us at the old house. Ah-Sam and Ah-Ming are very happy to hear he found a wife. I wonder where he found her. Do you think he had to look very hard?"

"I don't think he found his wife quite that way." Bethan pulled off her shoes and stockings and wriggled her toes in the warm sand. "You make it sound like they were playing a game of *hidey*."

"Uncle Hadrian used to play that game with me sometimes. He brought me treats, too—custard apples and mangosteens." The tip of Rosalia's tongue flicked over her lips.

The way she spoke of Mr Northmore reminded Bethan of the happiest years of her childhood. "Does your father play with you often?"

Rosalia shook her head, making the loops of her braids slap against her cheeks. "Papa can't play. His sore leg makes it hard for him to run."

Bethan understood how Simon's old injury might make it difficult for him to romp about with his small daughter. But surely he could find some other ways to provide Rosalia with the attention she clearly craved.

"There's nothing wrong with *my* legs." She lifted the hem of her skirts to give the child a peek. "And I can think of all sorts of games to play on the beach. We could race each other along the shore, jump the waves as they come in, build a sandcastle…"

Rosalia's face lit up more brightly at each suggestion. Then she looked down at her shoes and skirts with a dispirited grimace. "We might get dirty and I don't think I'm allowed to go barefoot like the Malay children."

"You most certainly are." Bethan planted her hands on her hips. "I'm allowing it and if we get dirty I'll take all the blame. Come on, now, we've only got an hour, remember?"

"All right." Rosalia balanced against a large, weathered rock to remove her shoes and stockings. "Uncle Hadrian used to let me do things I wasn't allowed. Ah-Sam grumbled sometimes, but she couldn't scold him."

"Let's go." Bethan hoisted up her skirts with one hand while holding her hat with the other. "See if you can catch me."

As they played together on the beach, Bethan mulled

over what Rosalia had said about her father. Thinking back over the days since she had come to Singapore, she realised Simon had spent hardly any time with his daughter.

He was a very busy man, she reminded herself. She hoped he did not feel obliged to spend time courting her that he might otherwise have devoted to his daughter. She would have to speak to him about it.

Perhaps his answer would help her reach a decision about whether to marry him.

The night after Ah-Sam left for Macau, Simon entered his house and immediately headed for the nursery. As he approached, peals of merry laughter floated through the villa like a cool sea breeze on a stifling day. Stopping by the open door, he peered in to find Bethan sitting opposite Rosalia at a small table.

"My tiger eats your leopard," cried Rosalia with a ring of gleeful triumph that surprised Simon.

He'd always found her a rather subdued child.

"My poor leopard!" Bethan gave an exaggerated sob that ended in a giggle. "I was very fond of him. In that case, I'm afraid my wolf will have to eat your dog."

"He can't!" Rosalia shook her head so hard, her dark braids swung in wide arcs. "Dog can eat wolf, not the other way around. You'd better move your wolf or my dog will eat him next."

"That doesn't sound right to me," Bethan protested. "Perhaps he isn't really a wolf at all, just a little fox."

She glanced up suddenly and spied Simon watching them. He gave a guilty start as their eyes met.

"Come in," she called. "Your daughter is teaching me how to play *Do Show…*"

"*Dou Shou Qi*. Yes, I heard." As he stepped into the

room, Simon felt his presence cast a shadow over their merriment.

"Would you like to play the winner of our match?" asked Bethan, with a subtle ring of challenge in her tone. "Your daughter's animals have been making a fine meal out of mine."

"Well done, Rosalia." Simon nodded to the child. "Another time, perhaps. I came to ask if you would care to take another drive with me before dinner. We could go down Beach Road to see the Sultan's *istana*."

"That sounds lovely!" Bethan scrambled up from the floor. "Can Rosalia come too? I'm sure she'd enjoy an outing."

This was what he'd been afraid of when Bethan offered to care for the child. Did she intend to use Rosalia as a little chaperon to keep him at arm's length? He must take a firm stand or who knew when he might get another moment alone with her.

"Then you must take her on one, by all means. I will put Mahmud and the gharry at your disposal. I would rather limit this excursion to the two of us. I spoke to Ah-Ming and she will be happy to give the child her supper and put her to bed. Is that all right with you, Rosalia?"

"Yes, Papa." She nodded obediently. "I hope you have a nice drive."

"Thank you, my dear." Simon had known he could count on her not to make a fuss. He would tell Ah-Ming to provide a special treat for her.

He turned his attention back to Bethan. "That's settled, then. After you finish your game, we can go."

"Very well." Her nose wrinkled as if she'd caught a whiff of putrid-smelling durian fruit. "Perhaps it is best if we go by ourselves. There's something I wanted to talk to you about."

Simon didn't like the sound of that. With a curt bow, he withdrew to wait for her in the gharry.

When half an hour passed and she still had not come, his patience began to wear thin. He was on the verge of abandoning the whole idea when Bethan appeared, looking every bit as vexed with him as he was with her.

"What took you so long?" he muttered. "I'm not accustomed to being kept waiting."

"I'm not one of your workers!" Her lips pursed until they looked like hard little nuggets of coral. "I didn't want to leave Rosalia until I was certain she was all right."

"Is she ill? She looked perfectly well when I saw her." Concern for the child overcame Simon's irritation. Tropical fevers could strike as suddenly as tropical storms, and wreak even greater devastation.

"It's nothing like that." Bethan shook her head. "But she misses Ah-Sam and now she thinks you're angry with her."

"That's ridiculous!" Simon slapped the reins against the horse's rump more sharply than he'd intended. "I can't imagine where she got such an idea."

"Just because you don't understand how your daughter feels doesn't make those feelings any less real to her." Bethan spoke in a pleading tone with an edge of exasperation. "Rosalia is so quiet, you don't realise how deeply she feels things."

"And you do, I suppose?" It troubled him to think that after less than a fortnight's acquaintance she might already know things about Rosalia that he'd never suspected.

"I do." Bethan crossed her arms in from of her chest. "And so would you if you cared enough to spend any time with her."

"That's not fair!" Simon protested. "I have a great many claims on my time. I've always made certain Rosalia was well cared for and wants for nothing."

"Nothing except a father's fondness and attention," said Bethan as Simon swung the gharry on to Beach Road. "That's not something you can buy with your fortune, but it's priceless all the same."

He did not want to hear such things, especially not from her. If they'd been back at the house, he would have walked away. Out here, he had no choice but to sit and listen.

His features must have betrayed more of his true feelings than he usually allowed, for Bethan's tone softened. "I'm not saying it's a bad thing you've provided so well for Rosalia. It's just that she needs more from you than a fine house and lots of servants."

She sounded as if she were trying to explain the simplest fact to some poor halfwit. "Who are you to tell *me* what Rosalia needs? You're not her mother and you never will be!"

Simon regretted the words even as they left his lips. He'd thrown in her face the real reason she was here—a reason she was still innocent enough to find shameful.

She sucked in a sharp breath as if he'd struck her with his fist.

"Forgive me." It was a struggle for him to get those words out. "That was uncalled for."

"I know I won't be Rosalia's mother." Her quiet reply only made him feel worse. "But that doesn't stop me from caring about her. I may not have been here long, but I understand her better than you think. Tell me, why do you suppose she's so well behaved all the time?"

Her question made Simon squirm. "There's nothing wrong with that, surely? It is Ah-Sam's influence, and I commend her for it. Her people set great store by raising children to be obedient and respectful."

"That may be part of it," Bethan conceded, "but the chief reason is that your daughter hopes she can be good enough to win your love."

"Nonsense!" If she'd thrashed his wounded leg with a bamboo cane, Simon would not have been more desperate to make her stop. "I've had quite enough of this subject for one evening. Can we talk about something else?"

He pointed towards a wall of wooden stakes that surrounded a vast cluster of buildings with shaggy attap roofs. Above those towered a new one of red tiles arranged in a tiered pyramid that looked as if it might have been transplanted from Chinatown.

"This is Kampong Gelam where the Sultan lives with many of his relatives and retainers." He rattled off the information, hoping it might distract her. "*Kampong* is the Malay word for village and the *gelam* is a kind of tree that is plentiful hereabouts. The *orang laut* people use its bark to repair their boats."

Bethan refused to be diverted. "Should I add your daughter to the list of things you refuse to talk about?"

"I don't know what you mean," Simon tried to dismiss her question. "See that new building with the red roof? That is not the sultan's *istana*, as you might suppose. It is a mosque, a place of worship for Muslims."

Once again Bethan ignored his effort to change the subject. "Your injured leg…your late wife…" She ticked off the forbidden topics on her fingers. "How many more are there? Perhaps you should tell me so I'll know to avoid them."

Coming here had been a mistake. Simon turned the gharry around and headed back towards his house. "If

I thought you would have the courtesy to refrain from raising those subjects I prefer not to discuss, I would certainly tell you."

Bethan shook her head. "I don't understand. I know they're not pleasant memories. But you act as if they'll go away if you never talk about them. They won't, you know."

Simon could barely unclench his jaw enough to growl, "I don't wish to discuss *that*, either."

How would she like it if he interrogated her about the man who'd ruined her and how it had come about?

"I don't care if you won't talk about those other things." Bethan heaved an exasperated sigh. "But don't expect me to keep quiet about your daughter. The poor child is afraid that if she steps a toe out of line you'll never love her. You must show her that's not true. And if it *is* true…well, it's just plain wrong, that's all!"

Of course it was wrong. Simon knew that from his own experience. But he hadn't given Rosalia any cause to believe such things…had he?

Haunted by that uncertainty, Simon refused to speak again until they reached the house. When he helped Bethan out of the gharry, the touch of her hand made his heart beat faster, but he stifled the urge to linger in her presence.

"Excuse me." With a curt bow, he turned from her and strode off towards the garden.

"Aren't you coming to dinner?" she called after him.

Simon did not look back. "I seem to have lost my appetite." He marched through the garden and down to the shore.

There he paced and listened to the muted crash of waves on the sand. He hoped the sound would scour his mind of all the maddening thoughts Bethan had stirred up with her intrusive questions and meddlesome opinions. But it did not.

He could not stop thinking about Rosalia and the possibility that what Bethan had said about her might be true.

Was Simon guilty of neglecting his daughter? Bethan asked herself as she ate a solitary dinner. Or had she been too hard on him?

Cook had prepared a fine meal, giving familiar European dishes an exotic twist with local ingredients. Yet tonight none of it tasted quite as good without the added spice of Simon's company.

If she'd stopped badgering him about Rosalia when he asked her to, he might be there now, telling her fascinating stories about the things they'd seen at the Sultan's compound. But she'd been so stubbornly determined to scold him for not paying more attention to his daughter that she could not recall anything he'd tried to show her.

Perhaps she should have shown Simon a little of the patience and understanding that came so naturally to her when dealing with his young daughter. He might have listened to her then. But his scowling defensiveness had provoked her to lash out with her blunt tongue, driving him away. How would she ever get him to heed her advice about Rosalia if she could not keep him within ten feet of her?

His maddening refusal to talk about anything that troubled him reminded Bethan of her mother, with whom she'd had a difficult relationship. *Things are what they are, girl. All the talking in the world won't change them.*

She hadn't been able to make her mother understand she wasn't trying to *change* the past by talking it over. All she'd wanted was a chance to sort out her feelings about it. Hugh was the only one who'd been willing to listen, until he went away to sea. She would give anything to have him with her now, listening to all her problems with Simon Grimshaw and offering brotherly advice.

What would Hugh say about all this? Bethan wondered as she gave up trying to eat and wandered out to the veranda. Might he suggest she try to see Simon's side of things?

It must have been hard for him to lose his wife and find himself responsible for a tiny daughter, all when he and his partners were working day and night to establish their business. Was it any wonder he'd placed Rosalia in the care of an experienced *amah*? Though he might not have showered her with treats and attention, he had done his best to provide her with a safe, comfortable life.

A sudden flash of lightning startled Bethan out of her woolgathering. The loud crack of thunder that followed made her quake. Her first thought was for Rosalia. What if the child awoke frightened by the storm, without Ah-Sam nearby to comfort her?

Bethan hurried towards the nursery. She had almost reached it when a flash of lightning revealed Simon standing in the darkened hallway just outside his daughter's room. He was no longer wearing his coat. His neckcloth was untied and his hair looked windblown.

For an instant Bethan wondered if she'd fallen asleep and dreamed of him, as she had so often since coming to Singapore.

"What are you doing here?" she demanded in a muted gasp.

"This is *my* house." More silver-white lightning flashed outside and in Simon's eyes. "I am not obliged to answer to you for my comings and goings."

"That's not what I meant. It's just that you hardly ever come here when Rosalia is awake. Why are you prowling around her nursery when she's sleeping?"

"I'm not *prowling*!" The rumble of Simon's voice was followed by an echo of thunder. "But since we are on the subject, what are *you* doing here?"

"I came to be with Rosalia in case the storm wakes her." Bethan listened for any sound of the child stirring.

"I doubt it will. She's a deep sleeper. It comes of living so long in our old house by the river, I suppose." With every word, the hostility in his tone faded. "If she could sleep through that racket, it will take more than a few claps of thunder to wake her."

Bethan was surprised he knew that about his daughter.

He expelled a slow, deep breath. "If you must know, I came to sit near her bed while she slept and think about what you said to me earlier."

"And…?" she prompted him after a long, expectant pause.

"I am grateful Rosalia is so well behaved." His voice blended with the haunting patter of rain on the tile roof overhead. "But I cannot imagine where she got the notion I might be angry with her. I've never once raised my voice to her."

"I'm sure you were never purposely unkind." Bethan moved a little closer, so Simon could hear her above the sound of the rain. "But children see the world in their own way. Didn't you have any foolish fancies or secret fears when you were her age?"

She didn't expect Simon to answer, given his stubborn refusal to talk about his past. But she hoped he would think about it at least and begin to understand.

Perhaps it would help if she told him something about *her* life. "I know how Rosalia feels. When I was only a bit older than her, my father left my mother and me. He travelled a lot for his work as an estate surveyor, but that time he never came back. I thought it must be my fault, because I was so full of mischief."

"Abandoned his wife and child?" The harshness of Simon's tone did not offend Bethan, for she heard his outrage on her behalf. "That is infamous!"

All these years later, she still felt compelled to make excuses for her father. "My mother wasn't an easy woman to live with. What hurt me worse than Daddy's going was that he left me behind. I used to dream of running away to find him."

"Is *that* why you were so anxious to get to Singapore?" asked Simon. "Did you think you might find your father here?"

For one mad moment, Bethan considered blurting out the truth, which was so close to Simon's guess. But after what he'd said about criminals and punishment, she couldn't bring herself to tell him. "That had nothing to do with it. A few years after my father left, we got word that he'd died. My mother thought he deserved it for turning his back on us, but I only wished I'd tried harder to go to him. His dying before I could see him one last time felt like a punishment on me."

That was something she'd never told anyone—not even Hugh. What possessed her to confide in a man she'd known barely a fortnight—a man who refused to tell her anything important about himself?

"I understand better than you might think." A sigh

escaped from Simon's lips. "I was seven when my mother died and ten when my father remarried. My stepmother was a neighbour of ours who'd fallen on hard times. I urged Father to assist her and he did, with an offer of marriage. She was very attentive to me until her own children came along. But with each new baby, her manner grew colder. She made an effort to keep on good terms with my elder brother who would inherit the estate. I assume she saw me as a threat to her children though I didn't realise it at the time. I thought it was because…I wasn't good enough."

Bethan could picture him, a quiet child whose grave manner hid a kind heart, too easily bruised. "Was that why you came to the Indies—to prove yourself by making your fortune?"

"Perhaps," Simon answered after a long pause. "Though, at the time, I only wanted to get as far away from my family as I could."

Once again Bethan wondered if she was dreaming. Could this guarded man really be telling her so much about his past and his most private feelings?

Before she could reply, Simon continued, "Perhaps, without meaning to, I've made Rosalia feel that way. I want to make it up to her, but I'm not certain how to go about it."

"You'll manage," Bethan reassured him. "I think you're a man who can do most anything you set your mind to."

"In business, perhaps." He sounded weighed down with regret. "But with people, especially those that matter most to me, I've made a great many mistakes. You get on with Rosalia so naturally. Could you help me get closer to her?"

"Of course!" She groped for Simon's hand and give

it a heartening squeeze. "I think I get on so well with children because I still have a bit of child in me. You sound like someone who was grown up from a young age."

She did not mean to cling to his hand, but her fingers refused to let go. "You need to spend more time with Rosalia. Talk to her. Listen to her the way you listened to me just now. Try to smile more…or at least scowl less."

Rather than taking offence at her bluntness, Simon gave a husky chuckle. "I will *try.* I find it easier to smile when you're around."

"That's the nicest thing any man's ever said to me."

The rain had stopped by now and the water falling from the eaves had slowed to a steady trickle. The quiet made Bethan more conscious than ever of Simon's nearness and the sensations he provoked in her, even when he wasn't trying.

Would he kiss her now? Her lips quivered with anticipation.

Instead he raised her hand and pressed his lips to it. "Thank you for your advice."

Before she could recover her voice, he was gone, leaving her aching with longing. But unlike the other times Simon had roused her desire, this time he had also stirred a sweet, brooding tenderness that she could not decide whether to welcome…or resist.

Chapter Seven

Last night would have been a perfect opportunity to further his slow seduction of Bethan. Simon pondered that thought at work the next day and tried to figure out what had made him hesitate.

He tried to persuade himself he'd fled because he did not want to take the chance of losing control and frightening her again. But that was only part of it. What he'd really been running from was the alarming urge to pour out his whole heart to her. Not only did Bethan threaten his self-control, she also posed a danger to his fiercely guarded privacy.

Last night, she'd somehow managed to open one of the heavily locked doors to his past and compel him to reveal things he'd never confided in anyone. The darkness and the sound of the rain had cast a curtain around him, making him feel as if he were alone with his memories. Yet Bethan's presence had been so close and vital. By sharing a glimpse into her painful past, she had opened a secret window into his.

He must not let it happen again.

He would avoid her for a few days, throwing himself into his work. When he felt it was safe to resume contact with Bethan, he would act as if his midnight confession had never taken place.

"Begging your pardon, Mr Grimshaw." The voice of his new clerk, Wilson Hall, intruded on Simon's thoughts, making him start. "You said you wanted to keep an eye on the lads while they load that cargo of sugar."

"I did?" Simon could not recall the last time he'd been so thoroughly distracted *from* business matters. Work was supposed to make him forget the troubles in his private life, not the other way around. "I mean…of course I did. Some goods that fall in the river can be fished out again with no harm done. Drop a load of sugar overboard and it's a different story."

He bustled off to the quayside, hoping to leave all thoughts of Bethan behind him. But they pursued him with the same relentless purpose she had shown chasing that thief into Chinatown. Her voice lurked in the back of his mind, ready to skewer his conscience with a few blunt truths if he let his guard down for even an instant.

She pointed out that no harm had come from talking about his past. Apart from the fear of where it might lead, he actually felt a little better after airing those long-festering wounds from his youth. It also made him think differently about his relationship with Rosalia—or lack of one.

He could see now that just because the child was as well behaved as he'd been at her age did not mean she was happy. Providing her with the finest material goods was not enough. She also needed someone to foster the well-being of her vulnerable young heart.

The former came easily to Simon. The latter did not. He had no idea where to begin and he was haunted by the fear that he would fail her. In his uncertainty he'd reached out to Bethan, who had generously agreed to help him.

Now he began to wonder if that was such a good idea. Since arriving in Singapore, she had assumed roles in his life that he'd never intended. She was acting nothing like a mistress and far too much like a wife.

"Are you certain Papa won't mind?" Rosalia clasped Bethan's hand tightly as they drove towards the Vindicara *godown*.

"Don't fret." Bethan strove to put aside her own misgivings. Simon had meant what he said last night, hadn't he, about wanting to get closer to his daughter? "It'll be fine, you'll see."

When they reached the office, she was delighted to find Wilson Hall sitting at a desk writing figures in a large book.

"Bethan!" he cried, laying aside his work. "It's good to see you. You look well. Singapore must agree with you."

"And you." She beamed with approval at the change in Wilson. During the past fortnight the awkward, bashful lad seemed to have found new confidence. "You look quite the man of business."

Wilson's lips spread in a sheepish grin. "I was so clumsy in the warehouse I was afraid Mr Grimshaw would sack me. But he let me try clerking instead and I like it. I've a lot to learn since I never had much schooling, but Mr Grimshaw says I've got a clever head for figures. The other lads like it here, too. Heaven this place is after the mines—so warm and sunny with plenty to eat.

We've picked up a few words of some other languages. Mr Grimshaw hired a man to teach us—the *munshi* they call him. He's the cleverest man I ever met. He thinks very highly of Mr Grimshaw."

Two weeks ago, Bethan might have been surprised to hear such nice things about Simon. But since then she'd glimpsed the generous heart he hid beneath his grave, sometimes gruff exterior. If he let down his guard a little, she felt certain he could be a good father. "I'm so glad to hear you're all getting on so well, Wilson. Is Mr Grimshaw around? Rosalia and I have come to pay him a visit if he's not too busy."

"He's out on the quay. Shall I fetch him for you?"

"If you wouldn't mind." Bethan glanced down at Rosalia, who still looked anxious about being there.

A few moments later, Simon strode in, his limp barely noticeable. "Good day, ladies. This is a surprise. To what do I owe the honour of your visit?"

The child tightened her grip on Bethan's hand and hung back as if she did not quite trust her father's cheerful greeting.

"Rosalia misses watching the boats on the river." Bethan cast Simon an encouraging look. "If you don't mind, we'll sit out on the veranda of your old house for a while."

The child summoned up her courage to add, "May we, Papa?"

"That sounds like a good idea." Without any prompting from Bethan, Simon sank into a crouch, though he gave a passing wince of pain. "There are a great many boats on the river today. If there were any more, I doubt they'd have room to move."

"Perhaps you could join us for a little while," Bethan suggested, "if you're not too busy."

For a moment Simon looked as if he might refuse, but then he rose and held out his hand to his daughter. "I could do with a little break from work. Ralph and the others seem to have grasped the importance of being careful when they load sugar."

Bethan caught Rosalia's eye, smiled and nodded. With that encouragement, the child took her father's hand. The three of them strolled next door to the simple timber house with its palm-thatched roof. A large open veranda at the front commanded a fine view of the busy Singapore River. Forgetting her bashfulness for a moment, Rosalia ran to the railing.

Leaning towards Simon, Bethan whispered, "That wasn't so hard, was it?"

He shook his head ruefully. "Not as hard as accepting what a poor excuse for a father I've been."

It could not be easy for such a proud, successful man to admit his mistakes. The fact that Simon had owned up and was willing to try to change raised him even higher in her eyes. "You did the best you could at the time, more than most fathers might have done. But with your wife gone, Rosalia needs you to be both father and mother to her."

Simon's jaw clenched at her mention of his late wife. It reminded Bethan of what he'd said about her not being able to replace Rosalia's mother. Had he been trying to warn her that she could never hope to take the place of his late wife in *his* heart, either? If so, it was another good reason to resist the feelings beginning to grow in her heart before they put down deep roots.

Leaving Simon's side, she joined Rosalia and tried to concentrate on what the child was saying. "All these boats that fetch and carry cargo from the big ships are called *tongkangs*. The lightermen are Chuliahs. Mahmud told me they pray to Allah like the Malays and Arabs do. When I was a little girl, I used to wave to them from the veranda. They would wave back and call out to me."

"Really?" Bethan tried not to smile at the child's mention of being a *little girl*, as if that was long in the past. "What did they say?"

"I didn't understand their language." Rosalia waved at one of the boats that passed directly in front of the house. "But I could tell from their voices it was something nice—a blessing, maybe."

As she watched the boats navigate the crowded river, Bethan wondered if any of those lightermen might have had contact with her brother when his ship was in Singapore. If they had, she wouldn't know how to ask them. And she didn't want to risk another incident like the one on her first day in Singapore.

Simon stepped up to stand beside his daughter. "Bethan tells me you miss this noisy old place—is that true?"

"Sometimes," Rosalia admitted reluctantly. "There were lots of things to see and do here. The market is close. I remember the lantern parade on the south quay."

"This place has come in handy to house my new workers from England," said Simon, "but you may visit here to watch the boats whenever you like."

"I can?"

He nodded. "I know we haven't seen each other as much since we moved to the new house. I think it's time we corrected that, don't you?"

"Yes, Papa." Rosalia sounded bewildered by this sudden change in her father.

Bethan hoped his daughter's hesitation would not discourage Simon. This problem had been a long time in the making. It would not be solved in a single stroke.

But Simon had not made his fortune by giving up easily. "We could go on some outings if you'd like. Is there anything special you'd like to do?"

Rosalia thought for a moment. "I've hardly seen Agnes and Alfie since they moved out to their new house. Could we go visit them?"

"I'll see what can be arranged," said Simon. "Anything else?"

Rosalia pointed toward the boats on the river. "I've always wanted to go for a ride in a *tongkang*. Could we do that?"

Bethan expected Simon to commend his daughter for such a good idea.

Instead, he looked as if the child had suggested going on a tiger hunt…without any guns. "Please excuse me. I just remembered an urgent business matter I must deal with straight away. Tell Ah-Ming I may not be home for dinner."

"Of course." Bethan tried to sound as if she believed him. "We'll stay and watch the boats for a while longer, if that's all right."

Wrapping an arm around the child's shoulders, she shot a puzzled look at Simon over Rosalia's head. He'd been doing so well. What on earth had got into him?

"Quite all right." He continued to back away. "I'm sorry to rush off like this. Enjoy your boat watching."

"Goodbye, Papa." Rosalia sounded subdued.

It was clear she sensed something wrong. Bethan was afraid the child might think it was her fault.

Simon did not help matters. Twisting his lips into a poor mockery of a smile, he waved his daughter farewell and strode away as if something dangerous was chasing him.

Bethan wished she could follow him and demand to know what was wrong, but she could not leave Rosalia. She would have to wait up for Simon tonight, and get to the bottom of this.

Simon returned to his office at a brisk march, trying to outrun the troubling memories that pursued him.

He should have known spending time with Rosalia was bound to rouse them. The child looked so much like her mother, after all. When she'd looked up at him with Carlotta's dark eyes and asked to ride in a *tongkang*, the best Simon could do was invent a transparent excuse to get away before he said something worse.

Who was he trying to fool? He'd known he was not cut out to be a doting father. He should have concentrated on the things he could do—protecting and providing for Rosalia—while leaving to others better able the challenging task of showing affection. Like Bethan. For her it seemed as easy as breathing. He envied her that natural ability.

Upon reaching the *godown*, he ignored a curious look from his clerk and demanded to see the accounts ledger. For the next several hours, he poured over the neat columns of figures, drawing comfort from their orderliness and simplicity, so at odds with his life. They also provided reassuring proof he could succeed at the one thing that mattered most in this town.

While he examined the accounts, Simon pulled out his flask and took several swigs of potent arrack. Though his leg was not troubling him much today, he had other wounds that cried out for relief.

* * *

It was after midnight when he returned home, expecting everyone else to be in bed. To his surprise, he found a lamp still burning in the sitting room and Bethan slumped in one corner of the sofa, fast asleep. No doubt she'd intended to ambush him and take him to task for his sudden, clumsy departure that afternoon.

Simon was strongly tempted to avoid that confrontation by dousing the light and leaving her to sleep. But he knew that would only delay the inevitable. Bethan Conway was one of the most exasperatingly tenacious people he'd ever met. If she were a man, that quality would be a great asset in business.

But she was not a man. No, indeed.

Gingerly, so as not to wake her, Simon sank on to the sofa and made the most of this unexpected opportunity to sate his eyes upon her fresh, vivid beauty. His gaze ranged over her untidy mane of auburn hair to her full pink lips, which fairly begged to be kissed. It lingered appreciatively on her lovely shoulders. There was something about that part of a woman's body that roused him as much as fine breasts or a shapely bottom.

Desire gnawed at him, eroding his virtuous resolve to keep his hands off her. Perhaps in her arms, at her breast and between her dewy thighs, he might find a more lasting forgetfulness than he had in the pages of a business ledger or at the bottom of a flask. How many more days must he wait to make her his?

"Bethan," he whispered. When she did not respond, he reached over and tapped her on the knee. "It's late. You should go to bed."

What would he do if he could not wake her—scoop her up and carry her to her room? In his present state, he did not trust himself to leave her on the bed and walk away.

Bethan settled the matter by stirring and turning towards him. Somehow, her movement shifted Simon's hand from her knee to her thigh. Through her light muslin gown, he could feel the sultry heat of her body. It ignited an answering fever in his. He pulled back his hand abruptly, for fear they might both get burned.

His sudden movement brought her more fully awake.

"Simon?" She stretched, pulling the fabric of her gown taut against her body in several intriguing places. "What time is it? Why did you rush away this afternoon?"

"It's too late to go into all that now. We can discuss it another time."

"When?" She yawned and rubbed her eyes. "It isn't something I want to talk about in front of Rosalia, even if you do come home earlier some other day. She was upset after you left, though she tried not to show it. She's a clever little thing and I know she didn't believe your excuse about forgotten business any more than I did. She thinks she must have done something to make you angry and I couldn't comfort her because I wasn't certain myself. Now I'm not going to bed until you give me an answer I can understand and explain to her."

"I told you I would *try* to be a more attentive father." Simon moved back to the other end of the sofa. What would Bethan do if he got up and left without an explanation? Would she follow him to his bedroom, trusting in his honour to keep her safe? "And I did try. But I fell short, as I knew I would. I feared nothing about children and I've never been a demonstrative person."

"But you were doing so well. Then all of a sudden

you started acting like a horse who'd been spooked. *Was* it something Rosalia did? Whatever it was, she didn't mean to. Is there something wrong with those children she wants to visit?"

"It's nothing to do with them!" Simon snapped. He was tired and aroused and annoyed with himself and Bethan. He knew she would keep on asking and guessing until she pried the truth out of him.

"What *does* it have to do with, then?" she demanded, just as he'd feared she would. "Something else on that list of things you refuse to talk about, I suppose. Your injured leg? Your wife?"

Her question made Simon wince.

Bethan seized upon that slip. "But Rosalia never said a word about her mother."

When he jammed his lips together in a stubborn barricade, her angry look muted into one of tender sympathy. "I understand if you grieve for your wife still. Young as she is, I know Rosalia would understand too, if you'd just tell her."

"I don't grieve for Carlotta—I never did!" The words burst out of Simon, driven by his desperation to keep Bethan from making any more false claims about his marriage. The things she was saying were so far removed from the truth they were almost obscene. "She drowned one night, while trying to board a *tongkang*. She slipped, struck her head and fell into the river. By the time they got her out, it was too late."

He bit down hard on his tongue to keep from saying more. He prayed Bethan would not ask why Carlotta had been trying to board a boat at night and where he'd been at the time.

Fortunately, her sympathy overcame her curiosity. "I'm sorry, Simon. It must have brought back such awful memories when Rosalia asked to go for a ride in one of those boats. But she had no idea. You must tell her. She needs to know why you acted the way you did so she won't think she was to blame."

Simon sprang to his feet. "You tell her, then, if you think she needs to know."

"It would be better coming from you," Bethan insisted gently. "You might tell her more about her mother, too—happy things. Rosalia doesn't have any recollection of her at all. If you think she can't miss what she doesn't remember, you're wrong. The poor child feels as if a part of her is missing."

Indignant rage blazed through Simon that Bethan dared to suggest such a thing. "I know you mean well, but what you are asking is impossible. Believe me when I tell you, the less Rosalia knows about her mother, the better!"

"Now will you tell me?" Rosalia settled on her bed the next evening, waiting for Bethan to arrange the tent of netting over it for the night. "You promised you would."

"So I did." Ignoring the netting for a moment, Bethan sat on the edge of the bed beside her small charge and considered how best to begin.

Her usual blunt speaking simply wouldn't do to broach this painful subject with such a sensitive child. She would have to choose her words carefully. Rosalia's dark, pleading gaze seemed to draw forth the difficult answers she craved.

"It's like this." Bethan took the child's delicate hand in hers. "Sometimes when things happen that make people very sad, they try as hard as they can not to think about them, so they won't be sad all the time."

Rosalia's fine dark brows knit in a looked of puzzled concentration. Clearly she was trying to work out what Bethan meant and how it applied to the recent incident with her father.

She needed an example she could understand, though Bethan feared it might upset her. "I know you must still miss Ah-Sam, though you don't talk about her much."

After a moment's reflection, Rosalia gave a solemn nod.

"If I started talking about all the things you used to do with her," Bethan continued, "things that *made* you think about her when you didn't want to, you might run away from me so you wouldn't have to hear what I was saying."

The child toyed with the end of her braid.

Bethan rubbed the pad of her thumb over Rosalia's knuckles. "I know this might be hard for you to believe, but grownups can feel that way, too. Even big, brave men like your papa. The other day, when you said how much you'd like to go for a ride on one of those river boats, it reminded him of something very sad that he didn't want to think about. That's why he went away so suddenly."

"Was he angry?" The child sat bolt upright, very agitated. "I didn't mean to make him sad."

"Of course he's not angry, *cariad*!" Bethan gathered the little girl into a reassuring embrace. "He knows you didn't mean to."

"What was the sad thing I made him remember?"

That was the question Bethan had been dreading.

"I'm afraid it will make you sad, too." She eased Rosalia back on to her pillow. "But it might help you understand some of the things your papa says and does. Are you sure you want to know?"

Her features tensed in an anxious look, the child whispered, "Yes, please."

"Very well, then." Bethan stroked her dark, silky hair. "You know your mama went to heaven—that's another way of saying she died. Some people die because they get very old or very sick. Others have accidents and get hurt so badly that they can't live. If a person stays under water too long, they can die by drowning. That's what happened to your mama."

Rosalia stared up at her with eyes as big as saucers, taking in every word. Fortunately she didn't seem too upset, perhaps because her mother was a vague, shadowy figure of whom she had no recollection.

As gently as she could, Bethan repeated what Simon had told her of his wife's drowning. "So you see, when you asked to go for a ride on one of those same boats, it reminded your papa of what happened to her. And perhaps it made him worry about you."

Rosalia looked doubtful.

Bethan felt drawn to this sensitive little girl far more powerfully than to any of the cheerful, boisterous youngsters she'd cared for in Newcastle. She understood the doubts and sorrows that beset Rosalia's small heart. And she could not help wanting to heal them, even though it might be beyond her power. "People have different ways of showing how they feel, you know."

"They do?"

Bethan nodded. "Some people find it hard to show their feelings at all. That doesn't mean they don't get just as sad or happy or loving as other people who make a bigger show." In an encouraging tone, she added. "Do you know anybody like that?"

Slowly one corner of Rosalia's mouth arched upwards.

"I know somebody like that, too," said Bethan. "Your papa. He has a hard time showing his feelings because he's used to keeping them to himself, just like you. But the reason he built this fine house and works so hard to make his fortune is so you can be well cared for and have everything you need. It's his way of showing how much he loves you."

What had made her put off this talk until Rosalia's bedtime? Bethan chided herself. How could she expect the poor child to go to sleep after all she'd heard?

"Would you like me to I sing you a lullaby?" She stretched out beside Rosalia and pulled the bed netting over them both. "I hope you don't mind if the words are in Welsh. It's a song my daddy used to sing to me."

There'd been a time she couldn't hear this song without weeping, but lately it brought her a kind of wistful comfort. Only in those familiar words could she properly recall the sound of her father's voice.

Softly she began to sing, all the while continuing to stroke the child's hair. That repetitive movement and the familiar melody lulled her, letting her thoughts drift in the direction from which she'd struggled to divert them since her conversation with Simon.

What had his wife done to make him want to forget all about her? Whatever it was, she must have hurt him very badly. Was that what made Ah-Sam work so hard to bring up Rosalia as a well-behaved child who would not dishonour her father? And could it be part of the reason Simon had trouble getting close to the little girl who bore such a strong likeness to her mother?

Rosalia seemed peacefully unaware of the turbulent thoughts racing through Bethan's mind as she sang the strange soothing words of the lullaby. Or perhaps it was the closeness and a woman's caring touch that relaxed her. In a very short time, her eyelids drooped and her breath came in slow, easy waves.

Bethan sang softer and softer until her voice died away altogether. Then, grazing her lips across Rosalia's brow, she whispered, "I believe your papa needs you every bit as much as you need him, *cariad*. I wish for both your sakes I could make him see that."

With all her heart, she longed to help heal this small family in a way she had been powerless to heal her own.

Chapter Eight

Standing in the hallway outside the nursery, Simon listened as Bethan spoke to Rosalia. A powerful sense of gratitude welled up inside him. If his stepmother had been half as understanding and open-hearted as Bethan Conway, his life might have taken a very different path. Catching himself, Simon roughly dismissed that thought.

He was *not* dissatisfied with his current situation, after all.

He'd come looking for Bethan, to apologise for the way he'd spoken to her last night and for yesterday's blunder with Rosalia. He owed the child an explanation too, though he wasn't certain he'd be able to express his feelings in a way she could understand. If he caught a glimpse of reproach in her dark eyes, so like her mother's, Simon feared he might say or do something to make matters worse.

Overhearing the simple, wise words Bethan used to enlighten and comfort Rosalia, he could not help but admire her understanding of things that had always puzzled him. How was it that after such a short acquaintance, she seemed to understand him so well, yet did not hold his mistakes against him? His prickly sense of privacy felt threatened by her perceptive insights into his character and feelings, but the neglected child that hid in the deepest recesses of his heart responded to her compassion.

Perhaps she understood him so well because they were more alike than he would ever have imagined. They had both been abandoned in various ways as children, growing up in an atmosphere of disapproval. Later they had known the bitterness of betrayal.

As she began to sing, the lilt of her voice reminded him of the sirens in Homer's *Odyssey*. Caution warned Simon he should not linger there and risk an encounter with Bethan when his feelings were so confused and dangerously close to the surface. But the mysterious Welsh lyrics of her song seemed to bind him in some kind of enchantment.

He was still standing in the darkened hallway a few minutes later when she emerged from the nursery. At the unexpected sight of him, Bethan jumped back with a startled squeak.

"Forgive me," Simon whispered, hoping he had not roused disturbing memories from *her* past. "This time, I must admit, I *am* prowling."

"Are you now?" she asked in a breathless voice. "Why is that, may I ask?"

"I want to apologise for the way I spoke to you last night." He beckoned her away from nursery door. "I'm not angry with you any more than I am with Rosalia. It was true what you told her just now…about not wanting to be reminded of painful events from my past."

He wished he'd never mentioned Carlotta last night.

His rancorous outburst was just the sort of thing to whet Bethan's curiosity and make her hound him with questions he did not want to answer. "Do you think Rosalia can forgive me for the way I acted yesterday? Or have I ruined any chance of becoming the kind of father she needs?"

"Children are willing to give many more chances than you think." Bethan reached for his hand. "If my father had ever tried to get in touch with me after he left, I wouldn't have turned him away. Even after all the hurt he caused me, I still wore that locket with his picture in it. I'd give anything to have it back again."

The locket that had been stolen her first day in Singapore—Simon had almost forgotten it. At the time, he'd doubted her story. Now he regretted his suspicions and wished he'd tried to retrieve it for her. Perhaps, like his efforts to get closer to Rosalia, it was not too late.

He could speak to one of the Chinese merchants about offering a reward for its return. That was the least he could do to atone for misjudging Bethan. He would not mention it to her, though, for he did not want to raise false hopes in case his efforts failed.

Simon sniffed the air. "Dinner smells good and almost ready. Perhaps while we dine you can give me some suggestions about how I might make up to Rosalia for yesterday. I have been working on my smile, though I fear it looks rather gruesome when I try to force it."

His wry quip made Bethan laugh and that made Simon smile without any effort at all.

To his relief, she did not ask him a single question about his late wife that whole evening. Instead they talked about Rosalia—little things Bethan had noticed about the child, suggestions for things Simon might do to bring them closer. "You need to do things *with* her, things that you can talk about together without feeling forced and tongue-tied."

Simon gave a rueful nod. "That is exactly how I feel when I try to talk to her."

"I meant Rosalia." Bethan grinned. "But I don't wonder you both feel the same way about it. Though she doesn't look like you at all, everything else about her reminds me of you. The way her smile comes and goes so quickly, but lights up the whole room for that instant. The way she tries so hard to keep her troubles to herself. The way she wants so badly to do what's right."

Her words touched Simon more than he could begin to tell her, soothing poisonous doubts about his daughter's paternity that had long haunted him. Gradually, he became aware of a sensation in his chest that was unfamiliar, but not unpleasant. It reminded him of half-forgotten details from his boyhood in Lancashire, like the prickling of icy toes, as they warmed in front of a cheerfully crackling fire. Or frostbitten fingers wrapped around a steaming mug of mulled cider. Could it be that his heart was beginning to thaw?

He wasn't certain that was something he wanted to risk, now especially. There were benefits to remaining frozen. Frozen flesh was numb to pain. Frozen ground was hard to break, yielding only with great difficulty to the prying picks and shovels that sought to unearth the secrets buried deep within it.

In spite of all that, Simon found himself tempted to escape the perpetual winter that had held his heart in its protective, stifling grip for so long.

Getting to know Simon's daughter was helping her understand *him* a great deal better, Bethan realised as they talked about Rosalia over dinner. It was also making the prospect of marrying him much more appealing.

The mention of her stolen locket made her realise how little progress she'd made towards finding out what had become of her brother. Such a bewildering number of ships had been through Singapore in the past three years, she wondered if anyone here would remember the Dauntless, let alone one young crewman. She'd been a fool to think she could accomplish such a task. Almost as daft was her belief that finding Hugh would somehow restore her family. The chance to do that had been lost long ago. Had she persuaded herself it was possible so she would not feel completely abandoned in a big, uncaring world?

Whatever the reason, she was not sorry she'd tried. The search for her brother had led to Simon and Rosalia—a family who needed her to make it whole. With them, she had a chance to create a new family and to gain the kind of comfort and security she'd never known.

"Thank you for telling Rosalia about her mother," said Simon as they headed toward their bedrooms at the end of the evening. "If my daughter does give me another chance, I shall have you to thank for it."

It occurred to Bethan that this was the first time she'd heard him refer to Rosalia as *his daughter*. Until now he'd always called her by name or said *the child*. This had to be a good sign for the future.

"I am not accustomed to being understood so well." His murmured words sounded like the sweetest endearment. "It is rather disturbing…yet strangely comforting, too. You've come to know me better in a few short weeks than anyone else has in years and years."

Some people might think it strange to call being

understood *disturbing*, but Bethan thought she knew what Simon meant. Understanding might mean prying into all those forbidden subjects he did not want to be reminded of. She had bitten her tongue more than once this evening to keep from mentioning Rosalia's mother, though her curiosity was like a bedevilling itch. In a way she was relieved to discover Simon had not adored his late wife so much that he had no room in his heart for a new love.

She smiled up at him. "That's the second nicest thing anyone's ever said to me. You're not an easy man to understand, Simon—there are so many different sides to you. Just when I think I've seen them all, another one surprises me. Parts of you I understand because they're a lot like me. But in other ways, we're as different as can be."

"That's not such a bad thing, is it?" He leaned towards her. "Some likenesses as a basis for compatibility, some differences to add a little zest."

Bethan hoped he wouldn't rush away without kissing her, as he had on the night of the storm. Her body responded to his nearness in a way that had become familiar in the past two weeks. Her pulse speeded up and her breathing with it. A mysterious heat hummed through her flesh while her skin became sensitive to the slightest touch. Now that she knew Simon better, Bethan did not fight to subdue those sensations. She was curious to discover where they might lead.

If only she had more experience with men, she might know how to send him a signal that she wanted to feel his arms around her again and taste his kisses. The best she could manage was to gaze up at him through the fringe of her lashes and whisper, "You make it sound very nice, indeed."

Then she held herself as still as possible, not wanting to make any move that might discourage his attentions.

It worked.

He bent a little lower, tilted his head and slowly approached until his lips came to rest against hers. Their touch was so mild, Bethan wondered if he was as worried as she about making the wrong move. She savoured the smooth, restrained warmth of his kiss, trying to be content with it when part of her was greedy for more.

Her patience was soon rewarded when Simon raised his hands to caress her shoulders. Many times in the past fortnight she'd caught herself admiring his large, powerful hands. Now the deft strength of his touch encouraged her to part her lips and invite his kiss deeper. The hot, slick caress of his tongue carried the mellow sweetness of coconut, from the little cakes they'd eaten to finish off their dinner. It fed a different kind of hunger that had gnawed at her for days.

Dizzy with desire, she raised her hands to grip *his* shoulders. Their broad strength helped steady her. Then one of his hands strayed upwards to entangle itself in her hair. The other skimmed down to fondle her breast. His thumb rubbed over the nipple, making it harden and push out against her bodice. Every stroke sent ripples of delight lapping through her. A soft purr of pleasure rolled in the back of her throat as she clasped Simon around the neck and melted against him.

Then suddenly he wrenched his lips away from hers and pushed her away. "Forgive me, Bethan! I promised I would control myself and not do anything to frighten you or bring back distressing memories."

Frighten her? What sort of timid mouse did he think she was to be frightened of a kiss? And what *distressing memories* was he talking about? Had the heat of passion addled his wits?

Before she could master her voice to ask, he continued, "I want you so much I got carried away. But I swear I will never press my attentions upon you against your will. I only want to bring you pleasure. Your previous experience may have made you doubt that is possible. But with the right man, I assure you it is."

Her previous experience? Could this be what he'd meant by those baffling words after their kiss on Government Hill, when she'd thought he was talking about her brother?

"It's all right, Simon. You didn't frighten me. I like the way you kiss." She gave a nervous trill of laughter, hoping he wouldn't think her next suggestion too forward. "In fact, I wouldn't mind going on from where we just left off."

In the long, uneasy silence that followed, she wondered if Simon disapproved of her brazen offer?

"I cannot deny I am sorely tempted." A shudder ran through him. "But I do not trust myself at the moment. I will wait until you are prepared to take that *big step*."

With a sudden movement, he thrust his bedroom door open and marched over the threshold. "Goodnight. Sleep well."

Bethan had no time to protest before his door swung shut, leaving her out alone in the hallway. After a few moments waiting in the hope that he might change his mind, she gave up and went to bed. Puzzled and consumed with yearning, she doubted she would sleep at all that night, let alone *well*.

His barely controlled ardour had not frightened Bethan. Simon considered that hopeful notion the next day as he returned home early. She'd claimed to like it and what he could recall of her response led him to believe her. Or was it only his longing for it to be true that persuaded him?

No, it was more than that. She'd invited him to keep on, after all, even when he'd made it clear that his self-control was tenuous at best. Did she know him well enough to sense he was a far more honourable man than the one who'd taken her innocence by force? Did she trust that no matter how deep the powerful current of passion carried him he would not let it sweep them into dangerous waters? If that was the case, she trusted him far more than he trusted himself.

Her lack of fear boded well for the future, though. It gave him hope that she would soon be ready to become his mistress.

To prepare for that, he'd spent part of the day trying to find a suitable woman to help her care for Rosalia. He'd also called on one of the Chinese merchants he knew well and asked the man's help to recover Bethan's stolen locket. They agreed that a reward should be offered and no charges brought against whoever turned in the stolen property. Though that chafed against Simon's rigorous sense of justice, he was prepared to make allowances for Bethan's sake.

Looking back over his day, Simon realised he had spent very little time attending to business matters. Yet trade at Vindicara had gone on as usual with no catastrophes. That encouraged him to head home early, hoping he might spend some time with Rosalia.

When he arrived home, Simon peeked into the nursery, only to find it empty. His disappointment eased when he heard the sweet harmony of feminine laughter rising from the garden. A moment later, he stole up behind Bethan and Rosalia, eager to share in their cheerful company without casting a shadow upon it.

They knelt in the shade of a laurelwood tree, digging with small spades in a circle of freshly turned earth around the base of the trunk.

Rosalia was chattering away with more animation than Simon had ever heard in her voice. "You'll like Chinese New Year, Bethan! Cook makes all sorts of special treats and there are parades and fireworks."

With a rush of sweet anticipation, Simon pictured the three of them watching from Government Hill next winter as sparkling explosions lit up the night sky.

"Look at you two," he called out. "Training to become *kebun*, are you?"

Rosalia jumped up, coming to attention like a miniature *sepoy* soldier. "Do you mind us planting the flowers, Papa? Bethan said it would be all right."

"Of course I don't mind." He glanced past the anxious child to Bethan, silently seeking some cue from her about how to reassure his daughter.

Her encouraging smile told him he'd made a good start.

Simon sank into a crouch so he would not tower over the child and intimidate her. "When I was your age, I wanted to be a gardener when I grew up."

Rosalia's dark eyes widened, as if she had trouble believing he'd ever been a small boy.

Behind the child, Bethan gave a nod of approval. He recalled the advice she'd given him the other night about finding subjects of mutual interest to talk about with his daughter. At the time he'd doubted they had any common interests. He was pleased to discover otherwise.

"What sort of flowers are you planting?" he asked.

"Kenekir." Rosalia seemed uncertain what to make of

her father's sudden interest in her doings. "Samad says they're easy to grow and they smell pretty."

Simon glanced toward the seedlings. "Excellent qualities in a garden flower. It's been quite a few years since I wielded a spade back in Lancashire, but I'd be happy to help, if you'll permit me."

"I say the more the merrier." Bethan slapped the dirt off her hands. "What do you think, Rosalia? Could we use an extra helper?"

The child replied with a nod that was not particularly eager, but not reluctant either. "Where is Lancashire, Papa?"

The question took Simon by surprise. Did his own daughter not even know where he came from? "It's in England, where I was born. Once we've finished here, I will dig out my atlas and show you where it is."

They spent a pleasant hour planting the seedlings while they talked about gardening and his childhood in the Ribble Valley. Afterward, they looked at maps, tracing the long sea route from England to Singapore with their fingers.

When he ventured to suggest that Rosalia might stay up a little later so she could join them for dinner, it was hard to tell who seemed more pleased—his daughter or Bethan. After a pleasant meal, he helped put Rosalia to bed. Then he and Bethan wandered back out into the garden.

It was an altogether different place at night. The rising moon bathed all the tropical greenery with a magical, silvery glow like one Simon had glimpsed in Bethan's eyes. The lush aroma of jasmine perfumed the sultry air. As silence fell between them and the warm, tropical darkness wrapped around them, Simon was more intensely conscious of her nearness. Her fresh, wholesome scent reminded him of a field of clover in a Lancashire meadow on a sunny June morning. It took him back to a time when his life had been so much simpler and sweeter, before he'd encountered things like rejection, cruelty and betrayal.

"Today went better than I expected with Rosalia," he said. "Far better than I had any right to hope. I know I still have my work cut out for me to become the kind of father she deserves, but I believe I've made a start. And I owe it all to you."

Bethan shook her head. "You give me too much credit. You heeded my warning and made the effort. Rosalia gave you the chance. All I did was give you both a little nudge toward each other."

"A *little nudge*?" asked Simon.

"Perhaps more like a great, rough push," Bethan admitted.

They both chuckled over that. He liked the way his laughter harmonised with hers.

"When you first arrived in Singapore," Simon mused, "I wondered what had possessed Hadrian Northmore to send you here. But more and more, I see what a shrewd judge of character he is."

Bethan stooped to pick a flower from a low shrub. "I recall him saying he thought I would suit you very well." One by one, she pulled off the petals, scattering them over the grass. "I wasn't so sure about that when we first met, but I'm beginning to think he was right."

That certainly sounded encouraging. Simon plucked a fragrant jasmine flower and tucked it into her hair. "In some ways the time since you arrived in Singapore has flown by. In others, it feels as though you've been here much longer."

His hand hovered near her cheek, reluctant to pull away.

Bethan looked up at him with a breathtaking glimmer of invitation in her eyes. Or was it only the bewitching reflection of moonlight? "It feels that way to me, as well."

"You asked for a month," he reminded her, his fingertips whispering down her cheek to rest beneath her chin, "to get used to this place and to me. I have tried to be patient, but I must confess I look forward to the day when a pleasant evening like this will not have to end with us in separate beds."

What would she say to that? Would she think he was putting pressure on her and take fright?

Bethan's gaze did not flinch. "Now that you mention it, I've been thinking a month is quite a long time. We still have a way to go before we know each other well. But I think we've made a good start. I think I'm ready to do what I came here for."

Simon's jaw dropped. "You mean...*now*?"

The growing desire he had struggled keep on a tight leash threatened to burst its bonds. But there was more to his delighted surprise than just the prospect of physical release. Though their acquaintance so far had held its share of difficult moments, Bethan had taken his measure and not found him wanting.

His surprise brought a flustered grin to her lips. "Not right this moment, of course. But as soon as you'd like to...if you still want me."

"If I—?" Simon swept her into his arms. "Good Lord, woman, have I not made it clear I want you more than ever?"

Spurred out of his usual restraint, he kissed her deeply and eagerly, his passion tempered with unexpected tenderness. Bethan responded with innocent ardour, as if she had no reason to fear betrayal or mistreatment at the hands of a man who desired her. Slipping her arms around his neck, she pressed her slender body against his, begging for the attentions he could hardly wait to lavish upon her.

Simon burned with the wild yearning of a young man for the first girl who'd caught his fancy. He wanted to touch every part of her and discover the sensations his fingertips could provoke in her. He longed to ignite a sizzling excitement in her to match his.

They kissed and caressed in the moonlit garden, becoming ever more daring, until at last Simon whispered. "Unless you want me to lose control altogether, I think we'd better continue this in bed."

Chapter Nine

In bed? Before they were married?

In spite of the delicious, new sensations rippling through her, Bethan could not forget the stern warning she'd been given on her first day in service: *A man and woman have no business being in bed together if they are not wed. Any maidservant caught entertaining a man in her bed will be dismissed at once without character.*

At the time she wondered what sort of *entertaining* might be done in bed, but had been reluctant to expose her ignorance by asking. Lately, Simon's thrilling attentions had given her a much better idea. They'd also made her eager to learn more.

She thought about asking him if they should wait until after the wedding but decided against it. She did not want to spoil this wonderful evening by seeming to question his propriety or honour. Simon had patiently endured being kept waiting this long. Though it was clear the delay challenged his self-control, he'd behaved like a gentleman, making no demands upon her beyond a few kisses. And those she had willingly given. It wouldn't be fair to put him off any longer.

As his hot breath gusted against her cheek and his powerful arms enfolded her, Bethan strove to forget the straitlaced rules of propriety that had been drummed into her. She was no longer a mere servant, obliged to do her employers' bidding in everything, including how she bestowed her favours. She would soon be the mistress of this fine house and one of the leading ladies in Singapore society. Who in this town would dare pass judgement on her for dallying in bed with her husband-to-be a night or two before their wedding?

"That sounds like a fine idea," she whispered, trying not to betray any uncertainty.

Simon must have sensed her misgivings, all the same.

Pressing his cheek lightly against hers, he spoke in a reassuring murmur. "I promise you won't regret it. This may not be the situation in which you expected to find yourself, but I will do everything in my power to give you a fine life."

What *situation* was he talking about? Bethan wondered as he led her back into the house. Living on the other side of the world from where she'd been born and bred, perhaps? Or being sent here by his partner rather than courted and proposed to in the usual way? Neither of those things mattered to her any more than Simon's wealth and position. What mattered was that she had found a family and a man who would always be there for her. A man whose kisses made her melt and whose touch filled her insides with fluttering butterflies.

At the threshold of his bedroom, Simon stopped.

When Bethan opened her mouth to ask why, he cradled her face in his hands as if it were as fragile as an eggshell. "Any troubling memories about your past experiences, any reservations, any fears, I want you to leave them outside this door. Tonight I mean to make you mine and bring you nothing but pleasure."

His consideration for her innocent uncertainty touched Bethan. Though she was not fully in love with Simon yet, her feelings for him were growing deeper by the day and she was confident she could win his love in return.

He pressed his forehead against hers. "Do you know the best part of all?"

His sensuous whisper sent shivers through her. "What is that?"

"This will be only the first of many such nights." He spoke as if he was sharing a delightful secret. "And they will only get better."

"I'm already looking forward to them."

"Then I won't keep either of us waiting any longer." Simon whisked her into his bedroom and shut the door behind them with muted finality.

Before any troublesome second thoughts had a chance to plague her, he led her to his bed and eased her on to it. After trimming the argand lamp, he began kissing her in a way that inflamed her desire and seared away her doubts. Meanwhile, he explored and caressed her body, making her wonder how many delectable flavours of pleasure she would experience in his arms.

Certain that this was what she wanted, Bethan gave herself up to his lovemaking with joyful abandon. It reminded her of the first time they'd dined together and he'd introduced her to so many dishes she'd never before tasted, or even heard of. The sensations she now savoured were each as delightful in their own way, such as when Simon caught her lower lip between his and began to suckle it with leisurely, sensual strokes. At the same time his hands ranged over her body, never lingering long on any one spot but teasing her with the promise of deeper pleasures to come. Then he began to remove her clothes to the accompaniment of light, whispering kisses strewn over her face...down her neck...over her shoulders.

"There we are," he announced in a husky whisper when the last of their clothes had been shed. "Just as we were made, like Adam and Eve in the Garden."

Smooth, warm skin slid over smooth, warm skin. Firm, lean flesh pressed against soft, rounded flesh. Even as Bethan relished the sensual attentions of his hands, lips and tongue on her bare skin, his mention of Adam and Eve nagged at her. Could *this* be the sin for which the first man and woman were sent away from Eden? Years of her mother's embittered mutterings flooded her memory, threatening to sully her innocent pleasure.

Simon seemed to sense the subtle change in her response to him.

"Are you having second thoughts?" He lifted his hand from her breast to cup her cheek. "If you want me to stop, I will...somehow. I may suffer torments of longing, but I'd rather have that than go ahead when you—"

"No!" Raising herself slightly, Bethan kissed the first part of him her lips encountered in the darkness. It felt like the hollow at the base of his throat. She could feel the fevered heat of his skin and the thundering beat of his pulse beneath it. She had lit that fire and unleashed that tempest with him—yet he would try to contain them for her sake. The realisation amazed and moved her. "If you stop now, I'm afraid I will suffer torments of longing, too."

Hers might be even greater than his, since she wasn't altogether certain what it was he made her yearn for with such ravenous intensity. "I was troubled by a bad memory from the past, that's all. You know what that's like."

"I do." He drizzled kisses over her brow as if they had some magical power to drive those dark memories away. "I should have known better than to think you could leave them all outside the door. But I will do everything I can to make you forget."

A moment later she discovered what Simon meant when he slid down the bed a little way so his lips could search out the firm, sensitive tip of her breast and close over it.

She gave a soft gasp of delighted surprise that melted into a deep purr of pleasure. "Much more of that and I'll forget everything I ever knew."

With what little of her thoughts that were not immersed in the wondrous novelty of lovemaking, Bethan resolutely turned from any notion of sin. She and Simon were going to be married, after all. This closeness between a man and wife was surely a blessing—a means of returning, however briefly, to their lost paradise. With that reassuring notion, she surrendered fully to the sultry enchantment of Simon's caresses.

His tongue glided over her nipple, sending a gush of liquid bliss rippling through her body. When he reached down and ran his hand up her leg, she writhed to meet his searching fingers. But he pulled them away, the tormentor, to caress her knee instead. That only stoked the mysterious throbbing heat that had become the core of her senses, the centre of her passionate hunger.

Again and again he approached, varying his touch from a lush stroke, to a trailing glide with the back of his hand, to the lightest flirting of his fingertips. Each seemed to pour a different kind of fuel on the blaze within her. Closer and closer he drew with each approach, always pulling back at the last moment, as if he was afraid her desire might scald his fingers. On his last attempt, Bethan wriggled her hips and let out a faint squeal of impatience.

A mellow chuckle vibrated through Simon's chest. Giving her breast a parting suckle, he slid up to graze his cheek against her shoulder and up her neck. Reaching her ear, he tickled it with a sly whisper. "I have waited too long for this to rush it. Besides, the greater the anticipation, the greater the pleasure."

"If you say so," she panted, "though I'm not sure how much more of it I can stand."

"Let's find out, shall we?" He returned to his tantalising caresses, this time moving in from above. He ran his hand down her belly and over her hips then slid it beneath her to fondle the lobes of her bottom.

After what seemed like hours of such toying, when she had begun to despair of him going further, Bethan felt such a delicate whisper of his fingertip between her parted legs that she wondered if she'd only imagined it. But the sensation was beyond anything she'd felt before.

As Simon continued to touch her in this most intimate of places, she realised how moist and slick those sensitive folds of flesh had become—as if they'd been anointed with warm oil. It made the seductive glide of his finger even more stimulating, urging her desire to glow hotter than ever.

Simon gave a deep, wordless murmur of approval. But Bethan could scarcely hear him over the galloping beat of her heart and the hiss of her racing breath. Something inside her felt as if it was swelling larger and larger until she could no longer contain it. What would she feel when that bubble of desire burst—pleasure or pain? It seemed impossible that she could know greater pleasure than Simon had brought her already.

Then suddenly her hips began to shudder, as coloured stars burst behind her eyelids and wave after wave of shuddering rapture engulfed her. She was vaguely aware of Simon looming over her, as if this was a signal he'd been waiting for. Something hard and smooth slid between her thighs to fill the moist passage where his finger had been a moment ago. As it plunged deeper than his finger had explored, a sense of pressure built and broke in a stab of pain. But before she could cry out, Simon's lips closed over hers.

So *this* was where the whole mysterious connection of men and women met with the familiar sights of country life—rams mounting ewes in the autumn pastures, birds joined together in such tight pairs that they looked like a single creature.

Simon began to move, his hips pulling back, then thrusting deep again. It gave Bethan a twinge in the spot where he'd first entered, but the pain was dampened by a pulse of warm satisfaction that coursed through her.

His thrusts grew faster and wilder, every muscle of his body clenched so tight she feared he would shatter. And then he did, in powerful shuddering heaves that tore a hoarse cry from his throat and left him spent and gasping. If she hadn't just experienced something like it herself, she might have wondered if he'd been hurt.

Twining her arms around him, she savoured the sweet fulfilment of being able to bring Simon an escape from his troubled past. Perhaps one day he would trust her enough to confide the secrets that haunted him, and she would feel secure enough in his regard to tell him hers.

* * *

When Simon woke the next morning, his heart felt unaccountably light and a bright little melody ran through his mind, begging to be hummed. Last night with Bethan had been well worth the frustration and thwarted longing he'd suffered since her arrival. She'd felt as wonderful in his arms as he remembered from that first evening—as wonderful as in his dreams!

To his surprise, her painful past experience had not made her skittish or reluctant to accept his attentions. Yet neither had she been coarsened by what she'd suffered. Every response had seemed natural and instinctive. Just as he'd hoped, Simon had found balm for his wounds in her kisses and blessed escape from his haunted memories in their blissful coupling.

He reached out to draw her closer, but his arm embraced empty air. His heart gave a sickening lurch and his eyes flew open. A wave of relief buoyed his spirits when he glimpsed Bethan beside the bed, gathering her clothes from the floor.

"Don't steal away without a kiss." He opened his arms to her.

At the sight of her naked body, which he'd only touched and tasted in the darkness last night, *his* body roused. Perhaps he could tempt her to more than a kiss.

Suddenly bashful, Bethan held her gown up in front of her. Lips swollen from kissing arched in a sheepish smile. "I didn't mean to wake you, but I have to get up. Rosalia will be waking soon and wondering where I am."

"Of course." Simon strove to hide his disappointment. He wished he'd been able to find another *amah* to care for the child. Now he vowed he would engage someone, no matter what it cost him. "Just one kiss, then I'll let you go to her…I promise."

"Very well." She cast him a playful glance that held just a hint of wariness. "Only let me put on my clothes first."

"I can help with that if you like," he offered. "It would be only fair since I was the one who took them off."

That sort of flirtatious jesting didn't sound like him at all, Simon mused. But something strange had happened to him of late. A sense of lightness had crept into his heart, like a stray morsel of yeast, and begun to make his whole outlook rise. He didn't entirely trust it. But after so many years of flat, often bitter, existence, he could not help but welcome the feeling.

An endearing blush crept into Bethan's fair cheeks. Even after having her virtue sullied and becoming his mistress, she still retained an air of winsome innocence. "I'm perfectly able to dress myself, thank you."

"As you wish." Simon gave an amiable shrug. "In this climate, with fashions what they are, dressing isn't a difficult business for a woman."

He watched with admiring interest as she slipped on her shift. "It's more of an undertaking for a man, I can tell you. On hot days, I often envy the Malays their white trousers and bare chests."

Pulling her gown on over her undergarments, Bethan chuckled. "I'm sure you'd look quite fetching in that sort of get-up."

"Until I burnt as red as a radish." Simon made a wry face. "I'll stick to my shirt, breeches and boots, thank you. You are more than welcome to help *me* get dressed whenever you fancy."

"That is a tempting offer." She perched on the edge of the bed beside him. "You're very good at making those.

But I'd rather be Rosalia's *amah* than your valet, if it's all the same to you."

She leaned over and gave him the kiss he'd asked for. Her lips tasted every bit as delicious as they had in the night. This kiss brought back memories he welcomed, for a change. The only problem was how briefly it lasted. Simon tried to draw it out, but all too soon Bethan pulled back, though she seemed almost as reluctant as he was to end it.

"I can dress myself perfectly well without a valet." He raised her hand to his lips. "And I will find someone to take over nursery duties so you can concentrate all your energies on being my mistress."

She gave cheerful shrug. "I wouldn't mind having a little help with Rosalia, but I still want to spend time with her and take her on outings—even after Ah-Sam gets back."

Perhaps she glimpsed a flicker of disapproval in his eyes. Before he could say anything, she added, "I may not be able to replace her mother, but I want to be a better stepmother to Rosalia than yours was to you."

"Stepmother?" That word made Simon's gorge rise and not only because of its unpleasant associations from his boyhood. "What are you talking about? You're not Rosalia's stepmother."

"Not yet, maybe." Bethan shrank a little at his sharp tone. "But I will be as soon as we're married. Speaking of that, when should we have the wedding? It ought to be soon, I think, now that we've…"

As she glanced toward the rumpled bed, she blushed again. This time it did not make her look so innocent.

…as soon as we're married…when should we have the wedding? Her words sizzled in his mind as if they'd been branded there with a white-hot iron. He'd gone to

such lengths to secure a woman who would not complicate his life and look what he'd got instead!

He felt like the biggest fool in the whole East Indies for letting Bethan Conway worm her way into his life with her pose of wide-eyed innocence. "I have no intention of marrying you! That was never part of our bargain."

"What do you mean?" She stumbled back from his bed in a dangerously convincing pretence of bewildered dismay. "You asked Mr Northmore to find you a wife and he sent me."

"Not a *wife*!" The word burned on Simon's tongue. "I told Hadrian to find me a mistress…as if you didn't know."

He could not confront her properly while lying naked in bed—it put him at too great a disadvantage. Simon scrambled up, keeping the linen sheet wrapped around him to hide his scarred leg and the straining evidence of his arousal. The last thing he wanted was to let her see the intensity of desire she provoked in him.

"Does it matter what name you give it?" Bethan asked in a tone of desperate entreaty. "Mistress of your house, wife—they're the same thing…aren't they?"

Her protestations of ignorance only fuelled Simon's fury. How big a fool did the woman take him for? "Do not insult my intelligence with this transparent playacting! I'm certain you know exactly what a mistress is and what she does. For all I know, you may have been kept by half the men in Newcastle."

"Kept?" Bethan seized on that word, which Simon thought strange considering some of the others he'd hurled at her. "You brought me here to be your kept woman? You think I've been kept by other men?"

"So you do understand." He tried to ignore the soft glow of her auburn hair in the early morning light and forget its silken warmth beneath his fingertips. "Of course I want to keep you. And in fine style, I might add. But that wasn't enough for you, was it? You want my name, too, and a claim upon my fortune. Tell me, when did you come up with this scheme to demand marriage? Was it after you saw the size of my house or did you plan it all from the beginning?"

If he expected her to break under his accusations and confess her deceit, he could not have been more mistaken.

"I've never been kept by a man in my life and I never mean to be!" Bethan took a defiant step toward him, her chin tilted proudly. "I thought I was coming to Singapore to be your wife. I would never have accepted Mr Northmore's offer if I'd known what you really wanted. Come to that, how do I know it wasn't *you* who tricked *me*?"

"*I* who—?" Her outrageous accusation struck Simon dumb for a moment, making it impossible to press his attack.

Bethan took advantage of his silence to continue her onslaught. "For all I know, you lured me out here, far from my home and friends, so I'd have no choice but to let you do what you wanted with me?"

She made him sound like a pirate, seizing a helpless woman from the protection of her ship to have his brutal way with her.

"That was *never* my intention," Simon protested, galled that she'd succeeded in putting him on the defensive. "I offered a fair, straightforward exchange—your exclusive favours for my protection and generous terms of keeping. I have never taken advantage of a woman in my life. But neither will I allow you to impose upon me.

I refuse to be lured or coerced into marriage. So I warn you, don't bother trying!"

Simon wished he was as certain of that as he strove to sound—the luring part, especially. In spite of his shock and suspicion, desire for her still racked his body like a tropical fever.

Bethan took another step towards him and another, forcing Simon to stagger back until he mastered his astonishment and willed himself to stand his ground.

"Save your warnings, Mr Grimshaw." She stood toe to toe with him and fixed him with a blistering glare.

Did she not realise the danger in which she'd placed herself? He had only to raise his arms and bend forwards a few perilous inches and she would be captive in his embrace again, his lips on hers, taking what they wanted.

Or did she know exactly what she was doing? Was she trying to provoke his lust to test how much power she could exercise over him? Every muscle in Simon's body tensed with the effort to keep his hands off her.

"I am not the kind of woman you think," Bethan insisted. "I would never have come to your bed last night if I'd known that was all you wanted from me. I suppose you assumed that once you ruined me I'd have to take what I could get from you, but you're wrong. I may have been a green little fool for trusting you, but I'll be no man's whore!"

"I didn't ruin you." Hard as Simon clung to that certainty, a treacherous qualm of doubt slithered through his belly. "That was some other man, back in England— he forced you. That's why you wanted me to take things slowly, which I did. We talked about it. I remember distinctly."

His words seemed to shake her fierce certainty. "I

never told you any such thing. I'd never…been with a man that way until last night nor even been properly kissed!"

With that, she stormed off, leaving Simon feeling as if he'd been lashed by a cyclone. What troubled him far more than her furious outburst was the mist of tears he glimpsed in her beguiling eyes when she fled from him.

What she'd said couldn't be true, could it? He expelled a shaky breath, torn between fiery outrage and icy foreboding. He plundered his memory for anything Bethan had said or done that would prove she'd been lying to him all along. Much as he hated to think he'd been duped, the alternative was far worse.

He gaze fell upon the bed, his delightful memories of their night together now tainted by dark doubts. The sight of a rusty red smudge on the bottom sheet made his lame leg go suddenly weak. For a moment he could not bring himself to acknowledge the truth of what he was seeing.

Not that he had any direct experience of such matters…until now. There had been no bloodstains on the sheets after his wedding night with Carlotta. Wanting to make their hasty marriage work, he'd tried explaining it away in a manner that did not question the innocence of his bride. But deep down, he had never believed those excuses. In that moment the suspicion that poisoned their marriage had been born.

Confronted with the irrefutable proof of Bethan's accusations against him, Simon was forced to consider whether the rest of what she'd told him could be true as well. Had she sincerely believed he wanted to marry her? Or had she manipulated him to unwittingly take her virginity—counting on his honour to make him marry her?

If that was the case, she'd been right. It was one thing to make an offer of keeping to a woman whose virtue was already compromised. But to deflower a virgin left him with no honourable course but to redeem her reputation.

Even at the cost of another wretched marriage.

Chapter Ten

Hateful man! Bethan ran from Simon before she further humiliated herself with an outburst of tears.

She'd woken from the sweet, wanton dream of last night's pleasures to a cruel nightmare. Simon, her gentle, considerate lover, had suddenly vanished, leaving in his place cold, contemptuous Mr Grimshaw. His ugly accusations had frayed her pride raw, while discovering his true dishonourable intentions towards her made Bethan sick with shame. All this time she'd been struggling to decide whether or not she could bring herself to marry him, when he'd wanted only to turn her into the kind of wicked woman she most detested—the kind who had stolen her beloved father and destroyed her family.

Hurrying blindly from his bedroom, she dashed next door to hers where she paced the floor and cursed herself for her wayward folly. What a gullible fool she'd been to surrender her body to a man like that! Her only relief was that she had not surrendered her heart to him as well.

From off in the distance came the muted rumble of waves striking the shore. Rather than calming her as it usually did, the restless ebb and surge of the surf only reminded Bethan how far she was from home and how completely in the power of a ruthless man who both attracted and repelled her. A few moments later, when she heard Simon's door open and his footsteps heading briskly away, she breathed a sigh of relief followed by whimper of vexation. There he went, off about his business as usual, only mildly inconvenienced by an event that had turned her whole life upside down!

Part of her longed to crumple on to the bed and sob out her fear, hurt and shame. Another part urged her to flee his house and never look back. Much as those impulses appealed to her, she did not have the luxury of indulging either of them just now.

Rosalia was depending on her and Bethan refused to punish the child for the sins of her father. With all the recent upheaval in her young life, the last thing such a sensitive little girl needed was to lose another care-giver without warning. She might blame Bethan's departure on some trifling misdeed of hers and feel worse than ever.

Determined not to let that happen, Bethan gathered the tattered shreds of her composure, cleaned up and changed her clothes. Then she went to the nursery and did her best to act as if nothing was bothering her. Fortunately, all the recent attention from her father had put Rosalia in high spirits. Chattering eagerly about her plans for future outings, she did not seem to notice Bethan's distraction.

"Can we go down to the beach and look for pretty seashells?" she asked at breakfast.

"That sounds like a good idea." Bethan seized upon the suggestion with desperate eagerness. An activity like that would keep Rosalia happily occupied, while giving *her* a badly needed chance to think.

* * *

As her young charge combed the shore that morning, Bethan scoured her memory in an effort to sort out the terrible confusion between her and Simon Grimshaw.

Had he brought her all the way to Singapore only to deceive and to use her? Though she'd accused him of it, she could not bring herself to believe it. She'd only wanted to give him a taste of the nasty lies he was heaping upon her, to see how he liked it.

She wondered if his partner might have somehow misunderstood what Simon wanted in a woman. Or...?

A spasm of guilt clutched Bethan so tightly she could hardly breathe. Had she brought this trouble upon herself, after all? Not from any devious purpose, but out of ignorance and desperation. The more she thought back on her interview with Mr Northmore and everything that had passed between her and Simon, the more likely it seemed.

Having no one but herself to blame did not make her situation any easier—quite the contrary, in fact. Now that she knew how this awful misunderstanding might have come about, she was forced to consider how she would deal with its consequences.

She'd told Simon she refused to be his kept woman, but would she have any other choice now that she had let him bed her? Even if she could bring herself to marry some other man, who would have her after this? Who would even be willing to give her a job or a place to live? She did not have a single friend in Singapore other than members of Simon's household or people who worked for him. She could not ask them to risk offending him by helping her.

And what if Simon had got her with child last night? That possibility almost knocked Bethan to her knees.

Much as she loved children and longed to be a mother some day, the thought of bearing a baby under these circumstances horrified her. She had no means of caring for a child on her own, which would leave her trapped in Simon's keeping for as long as he wanted her. And when he tired of her—what then?

Never in his life had Simon put in a longer day at work!

Usually there were not enough hours for him to deal with everything that needed to be done. Business occupied all his energy and all his thoughts. Since Bethan's arrival, he'd become more and more distracted until today he could not keep his mind on his work for five minutes together.

What a fool he'd been! Blinded by desire and his daft weakness for damsels in distress, he'd ignored all his suspicions about that infernal creature to cast her in the role of an innocent victim. He'd come to discover she was only innocent in a purely physical sense. And she had made *him* the victim of her scheme.

There was one thing she'd been right about, however. He should not have tried so hard to avoid any memories of his troubled past. To forget what he had suffered only doomed him to repeat his mistakes and reap the wretched consequences all over again.

All day he brooded about how Bethan had manipulated and duped him. He cursed himself for falling into her snare so easily. There was no question that she had him trapped. Like Carlotta, she'd quickly gauged his weakness and set about turning it to her advantage. Hard as he tried, Simon could see no way out—at least none that would allow him to face himself in the mirror every morning.

* * *

Heavy as the time hung on his hands at the office, he delayed returning to the house that evening. For one thing, he could not bring himself to capitulate to that woman a moment sooner than he had to. For another, he did not want to risk having Rosalia sense his seething frustration and rage. Only when he was certain she would be asleep did he venture home to confront Bethan.

She was waiting for him in the parlour with such a haunted look in her green-grey eyes that he'd have been tempted to pity her under other circumstances. Simon reminded himself that *he* was the one who'd been deceived and manipulated.

Resisting the inclination to take a seat, he crossed his arms tightly over his chest and scowled down at her. "I suppose we should get this sorry business thrashed out here and now. For the life of me, I cannot fathom how two people could come to such a vast misunderstanding in their expectations of one another."

Unless, as he was certain, one of them had been lying through her teeth.

Inhaling a deep breath, Bethan rose from her seat and met his baleful glare. "I know you think this is my fault and you're right."

The last thing Simon had expected from her was such a frank, disarming admission of guilt. It left him off balance and lost for words. But he maintained his rigid stance, certain she would exploit any sign of weakening.

"It's not what you think, though." She took advantage of his astonished silence to continue. "It was an honest mistake. I didn't mean to trick you and I swear I've never let a man bed me before last night. I only let you do it because I thought you were going to marry me.

Truly, I came to Singapore believing it was a wife you wanted."

What sort of riddles was she trying to spin? Simon steeled himself against the persuasive ring of sincerity in her voice. If she had not intended to deceive him, how could the situation be her fault?

Bethan must have guessed his thoughts for her gaze faltered. "It *was* a mistake, though it might not have been altogether *honest*. I should have told Mr Northmore when I met with him. But I was afraid if he knew, he'd choose someone else instead."

So she had managed to deceive Hadrian as well. That knowledge made Simon feel a bit less of a fool. "What was it you should have told my partner?"

"That I didn't understand everything he said to me." Bethan caught her lower lip between her teeth. "Back then, my English wasn't as good as it is now and Mr Northmore used some hard words I didn't know. I shouldn't have pretended I did."

"You claim you didn't understand what Hadrian meant when he told you I was looking for a mistress?" Simon wasn't sure which was worse—that she expected him to credit such a preposterous story or that part of him wanted to swallow it whole.

More contemptible than either of those was the wanton yearning for her that he could not suppress, in spite of the way she'd taken advantage of his desires. It enraged him to realise she still wielded that power over him and he could not break free.

"It's more than a claim," Bethan shot back. "It's the truth! Even this morning when you talked about me being your *mistress*, I didn't know what you meant. To me a mistress is the kind of woman I'd work for—the lady of the house, a gentleman's wife."

"You knew what a kept woman was, though." Simon seized on that damning inconsistency. "How is that?"

"Because that's what I've heard them called." The blush that crept into Bethan's pale cheeks made her look every bit as innocent as she professed—and far too appealing for Simon's comfort. "As well as some nastier names that I never wanted to be called. I suppose I'll have to get used to them, now."

Guilt gnawed at Simon's conscience and refused to stop. Even when he reminded himself that he hadn't intended to take her virginity and that she had confessed to being to blame for the whole misunderstanding, he could not escape the crushing weight of responsibility for what he'd done. No doubt she'd counted on that. Her wistful reproach was surely calculated to shame him into taking the action he'd been so desperate to avoid.

"Don't fret about your reputation." He spat the words out as if they were poison. "There is one of your assertions I am forced to credit. Much as it astonishes me, I cannot deny you came to my bed a virgin. After last night I have no honourable recourse but to marry you, so we might as well get it over with as soon as possible. I will speak to Reverend Turnbull tomorrow if that suits you. In a place like this, the church is not so particular about the niceties of banns and special licences. But it will all be perfectly in order, I assure you."

Bethan flinched from his scorn, but she could not conceal the avid glint of elation that flashed in her eyes at his mention of marriage. "You still want to wed me? Even after you got what you wanted and I've told you the whole mix-up was my fault?"

She couldn't resist gloating, could she?

"Of course I don't *want* to!" He'd rather leap into shark-infested waters than stand before Reverend

Turnbull exchanging vows of lifelong fidelity. "Have you not heard a word I've said? Marriage is the last thing I desire, especially to a creature of your ilk. But since I have unwittingly taken your virginity, honour compels me to make an honest woman of you."

"But you don't love me." She sounded bewildered, as if his actions were somehow inconsistent. Did she think he was entirely without scruples?

More than that implied insult, the word *love* horrified Simon. Bad enough she wielded such a dangerously intense attraction over him. The prospect of giving her power over his heart shook him to the core. "If you think last night had anything to do with love, you must be daft!"

"Daft, am I?" A blaze of passionate fury seared all traces of bemusement and regret from Bethan's face. "Well, maybe I am—daft enough to think you were a good man who wanted and needed a wife to care for him. Daft enough to believe you respected me and thought more of me than just a willing body in your bed!"

The force of her outrage hit Simon like a broadside of artillery to blast gaping holes in the barricade he'd spent so long erecting around his heart—a barricade she'd been busy undercutting ever since her arrival in Singapore.

Her accusations struck their targets with perilous accuracy, forcing him on the defensive. "What more do you want from me? I've offered to wed you, damn it! Are you going to accept or not?"

Bethan hesitated only an instant.

"No!" She hurled his honourable proposal back in his face. "Not if it's against your will and you think so beastly ill of me. How would a marriage like that be any better than keeping—just because we stand before a parson and sign a paper? Every vow we made would be a lie. I believe that's a worse sin than anything we did last night!"

Simon's jaw fell slack. Never for an instant had he imagined she would refuse him. A torrent of conflicting, confusing emotions ripped through him—astonishment, relief, regret, longing, shame—all far too intense for his comfort.

Before he could marshal his shaken wits to reply, she dashed past him, out of the sitting room and down the stairs.

When he heard the outside door slam, a spasm of panic gripped Simon. It had never occurred to him that she would be foolhardy enough to leave the house on her own after dark. Cursing himself and the hopelessly muddled situation between them, he set off after her as quickly as his protesting leg would allow.

Halfway down the stairs he met Ah-Ming coming up. "Where are you going, master? Dinner is ready."

"I'll eat later. I have to go out." He didn't dare stop to explain. Bethan had a head start on him and two sound legs to carry her.

Part of him was tempted to let her go and reap the consequences of her folly. But he knew the burden of guilt he would carry if any harm came to her. The shame of taking her virginity would be nothing compared with that.

Hurrying outside, he peered up and down the street until he caught a glimpse of her disappearing in the direction of the square. She had enough of a head start that he could never hope to overtake her on foot. Rather than trying, he called for Mahmud to saddle his horse at once.

A few moments later he rode toward the square at a full gallop. Peering into the moonlit shadows, he strained to catch a glimpse of Bethan's yellow muslin gown. All the while he struggled to understand what had made her reject his proposal. Her actions forced him to consider the disturbing possibility that he'd completely misjudged her.

Shame and outrage warred within Bethan as she ran up North Bridge Road. She had no idea where she wanted to go, except to get out from under Simon's roof. Discovering that he'd never intended to marry her had not humiliated her half as much as his hostile, demeaning proposal. He'd called her daft and he was right. What a green little fool she'd been to think he could care for her and they might possibly be happy together!

She could have understood him being angry over her lapse in honesty and how it had caused this terrible misunderstanding. But his reaction had been so much worse than that. Simon's marriage offer made it brutally clear that he mistrusted and despised her. He thought so little of her that he'd expected her to jump at his proposal even after he declared he had never loved her and never would.

Though part of her had been tempted to become his wife on whatever terms he offered, her pride refused accept a proposal that he'd tossed at her feet with such blatant contempt. To do so would only prove that she was as conniving a creature as he believed her to be.

But how would she survive if she did not wed him and how would she keep all this from hurting Simon's daughter?

Preoccupied with such thoughts, Bethan did not notice a pair of *sepoys* until she was almost on top of them. They seemed every bit as startled by her sudden appearance.

"Who is there?" one of the soldiers barked while both quickly raised their rifles. Their bayonets bristled in the dim light of distant street lamps.

She jumped back with a squeak of alarm. "My name's Bethan Conway. I...I look after Mr Grimshaw's daughter."

The moment she mentioned Simon, the soldiers hastily lowered their weapons.

"Pardon, *memsahib*!" they cried in a tone of frantic apology. "It is not safe for a lady to walk alone at night. You must go home now, please."

The thought of slinking back to Simon so soon after she'd flounced off troubled Bethan more than any danger she could imagine.

"I just want a bit of air." She backed away rapidly. "Don't fret about me. I'll be fine."

Slipping off into the shadows, she told herself the soldiers wouldn't dare risk firing at her. To her relief, she was right.

The encounter forced her to pay more attention to her surroundings. Thinking about her predicament would have to wait until she found a quiet spot to rest.

She gave the lights of the military encampment a wide berth and soon felt the ground beneath her feet sloping upwards. Trees loomed up around her and the scent of spices enfolded her. This must be the experimental garden she'd glimpsed that evening Simon took her for a drive up Government Hill.

Remembering it made her imagine she could hear the soft beat of a horse's hooves nearby. She realised it was more than a fancy when she heard the beast blowing out a loud breath.

As she hurried away from the sound, Simon's voice

rang out. "Stop, Bethan! I'll only follow you if you don't."

She knew him well enough to be certain he was not bluffing. Besides, he was mounted while she was already winded after running from the soldiers. If she *had* to talk to him, better here than back at the house, where he was master and she was only an unwelcome guest.

Her footsteps slowed until she came to rest against the slender trunk of a young tree, gasping in deep breaths of the warm spicy air.

Simon sprang from his saddle, landing with a muted thud and a half-stifled grunt of pain. He caught her by the arm and grasped it tightly, as if he feared she would take flight again.

"I don't care how angry you are at me," he growled. "Don't *ever* run off like that again. Do you hear me?"

"I may be daft, but I'm not deaf!" She wrenched her arm out of his grasp. "Why do you care what I do or where I go if you loathe me so?"

"I don't *loathe* you!" His fierce tone belied his words. "And I certainly don't want any harm to come to you."

"A little late for that, isn't it?" Bethan rubbed her arm in a fruitless effort to wipe away the tingling heat left by his touch.

Simon exhaled a deep sigh, heavy with regret. "I'm sorry for what happened between us. I swear I never meant to take your virginity. If I'd known it was marriage you expected, I wouldn't have—"

"I know." She cut him off sharply. Somehow it grieved her to hear he regretted the wondrous night they'd shared. In spite of everything that had followed and all it might cost her, she could not bring herself to wish it had never happened. Did that make her a wanton harlot, deserving of all the foul names she'd heard such women called? "That wasn't the kind of harm I meant."

"It wasn't?" He sounded baffled.

"I know you didn't take my maidenhead on purpose." Her eyes stung with tears she refused to shed. "But all the horrible things you thought and said about me, you can't claim you didn't mean them."

"Perhaps not." He sounded almost pained to admit it. "But I am beginning to suspect they may not be true."

"They're not!" she snapped, stung by the tepid nature of his doubts. "It doesn't matter now, though, for I don't care what you think of me."

Bethan *wished* that were true, but she could not afford to let Simon know how much his opinion of her still mattered.

"That may be," he replied after a long moment of tense silence, "but I still owe you an explanation for what prompted me to think and say those things. As you might guess, it has to do with my past."

"And you're willing to tell me about it?" she asked warily.

"If you're willing to listen." He sounded far from certain that she would be.

"I can't very well refuse, can I? Not after all the times I've pestered you about keeping secrets." She sank down at the base of the tree and wrapped her arms around her knees. "Go ahead, then. Have your say."

Simon dropped to the ground beside her. After a moment's hesitation, he took a deep breath and forged ahead. "Do you remember when I said the less Rosalia knows about her mother, the better?"

"Of course." Though she knew this must be difficult for him, Bethan did not feel obliged to make it any easier. "What of it?"

"If *you* know more about my late wife, perhaps you will understand why I am so determined not to wed again and why I suspected you of trying to trick me into marriage."

Bethan strove to stifle the itch of curiosity. An avid interest in Simon's past strayed dangerously close to *caring* about what had happened to him.

"You may have noticed," he continued in a wry, self-mocking tone, "I have a lamentable weakness for damsels in distress. I should have learned from my stepmother that such women are seldom as helpless as they appear. Carlotta certainly was not."

Perhaps not, but heroes weren't always as gallant as they appeared either. Even as that spiteful thought ran through Bethan's mind, she could not shake off the image of Simon striding to her rescue.

"I met her in Penang," he continued. "Her uncle was taking her from Macau to Lisbon for an arranged marriage. While their ship was having storm damage repaired, her uncle fell ill and could not keep her properly chaperoned. She begged me to help her escape…" His voice trailed off.

Overcome by the curiosity she had not been able to stifle, Bethan prompted him. "What did you do?"

"Married her, of course. Her uncle wanted to call me out for it, but Ford smoothed matters over somehow. For a while Carlotta was grateful and I was besotted. But her gratitude didn't last long. A few months later she humiliated me by running off with an East India Company factor. My partners dragged me away on Raffles's expedition to get my mind off her. It worked well enough until she turned up in Singapore a year later with a baby she claimed was mine. She begged me to take her back for the child's sake. Chivalrous idiot that I was, I agreed."

Bethan's mouth fell open when she realised what he was saying. "You think Rosalia might not be your daughter?"

"How can I ever know for certain? She is the image of her mother. I've never seen the slightest resemblance to me."

That resemblance must have made Rosalia a constant, painful reminder of her mother's betrayal. Simon had tried to be a good father.

In spite of all that had happened between them, Bethan could not resist the impulse to reassure him. "I'm certain you are her father. I told you all the likenesses I've seen between you."

"So you did." For the first time that day, his voice warmed. "That meant a great deal to me. Regardless of her paternity, I owe Rosalia a father's attention and affection. But knowing her feelings are like mine may make it easier to mend my past mistakes."

As silence fell between them, Bethan tried to keep her anger towards Simon burning hot. But thoughts of how Carlotta had abused his generosity and betrayed his trust fell upon it like raindrops. At first they only sizzled and evaporated, but gradually they began to quench the flames.

"You might as well hear the rest of the story," said Simon at last. "Carlotta did not remain content for long in a humble *kampong* house beside our *godown*. She died as I told you, drowned while boarding a *tongkang*. She was running away again—this time with the captain of a French ship."

Bethan risked a glance towards him. With his crisp, compelling profile lit by the silvery rays of the moon, he looked like a statue carved out of ice. "So that's why you thought I was trying to trick you into marriage. And why you don't want another wife."

"Carlotta was not the only reason. She was just the last and the worst of several women who deceived and betrayed me after I tried to help them."

"But I'm not like those other women, Simon! Why must you tar me with the same brush?" The moment those words left her mouth, Bethan's conscience hurled them back at her.

Was she so very different from Carlotta and the other women who had exploited Simon's gallantry for their own purposes? By misleading Hadrian Northmore to secure her passage to Singapore, she had cheated Simon out of the mistress he wanted. Since her arrival, she'd purposely misled him about her reasons for coming here. Even after he had confided in her some of the most painful secrets from his past, she still could not bring herself to trust him with her secret.

Her situation was different, Bethan tried to persuade herself. She had not acted from selfish motives. She had no designs on Simon's fortune and she would never desert him for another man. She was only trying to protect her beloved brother from people who might judge him as unfairly as Simon had judged her.

Her conscience refused to be soothed by those excuses.

Chapter Eleven

"I know you're not like those other women." Staring down the hill towards the lights of the town and the shadowy ships anchored off shore, Simon strove to ignore his nagging doubts. When Bethan had protested her innocence, she sounded as if she might be trying to convince herself more than him. "Part of me does, at least—the reasonable part, the fair part. But there's something else inside of me that's still bitter and certain of being betrayed again."

Telling her the sordid truth about his marriage had felt as if he were stripping off the hard protective shell he'd worn for so long. When it was gone, he'd stood before her with all his flaws and weaknesses exposed. Yet it had also been like lancing an old corrupted wound, draining off some of the resentment and self-doubt that was slowly poisoning him.

He owed Bethan a debt for that and for helping him form an attachment with his daughter. He wished she would let him repay her in the ways he was able, by offering her his protection, his passion and the best of everything his fortune could provide.

But when he tried to tell her so, his insidious doubts made him say something quite different. "There's one thing I still can't fathom. If your English wasn't good enough to understand Hadrian, how were you able to read the notice he put in the newspaper?"

He was afraid Bethan would resent his question, but she came back with an answer so readily, he knew it must be the truth. "Evan saw the notice and read it to me. Then he helped me write the letter to Mr Northmore."

The note of fondness in her voice vexed Simon. "Who's Evan?"

"He's a friend of my…a friend of *mine* from Llanaled." Her hesitation suggested there was more to it than that.

"How good a *friend*?" It shouldn't matter to him. Whatever the connection it was all in the past and he had no claim on her. In spite of all that, it *did* matter far too much.

"Good enough to help me find a job in service when I first came to Newcastle. If you must know, he wanted us to be more than friends. I told him I didn't feel that way about him and I wanted to see the world before I settled down. Evan was kind enough to help me make my dream come true."

Simon's lip curled. "Spurned suitors don't usually go out of their way to do favours for women who've rejected them."

"I don't know why you're asking about Evan." Bethan grew suddenly defensive. "What happened isn't his fault. It's mine. If I'd told Mr Northmore straight away that I couldn't speak English very well, I'm sure he would have made certain I understood that it wasn't a wife you wanted."

Was it possible Evan had been too simple to read between the lines of Hadrian's newspaper notice? Simon wondered. Or had her *friend* played a cruel trick on Bethan because she'd rebuffed his advances? It would never cross her mind that she might have been betrayed by someone she cared about. Much as Simon deplored her *naïveté*, something deep inside him envied her innocent belief in the goodness of others.

"You do believe me, don't you?" she pleaded. "That it was all a mistake and I never set out to trick you?"

"Yes, I believe you." Though there were parts of her story that still didn't ring quite true, a fragile seed of trust took root in Simon's heart. "If you'd wanted to trick me into marriage, you wouldn't have refused my proposal."

"I reckon that's true," said Bethan. "I don't want you to marry me against your will because of a mix-up that wasn't your fault."

The relief her answer gave Simon was not as overwhelming as it should have been. "In that case…is there any chance you'd consent to become…my mistress?"

Her whole body recoiled. "I may be daft and rash, but I do have *some* morals. If I let you keep me, I'll be no better than the woman my father left us for. No better than your wife. I'd only be using you to secure my comfort the same way she was. I'd deserve to be shunned by your neighbours and called filthy names."

"They wouldn't!" he insisted in a fierce whisper. "People here view that sort of thing differently than they do back home. Malay and Chinese men take concubines all the time and several of the Europeans have *country wives*."

"Country wives?" Bethan sounded doubtful. Perhaps

in spite of her reluctance to abandon respectability, she secretly wanted him to persuade her.

"That's what they call native or mixed-race women who live with European men during their time abroad. Our former Resident had a charming French-Malaccan lady. Everyone in Singapore accepted her and their children as part of the community."

If he thought his explanation would change her mind, he was mistaken. "What happens to these country wives when the men go back home?"

Her question made Simon squirm, but he tried to put a decent face on the practice. "Most make provision for them by deeding property or leaving money."

"They abandon them, you mean?" Bethan sprang to her feet.

"It isn't as bad as you make it sound." Simon's leg gave a twinge when he rose from the turf at the base of the nutmeg tree. "Besides, none of that matters to you and me. I have no intention of returning to England."

"No?" She didn't sound convinced. "But your partners did. I reckon the Indies is like one great bountiful mistress to some men. They come here and take what they want from her, then go away once they are satisfied. I won't let that happen to me!"

She was as afraid of being abandoned as he was of being betrayed. Simon longed to take her in his arms and promise her that he would always protect her and provide for her. But what if she asked for more than that—things he could not give?

"Where does that leave us, then, if you won't let me wed you or keep you?"

"I'll look after myself, of course, if you'll be gentleman enough not to boast of your conquest. If you can recommend me to another family who needs a nursemaid, I can earn the money to pay back what you spent on my passage to Singapore."

Simon's relief over his near escape from a forced marriage gave way to alarm at the prospect of losing Bethan. "That won't be necessary."

"Yes, it will," she insisted. "I don't want to be beholden to you. You paid to bring me here to be your mistress. Since I can't do that, it isn't fair for you to bear the expense. It may take me a while, but I'll repay every penny."

She was the first beautiful woman of his acquaintance who didn't want anything from him, not even the few guineas it had cost to bring her here. The thought of her leaving his household to strike out on her own troubled Simon deeply. He feared she might attract the admiration of ruthless men who would use whatever means necessary to get what they wanted from her.

"I don't need your money." He took a step toward her, but froze when she backed away. "You've seen how I live—I'll never miss it."

"That's not the point, Simon. I can't keep living in your house, on your charity, after what happened between us."

After what had happened between them, he couldn't bear to think of her living anywhere else. If ever a woman needed his protection it was Bethan Conway—as much from her own trusting nature and reckless impulses as from others who might exploit them. Unlike those who'd begged his help in the past, she truly deserved it, with her honesty and kindness.

"It wouldn't be charity. I owe you a debt for what you've done for me…and for what I've taken from you."

"You don't owe me anything!" Bethan insisted with

such fierce conviction, she almost persuaded him. "You didn't force me into your bed. What happened between us last night was my choice. I wanted it as much as you did."

"Only because you thought we were going to be married."

Bethan shook her head. "That was *my* mistake, not yours."

Her integrity and generosity took his breath away. She could have used his guilt as a bargaining tool to wring tough concessions from him. Instead she'd forfeited that advantage so he could make peace with what he'd done. That made Simon want more than ever to do right by her…if only she would let him.

Perhaps there was a way he could make amends to Bethan, while letting her believe she was repaying whatever obligation she felt towards him. It would test his self-control and perhaps place his heart in jeopardy. But when he weighed those costs against the prospect of letting her go, he could see no other choice.

What had made her insist she would leave Simon's house and find work elsewhere when she wasn't certain that was even possible? Bethan asked herself that question as they stood in the warm, spice-scented darkness of the experimental gardens arguing over her future.

Perhaps it was what Simon had told her about his late wife. She could not bear to use him as Carlotta had. Bad enough she was still keeping secrets from him after he'd risked confiding in her.

Or perhaps it was the renewed conviction that she must continue searching for her brother. She had been wrong to think she could forge a new family and forget the old one. Simon didn't want to create a family with her. He only wanted a willing partner to satisfy his desires, without making any demands upon him. Her brother was her only true hope for restoring the family she craved. If she left Simon's house, it would be easier to carry on her search without fear of rousing suspicion.

But what had made Simon resist the idea of her leaving? Was it only because he felt guilty for taking her virginity? Did he still have hopes of persuading her to become his mistress? Or could it be that, even after what had happened, he cared more for her than he dared admit?

"With all this talk of who is obligated to whom," he said "we're forgetting someone else to whom we both owe a duty."

"Rosalia?" Of course. She should have known Simon would be willing to abide her continued presence in his home only for the sake of his daughter.

"That's right. If you leave, who will take care of her until Ah-Sam returns?"

Once again, it occurred to Bethan how much her leaving might upset Rosalia, especially if she went to care for some other children in a house nearby. "I'm afraid if I go, she'll think it's because she did something wrong."

Simon gave a rueful sigh, echoed by a breeze rustling the leaves of the nutmeg tree. "It won't be easy to persuade her otherwise when she's was far too young to be told the true reason. That is why I want you to stay and continue caring for her. Once Ah-Sam returns in the autumn, you can decide how to proceed. If you choose to go back to England, I will arrange your passage and do everything I can to assist you."

"That's very generous but I don't want to be in your debt."

"You won't. I would consider the exchange a very

favourable bargain. Having Rosalia well cared for until Ah-Sam returns will be worth far more than that to me."

"I don't want her upset by all this, either, but I don't see how I can stay under the same roof with you after what happened between us." When Bethan's thoughts strayed to that blissful encounter, a tantalising heat crept up her thighs.

"Why not?" Simon's tone grew frosty. "Surely you don't believe you have anything to fear from me?"

"Not fear." At least not of *him*. "But you must admit it will be awkward. You brought me here to be your mistress and you've made no secret of…wanting me."

"I cannot deny I desire you." He leaned towards her, then pulled himself back. "But my sense of honour is stronger than that desire. These past weeks, when I thought you'd had a frightening experience with another man, I tried not to rush you into bed. I waited until you were ready. At least, I thought that's what you were telling me."

She could not help but be touched by his consideration. But how could she spend the next several months in his employ, trying to forget the taste of his kisses and the thrilling sensations he'd stirred in her body?

"It's not your honour I doubt, Simon. It's my virtue." Though she knew it might be a dangerous thing to admit, she owed him the truth about this at least. "I feel desire for you as well and after last night…I can't give in to that desire again. If I stay under your roof, I'm afraid I'll be tempted to."

"No, you won't, because I won't give you the chance. I'll keep my distance, I swear. Please don't make Rosalia pay for my blunder. I cannot deny I want you in my bed. But I need you in her life more."

How could she refuse such a plea and such a promise? This situation was her fault and she must make it right, whatever that took.

"All right, then. I'll stay." She tried to ignore a sly whisper in the back of her mind that accused her of seeking any excuse to remain near Simon. "But I warn you, if it gets too hard for me to resist these feelings, I will have to go."

"Fair enough," said Simon. "Now can we go home before the sentries spot us and think we're outlaws planning to attack the town?"

Bethan nodded. "I can go back now. But you're only joking about the outlaws, aren't you?"

"I wish I were." Simon caught the horse's reins and climbed into the saddle. "The jungle is full of the scoundrels. I've heard they belong to some sort of Chinese secret society. Until now they've been content to terrorise their own people, who are too frightened and mistrustful to go to the authorities. I fear it is only a matter of time until they grow bolder."

So that was why he'd come after her, because he felt compelled to protect her. Bethan stifled a pang of disappointment as she took his outstretched hand and let him hoist her on to the horse's back. He did not want to bear a greater burden of guilt if she came to harm, like his wayward wife.

On the ride back to the villa she clung to Simon's waist, greedily inhaling his scent, soaking up the close contact she must soon take care to avoid.

It wasn't only her physical yearning for Simon she would have to resist. She was afraid that last night she might have lost something to him even more precious than her virginity. It was something she'd never meant to surrender—a fragile piece of her heart that he might crush in his powerful fist or grind beneath his heel. She must guard against giving him any more, and somehow she *must* find out what had become of her brother.

If Hugh was still alive, she must go to him while she could still bring herself to part from Simon.

He'd assured Bethan his honour was stronger than his desire. But as the days passed, Simon discovered it was a far closer contest than he had reckoned.

His smouldering anticipation from the previous weeks gradually gave way to gnawing frustration. It had been easier to restrain his desires when he'd believed Bethan was fearful of intimate contact with a man. Now, by her own admission, he knew she wanted him as much as he wanted her, so much that she could scarcely trust herself under the same roof with him for fear of yielding to temptation. Knowing that made Simon yearn for her more than ever.

And he could no longer stave off that craving by looking forward to the day when she would become his mistress and he could enjoy her favours as often as he wished. The future held only the bleak prospect of Bethan sailing out of his life for ever.

For both their sakes, he resolved to keep his distance from her. But even from a distance, she plagued his thoughts and invaded his dreams. His senses practically quivered with awareness of her presence in his house—the lilt of her voice wafting up from the garden or a tantalising whiff of her scent. He even fancied the aftertaste of her kiss lingering on his tongue. In the sultry darkness he would wake from provocative dreams of her to tantalising memories of the night she'd spent in his bed. It felt so empty without her.

Then he would listen for any sound coming from the

next room and wonder if she was tossing and turning as well, thinking of him, longing for his touch. Such thoughts only stoked the heat of his now forbidden desire. They urged him to steal into her room and offer her anything in the world if only she would consent to become his mistress.

He understood her reluctance. No doubt she'd heard her mother vilify such women for years in the most shameful terms. How could he make her see that as long as they were both free and consenting, they were not harming anyone by indulging their desires?

He couldn't. Not without running the risk of driving her away. For her sake and for Rosalia's, he dared not let that happen.

Bethan was doing everything in her power to resist temptation. She no longer dined with him in the evenings; whenever he came to the nursery, she always found some excuse to slip away and leave him alone with Rosalia. By the end of the week, he was so desperate to exchange even a few words with her that he was ready to seize upon any excuse.

One presented itself when he returned home early from work and spied Rosalia heading out to the garden with Ah-Ming. Bethan was nowhere in sight.

Had she fallen ill? That fear sent him charging up the stairs and down the hallway with no thought for his leg. He burst through her bedroom door, which stood open.

His racing pulse slowed as he stared around the tranquil room. Rays of green-gold sunshine filtered through the blinds to fall in slender stripes across the bed. Though a beguiling hint of Bethan's scent hung in the still, humid air, there was no other sign of her—not even her trunk or clothes.

Could it be that, in spite of his best efforts, she'd found it impossible to remain in his house? Surely she wouldn't have gone away without telling him?

He was about to go seek out Ah-Ming to demand an explanation when the patter of approaching footsteps heralded Bethan's sudden appearance.

"Simon!" She shrank back against the wall, her hand pressed to her chest. "You gave me such a turn. What are you doing here?"

Ignoring her question, he countered with one of his own. "Where are your things? I thought you'd gone away. You haven't, have you?"

She shook her head. "Only as far as the little room off the nursery. That's where I belong now."

"Nonsense!" he cried. "You're not a servant."

"Yes, I am." Bethan straightened up and shot him a defiant look. "And proud of it. I'd rather earn my keep with honest work, than be a rich man's plaything."

Before he could stop himself, his voice dropped to a caressing, inviting tone. "I thought you enjoyed the way we played together."

Her face took on a dewy flush, which betrayed the truth even before she spoke. "So I did, but I've seen what happens to toys when their owners lose interest in them."

"I won't cast you aside. I swear!" That was perilously close to a vow, caution warned him. Hadn't he wanted a mistress so he could easily free himself if things went bad? He'd never stopped to consider the situation from the woman's side.

Bethan raised a hand to rub her temples. "I don't want to argue about this any more. We've said all there is to say. Besides, you promised me…"

"I know I did." How could she trust any future

promise he made after he'd broken that one? "I'm sorry. I'll watch my words more carefully from now on."

She edged towards the bed, keeping as much distance between them as possible. "I just came looking for a handkerchief of mine that I wanted to show Rosalia. My mother stitched it for me years ago. She was a fine needlewoman. When I couldn't find it in my trunk, I thought I'd check here."

Her words emerged in a high-pitched rush that went on and on, as if she were afraid to give him the opportunity to say anything more. But finally her breath failed her.

"What about you?" Simon moved to the opposite side of the room and joined in the search, though his gaze kept darting back to drink in the sight of her. "Do you like to sew?"

It bothered him to realise how little he knew about her, especially compared to the secrets she had coaxed out of him.

"I'd be a menace with a needle." Bethan gave a winded chuckle that set his blood humming. "I'd prick more holes in my fingers than a pincushion and bleed all over the cloth I was trying to sew."

"There it is." With a rush of triumph, Simon seized a wad of cloth wedged behind the washstand.

Shaking out the flimsy square of embroidered linen, he offered it to Bethan with a flourish. An image ran through his mind of gallant knights accepting such tokens of favour from their ladies. When Bethan reached for it and her fingertips brushed his hand, he could not bring himself to loosen his grip on the handkerchief at once.

"Thank you," she murmured. "You have good eyes. I'm not certain I'd ever have found it."

The silver-green shimmer in *her* eyes gave Simon just

enough encouragement to suggest, "As a reward, would you consider dining with me tonight? I've missed having someone to talk to."

She twisted the handkerchief in her restless fingers, clearly torn between inclination and caution. "Couldn't you just invite one of the other businessmen? Or one of the lads from Durham? I'm sure they'd enjoy Cook's fine meals."

"Perhaps I did not make myself clear. I've missed having *you* to talk to."

"I think it's better if I take my meals in the nursery with Rosalia." Swiping the handkerchief over her glowing face, she seized upon an opportunity to change the subject. "Is it going to get much hotter than this over the summer? I feel like a Christmas pudding steaming in the copper!"

She did look good enough to eat and there were parts of her he would love to nibble. It took every ounce of restraint Simon possessed to keep from uttering those errant thoughts.

"Singapore is so near the equator, the temperature never varies much throughout the year." He'd thought his long sojourn in the East had inured him to the climate, but a trickle of sweat down his back suggested otherwise. "Now that you mention it, though, today does feel hotter than usual."

They exchanged a furtive glance in which Simon sensed they were thinking the same thing. The tropical climate was not to blame for the feverish heat that tormented them at the moment. Suppressed desire was like a banked blaze. The dancing, licking tongues of flame might be stifled, but the coals continued to glow hotter than ever.

Abruptly Bethan drew away from him as if scorched

by the dangerous heat that smouldered between them. "I should get back to Rosalia. I think I'll take her for a walk on the beach. The breeze is always a bit cooler down there. If that fails, I may just plunge into the water."

Simon pictured her rising up from the surf, her auburn hair whipped out by the sea breeze and her pink muslin gown plastered to her skin, making her look deliciously naked. Botticelli's bland-faced Venus would pale in comparison.

"That sounds wonderful." He sighed. "May I come too?"

For moment he feared she would refuse. Then her wary look softened. "We'd be glad of your company."

Perhaps she'd taken pity on his sweat-misted face. Or perhaps she thought it would be easier to keep her distance from him out of doors. Whatever the reason, a wave of gratitude lifted Simon's spirits. "Let's go then, before we melt into a pair of puddles on the floor."

As they headed off to collect his daughter, the realisation struck Simon hard that he enjoyed Bethan's company in more than just his bed.

Chapter Twelve

Had she been wrong, letting Simon persuade her to stay and continue caring for Rosalia? As the days passed, Bethan asked herself that question more and more often.

She'd hoped that keeping him at a distance would nip her feelings for Simon in the bud. Instead she found herself touched by the concern for his daughter's welfare that had forced him to endure this awkward arrangement. She appreciated the restraint and respect he'd shown her after all the trouble she caused him. She pitied his loneliness and the festering wounds of the past that made it so hard for him to love or to trust a woman.

Now, as much as she longed to feel Simon's arms around her and his lips upon hers, she also yearned to laugh with him, comfort him and remain faithful to him until he learned he could trust her. After the betrayals he'd suffered, she doubted he would ever let her get that close to him. And she could not give herself to him, either as mistress or wife, in a heartless exchange for the material comforts his fortune could provide. It must be for love or not at all.

That did not make her immune from temptation. The longer she stayed under Simon's roof, the more it felt like home. She had to remind herself constantly that it was not and could never be. The stronger the bond she helped him forge with his daughter, the more she yearned to be part of it. She must not forget she was only a servant in this house, not a member of the family.

The only true family she had left was her brother and she could not afford to waste any more time in trying to locate him. So far her few, furtive inquiries had led nowhere. Caring for Rosalia left her no time during the day to pursue her search and Simon had made it clear he didn't want her going out by herself at night. If only there was someone she could trust who knew Singapore well and might be willing to help her.

What about the harbour-master Simon had mentioned?

"Would you like to go pay a visit to some of your friends?" she asked Rosalia one morning while braiding the child's hair. "Perhaps those people who live up on the hill?"

"I used to visit the Flynns before Willy went away with his aunt and uncle," Rosalia replied in a wistful tone. "Now there's no one to play with. Charlotte is all grown up and Baby Sophia is too little."

As Bethan strove to hide her disappointment over having her thwarted plan, Rosalie chattered on, "I'd much rather go see the Bertrams. Alfie and Agnes are almost my age. We used to play together all the time. Their papa writes the newspaper."

"Does he?" Bethan's spirits lifted. Rosalia had mentioned wanting to visit these children before. Their father might be a source of useful information about the *Dauntless*. "Let's go pay them a call then, shall we?"

Rosalia heaved a dispirited sigh. "They moved to a new house, way down past the Sultan's *istana*."

"That's not very far." Bethan tied a blue ribbon around the end of Rosalia's thick, dark plait. "We could walk there if it wasn't so hot. I'm sure Mahmud would be happy to drive us."

"Oh, no!" Rosalia whipped around with a look on her small face as if Bethan had suggested they play with a spitting cobra. "The sultan might catch us and make us his slaves, like those poor girls Papa rescued!"

"Don't fret." Bethan knelt and clasped the child's hands. "I'm sure the sultan wouldn't do any such thing. Your papa took me for a drive to see that *istana* place and no one there paid us any mind."

Partly to distract Rosalia and partly out of curiosity, she asked, "Did your papa really rescue some slave girls?"

Rosalia gave a grave nod. "I heard Ah-Ming and Ah-Sam talking about it. They said it was a brave deed."

"I'm sure it was." Bethan longed to hear all the details of this modern-hero story. She could easily picture Simon in the leading role. "Your papa is very good about helping people in trouble, isn't he?"

She recalled something he'd said about a weakness for damsels in distress. But it went further than that. He'd been so kind to the lads from Durham, especially Wilson—boosting his confidence by making him a clerk and hiring someone to teach him.

"Yes, he is," Rosalia declared proudly. "Ah-Sam said Sultan Shah was very angry and tried to make trouble for Papa's company."

Simon wouldn't have backed down, though, Bethan mused with a warm mixture of admiration and pride, as if he somehow belonged to her. He was the kind of man who stood up for defenceless folk, mistreated by those in power. Might that include a ship's wretched crew tyrannised by a cruel captain?

Perhaps she'd been looking in the wrong place for help to find her brother. Perhaps the time had come for *her* to trust Simon enough to confide in him.

Simon returned from work that night in a foul temper. He'd got little sleep the night before, thinking about Bethan and this frustrating impasse between them.

Why couldn't she see that, no matter what happened between them, he would never think of leaving her destitute? He was nothing like her father. Hadn't he gone out of his way to prove, again and again, that he was a man of honour?

When she had first arrived in Singapore, he'd granted her request for time to get to know him. After unwittingly taking her virginity, he'd made her a proper offer of marriage, even though it was the last thing in the world he wanted. When she threw his proposal back in his face, he'd insisted on giving her sanctuary in his house to protect her from those who might take advantage of her impulsive *naïveté*.

Like the two merchants who'd quizzed him about her in the most impudent way that afternoon. They'd pretended to have a wager they wanted settled. One claimed to believe the beautiful young woman sharing Simon's house was his daughter's new *amah*. The other insisted she must be his mistress. Simon had informed them in no uncertain terms that his domestic arrangements were none of their business. At the same time he made it absolutely clear Miss Conway was under his protection and he would not tolerate any interference with her. Let them make of that what they would.

Shutting the door hard behind him, Simon stalked into the house and went straight to the dining room where he dropped on to his chair.

His bottom had barely touched down when Bethan peeped into the room. "Would you mind if I join you for dinner? I've missed having you to talk to as well."

He knew he should refuse, as courteously as possible. There was nothing to be gained by tormenting himself with hopes of something that could never be. But one look at Bethan and he could not send her away.

Against his better judgement, he motioned her to take a seat. "I warn you not to expect brilliant conversation from me this evening. It's been a long day."

"I'm sorry." A soft glow of concern in her eyes soothed his vexation. "You needn't feel obliged to entertain me. I just wanted to ask if I could take Rosalia to visit some friends of hers. I think it would do her good to spend more time with other children."

Simon nodded. "I agree. By all means take her."

Ah-Ming appeared just then with their dinner. Somehow she'd guessed Bethan would be joining him. Her smug look was almost more than Simon could bear.

"There's only one problem." Bethan explained Rosalia's reluctance to drive past the Sultan's *istana* to reach the Bertrams' house.

"Where did she hear about that business with the slave girls?" Simon glowered at Ah-Ming, who pretended not to notice.

Bethan shrugged. "You know what they say about little pitchers having big ears. She's very proud of what you did."

"It was nothing," Simon muttered, addressing himself

to his dinner. "On my way to work one morning, I met a crowd of young women coming down the road from Kampong Gelam. I know enough Malay to understand they'd been cruelly mistreated and needed help, so I took them to the police station and told the Resident of their plight."

"Not *nothing*," huffed Ah-Ming. "Others were too afraid of Sultan Shah to help."

"Rubbish." Simon signalled his housekeeper to leave. He hated to be thought some kind of hero when the truth was so very different. "There was no one else around at that hour."

He could not silence Bethan so easily. "Rosalia told me the Sultan tried to make trouble for your company."

"Idle threats." He dismissed them with a flick of his hand. "The Sultan gave me more blame than I deserved. The Resident was looking for any excuse to demonstrate he is the new master of Singapore."

Bethan did not appear convinced. She flashed him a teasing grin. "You do make a habit of rescuing ladies in distress."

"And it never turns out well." His lips pursed in a wry grimace. "The Resident used that incident as a pretext to humiliate the Sultan, which caused bad feeling among the Malays."

Bethan froze with a forkful of food halfway to her mouth. "Are you saying if you had to do it again, you wouldn't have helped those poor girls?"

"Of course not!" Simon was more than eager to change the subject. "I'd have gone about it differently, that's all."

"That's one of the things I've come to admire about you, Simon. You believe in fairness, that powerful people should not abuse the weak or take advantage of them."

Much as it gratified Simon to hear her say such things about him, her admiration made it all the more difficult for him to control his dangerous feelings for her. "That's the British way, isn't it?"

"Is it?" She looked doubtful. "I've heard how seamen on British ships are often ill treated by their captains. You wouldn't agree with that, would you?"

Why on earth had she chosen that example? His leg began to ache just thinking about it. "That is a different matter entirely. Discipline at sea must be maintained. Which sometimes requires harsh measures."

The reverent glow in Bethan's eyes dimmed and her lips tightened in a defiant frown. "But you can't think it right for a captain to treat his crew like slaves or worse? Surely they should have the right to stand up for themselves and—?"

"And mutiny?" Simon slammed down his fork so hard it made her jump. "Is that what you'd advocate?"

Her fair skin grew so pale, the freckles on her nose stood out starkly. But she refused to back down. "If the captain was enough of a tyrant, why not? What other remedy would those men have, far out on the ocean with no one to appeal to?"

His thwarted longing, his confused feelings towards her and the bitter ire that had long gnawed at Simon all came together in an explosive brew. "If you expect me to have an ounce of sympathy with mutineers, you are mad!"

"I don't see how they are so different from the sultan's slave girls." She seemed strangely puzzled by his reaction and far angrier than she had any reason to be. Perhaps *her* conflicted feelings were looking for an outlet, too. "Is it because mistreated sailors aren't helpless women looking for you to save them?"

"No!" Simon's chest felt like a jug of fermented cider that had just been roughly shaken. The pressure building up inside him was more than he could contain. "It is because those slave girls did nobody any harm when they ran away. Whatever excuses mutineers give themselves, the truth is they're nothing but a pack of bloodthirsty animals, led by damned troublemakers!"

"But—"

"Don't try to defend them!" He shot out of his seat. "Because you have no idea what men like that are capable of."

He marched around to her side of the table, making no effort to spare his leg, which now throbbed with pain that was half-real and half-remembered. "You once asked me how I injured my leg. Perhaps it's time I told you."

Bethan shrank back in her chair. Her eyes were wide with alarm, but they also ached with sorrow and reproach.

Simon did not want to make her feel that way, but he was caught in a riptide of fierce, dark emotion. If he tried to fight the powerful current, it might drown him.

"There was a mutiny aboard the ship that brought me from England, ten years ago." Reaching down, he gripped the left leg of his breeches with both hands. "I tried to assist the officers and other passengers. For that, I was beaten, shot and left to die!"

With a violent wrench, he ripped the leg of his breeches apart to reveal the scarred flesh beneath.

The sight forced a strangled cry of horror from Bethan.

"I believe any crewman who even *thinks* of mutiny should be hanged!" he thundered.

With her hand clamped over her mouth, she stared at his mangled leg in horror. Simon told himself it served her right for making him remember things he didn't want to remember and feel things he didn't want to feel.

What had they done to him?

As she stared at Simon's scarred leg, Bethan pressed her hand to her lips to stifle a cry of anguish.

She'd known about his wound since their very first meeting. At times she'd noticed him walking with a hitch in his brisk stride. Now and then she'd glimpsed a fleeting grimace of pain contort his handsome features. Yet most of the time she'd forgotten about his old injury, never thinking that he might irritable because his leg ached or tired because it had kept him from sleeping.

The shock of seeing that limb, pitted and seamed with scars, reminded her of other wounds he bore—deep ones that had never healed properly. Wounds that had maimed his heart, making it as difficult to love and trust as this one made it to walk at times. How often during the past weeks had she dug at those wounds with her prying questions and meddlesome demands?

Just now, for instance.

As she tried to find the words to tell him how sorry she was, Ah-Ming appeared, wringing her hands. Clearly something had jarred the housekeeper out of her usual calm, capable manner.

"Master, you must come!" she cried, her voice shrill with alarm. "Padre Marco's cook is here, very frightened. Aiyah! He says outlaws broke into the priest's house."

Simon recovered from the shock of the news more quickly than Bethan. "What about Father Marco, where is he?"

"Still at the house." Ah-Ming pointed towards the inland part of town. "The cook is afraid they will kill him!"

"But God forbid he should summon the police," Simon muttered.

"He knew our cook from Macao." Ah-Ming beckoned her master. "That is why he came here."

Simon started for the door, then glanced down at his torn breeches. "I'll be with you in a minute. Have Mahmud saddle my horse, then send him to summon the *sepoys*."

To Bethan's surprise the housekeeper did not rush off at once to do Simon's bidding. "What will you do, master?"

"Go to the priest's house, of course," he snapped as he limped past her. "Do what I can to help him."

Ah-Ming shook her head. "Aiyah! You should wait for the soldiers."

"There isn't time," Simon called back as his footsteps retreated down the hall. "Now go do as I told you."

Fighting off the twofold shock that froze her in her chair, Bethan lurched to her feet. Ah-Ming's words stirred disturbing memories of her misadventure in Chinatown, the day she'd arrived in Singapore. Simon had managed to talk his way out of that tense situation, but those people had been ordinary townsfolk, angered by the ignorance of a foreigner. What if they'd been armed outlaws who meant to do her harm?

"Talk to him," Ah-Ming pleaded. "He might listen to you."

Before Bethan could deny it, the housekeeper hurried away.

After what had just passed between them, she was surely the last person Simon might heed. But she had to try.

She'd barely reached the hallway when Simon

came toward her, tucking his shirt into a fresh pair of breeches.

Bethan stepped into his path. "Ah-Ming is right. You *should* wait for the soldiers or the police. This kind of thing is their job."

"And what harm could come to Father Marco in the meantime?" Simon pushed past her to the stairs. "What would have happened to *you* that day if I'd waited for the soldiers?"

"You can't resist an appeal for help, can you?" she called after him, hoping it might make him stop and think. "Not even after all it has cost you?"

At the foot of the stairs, Simon spun around to glare up at her. "Do you think I'm too feeble to be of any help?"

"No, I just…"

She wanted to explain that she couldn't bear it if any harm came to him. He'd suffered far more than he deserved already. But the words froze on her tongue. She didn't have any right to say such things to him.

"What about Rosalia?" Bethan clutched at straws for anything that might keep him out of harm's way. "What if the outlaws come here? Shouldn't you stay to protect *her*?"

"Rosalia is not in any danger, nor are you." Simon bristled at her suggestion that he might be neglecting their safety. "The outlaws wouldn't dare venture this far. Besides, the *jagga* man is on duty. I will have Samad and Cook join him if it will make you feel better."

She had no doubt the big, burly watchman, who haled from northern India, would be more than a match for any number of outlaws. But it was not herself, or even Rosalia, whose safety concerned her just now.

"Please be careful!" she called after Simon as he

headed off into the night without even acknowledging her warning.

A wave of guilt and dread broke over Bethan as she watched him go. Clutching the handrail, she sank on to the top step. Had Simon rushed headlong into danger to escape from her and the wrenching memories she'd stirred up? Had her shock at the sight of his injured leg made him feel he needed to prove himself?

For the next hour she sat there waiting and praying for him to return. Time slowed to a crawl, measured by the frantic drumming of her heart and the terrifying scenes running through her mind. Her imagination tormented her with lurid visions of what might be happening to him. She was far more terrified on his behalf than she had ever been for herself or anyone except her beloved brother.

Thinking of Hugh brought back her whole quarrel with Simon about mutineers. Was it some malicious trick of Fate that her quest to find her brother had led her to a man who would want him hanged? Thank heaven she'd shown a little caution for once and not told Simon all about Hugh. Rather than sympathising with her brother, as she'd hoped, Simon would be the first to betray Hugh to the authorities if she ever managed to find him.

But could she blame Simon after what he'd suffered at the hands of mutineers? She found herself imagining Simon's mutiny with her brother as one of the murderous crewmen. But that was madness. Hugh would never attack an innocent man and leave him to die. Would he?

Bethan wished she could be certain.

Her bottom was growing numb from sitting on the stairs when at last she heard movement and voices outside. She sprang up and flew down the stairs just as Simon staggered in, his arms around the shoulders of his driver and the gardener. All the tension that had been building inside of her during the past anxious hours shattered at the sight of Simon, injured but alive. It was everything she could do to keep from hurling herself upon him and sobbing out tears of relief.

"Is he very badly hurt?" She forced the words out past a choking lump in her throat. "What happened to him?"

"I'll be fine." As he hobbled past, Simon raised his head to meet her worried gaze. His mouth was set in a grim line and a trail of blood trickled down the side of his face from the hair above his right temple. "The outlaws took to their heels when they heard me coming. I made the mistake of getting in their way. Father Marco was more shaken than hurt, though I fear it would have gone worse for him if help had arrived any later."

In an effort to curb her turbulent feelings, Bethan sprang into action.

Catching sight of Ah-Ming, she called, "The master has been hurt. Fetch the medicine chest."

Then she hurried to Simon's room where the two servants were easing him on to his bed. "Mahmud, please go fetch Dr Moncrieff."

"Let the poor man sleep," Simon growled through clenched teeth. "I don't need a surgeon at this hour of the night. A swig of arrack and some sleep will put me right."

He spoke a few words to the servants in their own language. They nodded and bowed, then left the room.

"You've got a head wound." Bethan flew to Simon's side. "That could be serious. What if it needs stitching?"

Simon lay back on the pillows, his eyes closed. "Then I'll see the doctor in the morning. Don't fret. I've survived a good deal worse than this."

The thought of what he'd suffered in the past twisted her insides. What could she do for him *now*? "I wish Ah-Ming would hurry with the medicine chest."

"I doubt she's dawdling." Simon did not open his eyes. "Why don't you go back to bed?"

Bethan didn't budge. "I wasn't in bed. Do you think I could sleep while you were out risking your life? I'm not going anywhere until you've been tended to."

Wanting to make him more comfortable, she began to pry off his boots. "Was it those same outlaws you told me about? Why would they attack a priest?"

"The very ones." He stretched his stocking feet and began to tug at his neck cloth. "They must have been after the silver and gold of his communion plate."

"Lie still." Bethan perched on the edge of his bed. "I'll get that."

Her fingers brushed his as she untied the lightly starched fillets of linen. She had to concentrate fiercely to keep them at their task. They itched to stray upwards to caress Simon's cheek.

Fortunately, before she yielded to that temptation, Ah-Ming arrived with the medical supplies. Together the two women stripped Simon of his coat and waistcoat.

"You wash the wound." The housekeeper thrust a cloth and a basin of water into Bethan's hands. "I will go brew herb tea."

Before Bethan could protest, she was gone.

Simon made a sound like a soft moan crossed with a wry chuckle. "I've gained a healthy respect for Chinese medicine over the years. But the brew I need at the moment is good old Batavia arrack. It does an excellent job of relaxing muscles and relieving pain. You'll find a flask in the pocket of my coat."

As Bethan set down the basin and fetched the flask, he added. "It calms the nerves too. You should take a drop after I'm done."

She shook her head as she raised the flask to his lips. "You need it more than I do."

After Simon had taken several long sips, she gave him the flask to hold. Then she wet the cloth Ah-Ming had given her and began to bathe his head. "There's quite a bump but it's not bleeding much any more."

With a gentle, caressing touch, she washed away the trail of dried blood down the side of his face. "I'm glad you weren't hurt any worse. I was beside myself with worry."

"No need." Simon raised the flash for another sip. "I told you, I'm a survivor."

From what she'd learned of his past, Bethan suspected he wasn't used to being worried about and fussed over. "You've been through a great deal over the years."

The blood was all washed off his face. But still she could not stop grazing the soft, moist cloth over his cheek. "I'm sorry I reminded you about that awful mutiny. If I'd known—"

"I should beg *your* pardon." He raised his hand to cover hers, pressing it against his cheek. "I had no call to rage at you like that. You couldn't have known what I refused to tell you."

Hovering over him, Bethan gazed into his eyes. The unyielding blue ice seemed to have melted from them, revealing crystal-clear pools of intriguing depth. She leaned closer, yearning to explore.

"Here is your tea, master." The housekeeper's sudden entrance made Bethan spring back with a guilty start.

"I washed the cut on his head." She dropped the bloodstained cloth into the basin and edged away from Simon's bed. "It wasn't as bad as it looked at first."

"He is lucky not to be hurt worse." Ah-Ming gave no sign of having noticed anything untoward between them. "Those outlaws stop at nothing. They take only men whose parents are dead, so they will not fear disgracing their families with their crimes."

She held out a tea bowl to Simon. Wisps of steam rose from the surface, releasing a pungent aroma. "Sit up and drink this. It will do you more good than arrack."

Simon grumbled a little, but did as he was told.

"Sleep now," Ah-Ming decreed after he had swallowed the last sip. She pulled the netting over Simon's bed and beckoned Bethan out of the room. "Aiyah! Such a night."

As Bethan headed towards the nursery, her feet felt heavier with each step. What if Simon needed something before morning? What if he took a turn for the worse? She still could not shake the feeling that she was to blame for his injuries.

She wasn't certain what made her turn and creep back to his bedchamber. Was it that sense of guilt or the growing feelings for him that she'd been trying to suppress?

Perhaps the time had come to stop fighting those feelings and tackle her fears, instead.

Chapter Thirteen

His wounds throbbed—his face, his ribs and especially his leg. But none of them pained more than his conscience.

Simon tried to pry open his swollen eyelids, but the lashes were gummed together with dried blood. What little he could make out, as the *Sabine* sailed away, was awash in a sea of lurid red. His ears were filled with the thunder of waves pummelling the sand. But even that could not drown out the piercing shrieks. Was it only the gulls or the anguished cries of women beyond rescue?

An answering cry swelled up from deep inside, begging for release. But his jaws were clenched tight and his lips locked. With no outlet, the pressure in his chest threatened to crush his heart.

"Simon?" The sound of his name, spoken in that charming lilt, loosened whatever was gagging him.

A cry broke from his throat—a shriek of torment mingled with a bellow of helpless rage and a wail of bottomless guilt.

"Wake up, Simon!" the same voice summoned him

back from that lost, hopeless place. "You're safe now. It was only a bad dream."

He struggled to sit up, breathing in ragged gasps. His heart hammered so frantically against his ribs, he feared they might crack. The only thing that sustained him was a woman's arm, draped around his shoulders. It felt as soft and warm as a familiar blanket on a cold night, yet strong and steadfast as an anchor in rough seas. The fingers of her other hand swept over his hair in a steady, soothing rhythm.

"Your nightmare must have been a dreadful one. But it's over now and none of it was real." She comforted him as if he were a frightened child.

Part of him resented that, but he could not bring himself to pull away. For years he'd resisted the urge to confide in anyone or seek consolation. Now, as he surrendered to the tender sympathy Bethan offered, he began to see what a foolish error that had been.

"I know it was a nightmare." He canted his head to rest against hers. "It is over, for now, but it *was* real."

Even though he was now clearly awake, Bethan did not let go of him. "Were you dreaming about what happened tonight?"

Simon shook his head. "Ten years ago, aboard the *Sabine*."

"Do you often have nightmares about it?"

"I used to, but not so much lately. When I kept myself occupied with business and refused to dwell on the past, they didn't trouble me as much. But lately…"

Bethan sighed. "Lately I've been pestering you with questions, stirring up memories you wanted to let sleep."

"You aren't to blame." His arm encircled her waist.

"Any more than Rosalia was when she asked to go for a boat ride."

"Now that I know, I won't bring it up again," she promised.

For some reason her promise troubled Simon. "What will you do? Tiptoe around watching every word so that you don't remind me of something I'd rather forget?"

He didn't want that. He preferred her the way she was—spontaneous, curious and forthright.

"I could try." It was clear she realised the task would not be an easy one. "At least I could bear your feelings in mind a bit more—not blunder along saying whatever comes into my head."

"But those things are often interesting or amusing. I'd hate to lose them all because you were trying to avoid anything on my lengthy list of forbidden subjects."

She had no ready quip to answer that.

The compulsion to confide in her battled against Simon's deep-seated reluctance. Being reminded of all his mistakes and failures would make him feel even less worthy of whatever misplaced admiration she might feel for him. Knowing them would give her a potent weapon against him, if she ever chose to use it.

Bethan would never do that, his fragile but stubborn faith in her insisted. After all, she could have exploited his sense of honour and feelings of guilt to make an advantageous marriage, but she had not. She had only ever used her knowledge of his secrets to loosen their power over him and leech away some of their bitterness.

"The worst of the mutiny was not my wounded leg," he began in a hoarse murmur, "though the scars and the pain are a constant reminder. Mrs Mordaunt's betrayal was not the worst either, though I fear it may have left a different kind of scar."

"Who is Mrs Mordaunt?" asked Bethan in a tone of protective anger. "And what did she do to you?"

"The captain's young wife aboard the *Sabine*." It disgusted him to remember. "She sparked the mutiny by carrying on with one of her husband's officers. I might have prevented it if I'd gone to the captain with my suspicions sooner. But she begged me not to, and I was fool enough to listen."

Bethan's head moved in a knowing nod. "Another damsel in distress calling on your protection."

"The wicked irony is what happened to the other women aboard on account of my misplaced chivalry." Simon drew several deep breaths, nerving himself to go on. "While the mutineers abandoned all their male victims on the northern coast of Ceylon, they took the women with them to endure a fate that haunts my nightmares to this day."

Feeling a shudder run through Bethan, he braced himself for her response. Would she condemn him as bitterly as he had often denounced himself?

"That was a terrible thing!" She clasped him tighter. "But you were not to blame. You were unarmed, outnumbered and wounded. You could not have stopped them."

"I know." Somehow, hearing that reassurance from her lips made it easier to believe. "The same way I know I can trust you. Reason tells me so, but my conscience and my nightmares tell me something different. And they are harder to ignore."

"I *do* know," she whispered and he sensed she was speaking from her own dark place of self-doubt.

There was nothing either of them could say to comfort

one another. Words were the language of reason, which needed no persuasion. Instead Bethan tried to soothe him as she might Rosalia, with the tender warmth of her touch.

It did help.

"Stay with me tonight?" He nuzzled her neck with his cheek. "Not in the way you did before. I only want to be near you. You make me forget the troubles of my past. At least you make it hurt less to remember them, which is even better."

"I wouldn't leave," she replied in a fierce whisper, "even if you told me to."

Easing him back down on to his pillow, she nestled in the circle of his arms. The rest of that night, they held and caressed one another in a chaste, tender way that felt more intimate than their earlier night of passion. It fed a hunger within Simon that went even deeper than his desire.

Bethan woke in the pearly glow of dawn to find herself in Simon's bed. She did not feel strange or taken by surprise. She knew why she was there and it felt perfectly natural.

She didn't know what she would say to him when he woke. No doubt it would be more awkward between them when she had to meet his penetrating blue gaze in the unsparing light of day, rather than exchanging whispers and caresses in the darkness. But for now she would savour the chance to watch him at the only time he was completely unguarded.

There was nothing severe or forbidding about his face when he slept. His strong jaw was no longer clenched tightly. Gone was the stern crease between his brows that deepened when he scowled. The resolute line of his lips was relaxed enough that it might easily arch into a smile without danger of breaking.

In his peaceful face, she glimpsed the boy who longed to make his mark in the world and perform a thousand heroic deeds so that someone might love him. How she wished the man he'd become could learn to recognise and accept love when it was offered, rather than settling for a heartless exchange that would only cheat both parties.

She yearned to trace the jutting ridge of his chin with her fingertips and graze her lips over his brow until she washed away all his painful memories. That wish reminded Bethan of something he'd said in the night about her making it hurt less for him to remember. It touched her to think Simon believed she had that power. She recalled the events of last night—Simon's brush with danger, the deep secrets he'd confided in her and the need for her he'd confessed. Taken together, they made her realise the true nature of the feelings for him that she'd been trying to resist.

She understood now why he'd needed to put up such daunting defences around his heart. But the walls that protected also imprisoned, robbing him of the freedom to trust and love. Though they shielded his wounded heart from further injury, they also kept it locked away from the fresh air and sunlight it needed to heal properly.

If she'd accepted the grudging proposal of marriage he had made out of guilt, he would always suspect and resent her. He would never permit himself to care for her. Though honour would compel him to remain with her in body, any hope of love would be abandoned. That would be far more painful than if he simply went away, as her father had. She would be constantly tormented by his presence—near enough to touch, but with his heart a thousand miles away.

If instead, she freely gave herself to him, without expectation or conditions, it might lull his suspicions and set his heart free to reach out in love.

It was not an easy decision to make. She still had her doubts—fears of rejection and abandonment, conflict between her desire to be honest with him and her desperate need to protect her brother. She knew that sharing his bed, perhaps one day bearing his child out of wedlock, would make her question her worth in his eyes and fear for the future. Yet it was a risk she *must* take if she ever hoped to win his love.

At that moment Simon's eyes opened.

For an unguarded instant, Bethan glimpsed a promise of what she might gain if she succeeded in what she'd resolved to do. Then, as it dawned on him that she'd been lying there watching for some time, an invisible shield went up between them and his features tensed. Bethan told herself she must not let the sting of his mistrust deter her.

"Good morning." She tried to reassure him with a smile. "You asked me to stay with you last night. Or was that just the arrack talking?"

"It would take more than a bolt of arrack and a knock on the head to make me forget something like that." Before Bethan could ask if his head wound still pained him, he continued. "It was kind of you to stay, but now I think you'd better go."

"Why?" Had he changed his mind about wanting her? Or could he not bear to face her after she'd seen the scars he tried to hide behind an outward show of severity and success?

"Because..." his hand rose to twine a lock of her hair

around it "…a man can only exercise so much restraint when he wakes to find himself in bed with a beautiful woman. And I fear mine is taxed to the limit just now."

Bethan sensed the gentle touch of her hair was half against his will and that he was using all his self-control to keep from taking any greater liberties.

"What if I don't want to go?" This was harder than the first time she'd given herself to Simon. Then, she'd believed he was going to marry her. Now she was fully aware that might never happen. "What if I want to stay, at least until I need to go tend to Rosalia? And what if I want to come back again tonight and tomorrow night and all the nights after that?"

She tried to ignore the vicious hiss in the back of her mind, calling her vile, filthy names. As long as she was doing this out of love for Simon, and not for the things he could give her, she could cling to her self-respect, no matter what the rest of the world might think.

A searing haze rose in his eyes, like the kind she'd seen over the coast of Africa on her voyage here. "Please don't taunt me with such questions unless you are quite certain it *is* what you want."

"I am," she whispered. "I've given this a great deal of thought and I've decided I want to be with you for as long as you'll have me. I know I can trust you to do right by me."

Then, to keep him from looking too deeply into her eyes and perhaps glimpsing the shadows of doubt that lingered there, Bethan leaned towards him and pressed her lips to his. Simon yielded to her kiss with a sigh that seemed to rise from the hidden depths of his heart.

She wished she dared tell him that she loved him and wanted nothing from him except the chance to be loved in return. But she was afraid he might see that as an obligation or a threat and retreat once again behind his defences. She would have to be patient, to wait and watch for the moment when he was ready to hear and believe how much she cared for him.

What had made Bethan change her mind about becoming his mistress? That question flitted through Simon's thoughts as he sank into the moist, velvet depths of her kiss.

He'd planned for this moment, dreamed of it, despaired of it. Now, suddenly, he was getting what he wanted and so much more than he'd ever dared hope for. His pent-up passion surged towards the promise of release, while a wild rush of triumph sent his spirits soaring. Yet deep beneath all that ran an insidious undercurrent of doubt.

It might have been different if he had won her over by countering her arguments, soothing her apprehension and persuading her this would be best for them both. But he had not been able to do any of those things for fear of driving her away. He could not understand why she had altered her choice so completely without any urging from him. And what Simon did not understand, he could not trust.

But his desire refused to heed any whispers of suspicion that threatened its anticipated pleasure. Just because Fate had dealt him so many hash blows should not make him resist a piece of unexpected good fortune. Bethan must have sound reasons for her decision and he could ask her all about them later. For now, he must concentrate on the softness of her skin beneath his hands, the thrilling flick of her tongue over his, the subtle pressure of her thigh against his loins that made him ache with need.

This delicious morning tryst promised even greater delights than their first night together. There would be no murky shadows of misunderstanding between them followed by the harsh glare of disturbing revelations. Instead, their eyes would be open in the tranquil glow of daybreak. Rather than merely imagining his naked Venus as he admired her beauty with his hands, he could feast his eyes upon her along with his other senses.

Raising his hands to cradle her face, he parted reluctantly from their kiss to reassure her, "Whatever has changed your mind, I will do everything in my power to see that you never regret your decision."

"Not for…" he feathered a kiss on her forehead "…a single…" his lips playfully grazed the tip of her nose "…moment," he breathed, capturing her lips again with lusty abandon.

Anxious to view his prize, he slid one hand behind her back and deftly unhooked her gown. Then he eased the brief sleeves over her slender shoulders and tugged the bodice down to reveal the fine linen shift beneath. Plucking one end of its drawstring ribbon, he pulled in a slow, fluid motion until it came undone.

A wordless murmur of admiration rose in his throat when he had peeled the shift down, baring her breasts to his appreciative gaze. When he stroked one with the back of his hand, her nipple tightened into a nugget of dark coral, demanding the attention of his lips and tongue. He was delighted to oblige. While he kissed, licked and sucked the tender morsel, he watched Bethan's face through half-closed eyes, relishing the looks of pleasure and sweet yearning that gripped her features.

Whatever she wanted from this liaison with him, Simon knew it was not the material gifts he might lavish upon her. That precious certainty made him more determined than ever to sweep her from the giddy, breath-taking heights of bliss to the wet, writhing depths of ecstasy.

To that end, he despatched her rumpled gown and her undergarments until he could gaze to his heart's content upon her naked body in all its rounded, dewy splendour.

"You are a living work of art," he breathed, anxious to explore every tantalising inch of her. "No painting or sculpture could begin to capture your beauty."

His blatant admiration made Bethan hide her face against his shoulder. "You're the only man who's ever seen me without my clothes on."

"You may be certain I cherish the privilege." Simon stroked her rich, lustrous hair and pressed his cheek against the crown of her head. If he had not bedded her himself, he would have thought her perfectly innocent.

He ran his hand down her belly, over the exquisite curve of her hip, veering in to the enticing tangle of downy curls that crowned the cleft where her legs met. Soon arousal overcame her bashfulness and she slipped her hand beneath his shirt to caress the firm flesh of his torso.

"What about *your* clothes?" she asked in an impudent whisper. "What's sauce for the gander is sauce for the goose, don't you think?"

"Help me finish what you started last night, then." Simon tugged up his shirt. "Though I fear I am getting the best end of this bargain."

Hard as he tried to make light of it, he was not altogether comfortable baring his scarred body to the gaze of such a goddess.

"You're too modest," Bethan pronounced when she had helped him shed his shirt, breeches and drawers, "as you are about your courage and so many other things. Just looking at you like this makes me feel the way I do when you touch me or kiss me."

"How is that exactly?" asked Simon, captivated by her artless innocence.

"It's hard to say, really. I never felt anything like it before I met you." She touched her breast. "I feel it here and here." Her hand slid lower. "It's like an ache that doesn't hurt but hums under my skin."

Her words worked a sensual magic, easing Simon's self-consciousness while stoking his arousal.

"You like that feeling, do you?" He raised himself on one elbow, the better to gaze upon her while running his hand up and down her body as far as he could reach.

She nodded, her misty-green eyes wide with wondrous anticipation, as they had been when he introduced her to the exotic sights and tastes of Singapore. Her lips parted in a wordless plea to be kissed again. Simon could not resist, nor did he want to.

As he plundered the lush depths of her mouth, his fingers ceased their pleasant but aimless roving to concentrate upon the other lush depths of her passage, priming her to receive him. One dip of his forefinger was all he needed to be certain she was a ready and eager to receive him.

Much as he'd enjoyed making love to her the first time, he wished he had not waited quite so long to bury himself inside her and savour the snug silken grip of her flesh on his. This time, rather than bringing her to release in advance, he wanted to feel her tighten around him as each stroke nudged her closer to the brink of rapture.

Still locked in their kiss, he raised himself and slid over to pin her beneath him. She seemed to sense what he wanted, or perhaps she wanted it just as much. Her thighs parted in an invitation he was impatient to accept. With slow, deliberate pressure, he mounted her, concentrating on the subtle change of sensation he experienced the deeper he pushed. When he had sheathed himself to the hilt, he paused for a moment, holding quite still, to soak in the incomparable harmony of their joining.

"It doesn't hurt at all this time." Bethan sounded surprised but delighted by the discovery.

A stab of shame tempered Simon's pleasure. The last time they'd been together like this, he had hurt her without even knowing it. Afterwards he'd been so consumed with her "deception", he hadn't even said he was sorry or stopped to wonder if she was still in pain.

Yet here she was beneath him again, having opened the most private, vulnerable part of herself to receive him, prepared to take the pain with the pleasure.

"It won't hurt again," he promised, gazing deep into her eye as he moved his hips in a controlled stroke.

Hot shards of delight ripped through his loins, but he was more concerned with Bethan's pleasure than his.

She left him in no doubt.

Her eyelids slid half-shut as her tawny brows came together. Her lips parted to release a gush of breath that was part-sigh and part-purr.

On his next thrust, she moved too, in perfect accord that heightened the sensation for both of them.

With each stroke it built and built like a powerful wave on the vast ocean—rolling, curling, foaming as it raced to break upon the shore. That wave drove everything before it—suspicion, bitterness, regrets.

It swept over Bethan first, making her arch towards him while her hips writhed and a wild, keening cry broke from her lips. Her passionate spasms plunged

Simon over the edge at last, demolishing the iron self-control that held him together and shattering him into a million pulsing pieces.

Later those broken fragments reformed stronger and better.

Chapter Fourteen

The rest of that day, whenever Bethan recalled how it had begun, echoes of pleasure rippled through her body, followed swiftly by a tremor of misgiving.

She'd been so certain her decision to become Simon's mistress was the right one. But as the intense emotions of the previous night wore off, second thoughts began to haunt her. He had swept her up to paradise that morning in his bed. But afterwards he'd dropped her back down to earth when he'd gone to work, warning her to keep Rosalia inside the house until he returned. Was she a fool to hope that he would come to love her in time? Or would he never think of her as anything more than a pleasant diversion from the pressures of his business?

"Can we please go out?" Rosalia reached across the table where they sat playing *Dou Shou Qi* and squeezed her hand. "Just for a little while?"

Though the child's beseeching gaze was as hard to resist as her father's, Bethan shook her head. "I've told you, we have to stay inside today. Orders from your papa."

She invoked the possibility of Simon's displeasure reluctantly. The last thing she wanted to do was make Rosalia fear losing the affection her father had recently begun to show. "When he gets home I will ask him about tomorrow."

"Ask me what?" Simon appeared in the nursery door, as though summoned by her longing to see him.

"Papa!" Rosalia jumped up and rushed towards him then froze. In a more guarded tone, she added, "You're home early."

"So I am." Simon scooped Rosalia into a hesitant but affectionate embrace. "Which means you can ask me whatever it was you were going to ask me."

"Go ahead," Bethan prompted the child. "You've pestered *me* about it often enough today."

"Well," Rosalia began at last, "we've been inside all day and it's so hot. Can we out go into the garden for a little while?"

"What about down to the beach?" Simon directed his suggestion to Bethan as well as his daughter. "I hear the two of you like to go for walks there."

Bethan nodded her approval while Rosalia threw her arms around his neck, "Oh, yes, Papa, that would be lovely!"

A short while later, Bethan and Simon strolled barefoot over the sand while Rosalia skipped on ahead searching for pretty shells or interesting bits of driftwood to show them. As the waves caressed the shore, leaving lacy traces of foam in their wake, a cooling breeze blew from the darkening eastern horizon.

Pitching her voice low so as not to alarm the child, Bethan asked, "Has your head been bothering you today?"

Simon seemed touched by her concern. "To tell you the truth, I've been too busy to notice."

"Did they catch those outlaws?"

He shook his head. "I never expected them to. Those scoundrels melt back into the jungle secure in the knowledge that they can't be followed by a force large enough to apprehend them."

"Are we in any danger?" It seemed hard to imagine on this tranquil beach.

"The Resident is convinced the attack on Father Marco was an isolated incident, but I am not so sure. He promised to put more *sepoys* on night patrol, but that is a stopgap at best. What's needed is a road into the jungle so the soldiers can pursue the outlaws and root them out of their hiding places. We might as well put our convict labour to good use."

Hoping to lighten his spirits a little, Bethan quipped, "So you want to use one group of outlaws to protect Singapore from another?"

"Quite an irony, isn't it? Or perhaps natural justice. I don't much care which as long as there are no more attacks."

"How long do you think it will be until Rosalia and I can go for outings again?" Though she'd tried not to let the child see, being confined to the house all day had made her feel trapped.

The sound of her name must have caught Rosalia's attention. Before her father could reply, she called out, "Bethan was going to take me to see Agnes and Alfie tomorrow. Can we still go?"

"I'm afraid you'll have to postpone your visit for a little while." Simon sounded reluctant to disappoint the child, but Bethan knew he could not bear to risk her safety.

"Perhaps we could invite your friends to visit us?" Bethan suggested when Rosalia's face fell. "Or…"

"Or what?" Simon sounded a trifle wary of what she might propose.

"I was just thinking if the other women and children have to stay close to home as well, perhaps we could raise everyone's spirits by inviting them to your house for a little party. Preparing for it would make the time pass more quickly for Rosalia and me."

"Oh, yes!" cried Rosalia. "Agnes and Alfie could come, and Charlie and Catherine. Can we have a party, please, please, please, Papa?"

"It might provide an excellent diversion for everyone," Simon replied after a slight hesitation. "May I come too? It sounds a good deal more entertaining than those tiresome balls our Resident hosts."

"Of course you can come!" Delighted out of her usual reticence, Rosalia charged towards her father and flung her arms around his legs. "Thank you, Papa!"

"You're welcome." Stroking her dark hair, Simon seemed pleased by his daughter's affectionate outburst. "Now we'd better head home before it gets too dark."

After their romp on the beach, Simon hung about the nursery and helped put Rosalia to bed. He even told his daughter a story about his childhood back in Lancashire. Rosalia seemed amazed to learn her father had once been a small boy. Perhaps from all her laughter and exertion in the sea air, she drifted off to sleep before he finished.

When Simon stooped to press a kiss upon her forehead, the sight lit a brooding glow deep within Bethan. His obvious love for the child gave her hope for herself.

He had been willing to recognise his mistakes and make the difficult effort to change.

He glanced up to catch her smiling down at them. "Rosalia hardly seems the same child she was when you arrived. I was so concerned with her being biddable that I didn't stop to wonder if she was happy. You've done wonders for her."

The gratitude in his tone warmed her. She must be patient with him and not expect miracles overnight. It had taken many years and many wounds to make him close off his heart. "Done wonders with *you*, you mean. Once I bullied you into paying her more attention to her and not being so stiff and stern around her, she stopped worrying so much about always behaving properly."

"You have indeed done wonders for me." Simon rose from his daughter's bedside and took her in his arms. "I've been wanting to do this since the moment I got home. The other merchants were puzzled how I could be in such cheerful spirits after what happened last night."

He kissed her as if it had been weeks since he'd last bedded her, rather than hours. "Little did they know I was thinking far less about *last* night than looking forward to tonight…with you."

She had attracted his desire, Bethan reflected as they strolled toward the dining room arm in arm. She had secured his gratitude and perhaps a measure of respect. Was it too much to hope those feelings would one day ripen into love? Or had she squandered any hope of respectability in a fruitless bid for the one thing Simon could not give her?

"To think Singapore would ever see Senhor Grimshaw host a children's party." Carlos Quintéra quipped to the other men who'd accompanied their families.

While Bethan led the youngsters in a series of games in the sitting room, and their mothers sat out on the veranda gossiping over cups of punch, the men had congregated in Simon's dining room.

"I think it's a canny plan," replied Denis Nairn. "This gives us a chance to gather and discuss what to do about these infernal outlaws without our esteemed Resident getting wind of it and imagining we're plotting his overthrow."

Simon did not deny the claim, though it wasn't strictly true. His chief motive for hosting this party had been to please his daughter and Bethan, and to make up for the restrictions he'd placed on them. This opportunity to meet with some of the other merchants and officials was an unexpected windfall.

"Speaking of the outlaws," said Captain Flynn, "did you hear about last night's raid on the *dhobi* lines? I heard the commotion from my hill. If any of you had clothes out being laundered, you may never see them again."

"What was the point of that?" demanded Quintéra over the outraged muttering of the others. "Do these savages mean to parade around the jungle in our shirts and waistcoats?"

Simon wondered how many items of his had been lost. "I think they did it to tweak our noses and show just how much they can get away with. Perhaps if they stole enough pairs of the Resident's trousers, he might take the situation more seriously."

"I agree." Quintéra nodded. "We need to set those convict crews building a road into the jungle so the outlaws cannot slip away after their impudent attacks."

"In the meantime," said Simon, "I suggest we all increase our contributions to the Night Watch Fund and have extra men patrol the European Quarter in addition to the Commercial District."

Nairn and one of the other Scotsmen shook their heads at the suggestion of an additional expense, but Quintéra endorsed it readily. "An excellent idea. The Resident can hardly interfere with a project we are funding ourselves. Perhaps it will embarrass him into agreeing that we need that road."

As the discussion continued, Simon found his attention distracted by the sound of Bethan's voice from the sitting room. "Remember, when you spot the thimble, call out *huckle-buckle-beanstalk* but don't tell the others where you've seen it."

Edging towards the doorway, he glanced in to watch the children at play. Rosalia was holding little Mary Flynn by the hand and beaming with excitement. His daughter's smile reminded Simon of the way Carlotta had looked once, when he'd bought her a present. He braced himself for the sharp sting that always accompanied memories of his late wife, but he felt only a faint twinge of regret.

Had his desperate efforts to suppress those memories given them more power over him? Now that he'd dared confront them, with Bethan's help, was it possible his old wounds might finally begin to heal?

As he continued to watch the children scramble around the room searching for the tiny thimble hidden in plain sight, he saw what Bethan meant about Rosalia's resemblance to him. His daughter was always the first to run and help a younger child who fell down. She encouraged a bashful latecomer to join in the game. When one of the boys teased his clumsy little brother, she had a few choice words for the bully.

Simon's chest swelled with pride to see how readily

his daughter helped those who needed it. His heart warmed with a sense of deep kinship unlike anything he'd felt for her before. Grateful to Bethan for fostering that bond, he sought her out with his gaze. For an instant, their eyes met over Rosalia's head. From the brooding softness of her smile, he sensed she'd been thinking the same thing about his daughter.

A rush of tenderness toward her welled up in him.

"I congratulate you on a splendid acquisition in Senhorita Conway." Carlos Quintéra suddenly appeared at Simon's elbow, interrupting their intimate gaze.

"My daughter thinks the world of her," he answered stiffly.

He'd never much cared for Quintéra, who used to infuriate him by speaking Portuguese to Carlotta so he could not understand what they were saying.

Now the man appraised Bethan with an exasperating little smirk. "You may have started a new fashion. My wife says we should hire a European *amah* for our boys. She claims they speak Cantonese better than their mother tongue. Don't be surprised if she or one of the other ladies try to lure Senhorita Conway away from you."

"If they do, I will find out the highest bid for her services, so I can top it." Simon tried to sound jocular, but the words came out in tone of deadly earnest.

Quintéra gave a low, suggestive chuckle. "I suspect another reason you chose to host a *children*'s party."

"Do you?" Simon forced the words through his clenched teeth.

"But of course. This way, none of Singapore's bachelors are on hand to gain introductions to the lovely Senhorita Conway. What sort of bids do you suppose they might make for her services?"

"What is that supposed to mean?" Simon's right hand clenched into a fist that he had trouble restraining.

"Come, come, man. Nothing to *fash yourself over*, as your partner Northmore used to say. I am only suggesting it might require a different sort of gold to counter their bids. In the form of a ring, perhaps."

The veiled suggestion that one of his competitors might make Bethan an offer of marriage stole the breath from Simon's lungs. A similar thought had troubled him when she'd threatened to leave his house. At that time he'd only been concerned with protecting her. Now his feelings were much more intense and personal.

It suddenly occurred to him that the freedom of their arrangement cut both ways. If Bethan received a better offer from another man, she would not be legally or morally bound to him in any way. Indeed, any respectable clergyman would urge her to abandon a life of sin for the sanctity of wedlock. Simon could not abide the idea of her remaining in Singapore but living in another man's house, bearing his name and perhaps his children. Not after the intimacy they'd shared. When Carlotta had betrayed him, at least she'd gone away, not stayed to flaunt her new liaison and mortify him in the eyes of the entire community.

And yet…he felt like the meanest dog in the manger for begrudging Bethan the chance to make a truly respectable life for herself. How dare he resent her accepting from another man the one thing he could not give her?

Simon reminded himself that he had made her an offer of marriage, only to have her refuse in the most insulting terms. Then again, it had been a most insulting offer.

As he watched Bethan gather his daughter into a

fond embrace, Simon wondered if perhaps the time had come to reconsider the part he wanted her to play in their lives.

Was this the reason Simon had seemed reluctant to host the party? Bethan wondered as she led the children through their games. Because he knew how awkward her position would be?

It was clear their guests did not know how to treat her. Was she the hostess or a mere servant? Was she Rosalia's respectable care-giver or Mr Grimshaw's secret mistress? The uncertainty about her place made everyone uneasy. The ladies were careful to be civil but not too friendly. The moment she was out of earshot, she was sure they started gossiping about her. Their husbands were rather *too* friendly, making her skin crawl with their leering looks. Only the children behaved naturally towards her. They did not care whether she was wife, nursemaid or mistress as long as she kept them entertained.

Had Simon deceived her with his assurance that mistresses were accepted in Singapore society? Or did men take no notice of the subtle signs women used to shun outcasts? Even if he did come to love her in the future and offer to marry her, could she ever expect more than grudging tolerance from the people among whom she must live?

In spite of those qualms, she was not sorry she'd suggested Simon host this party. The reason for that was one particular guest. Captain Flynn, the harbour-master she'd long been anxious to question about her brother's ship, had accompanied his wife and daughters to the gathering. Though the things she'd learned from Simon about his mutiny had shaken her absolute faith in Hugh, Bethan still could not rest until she knew what had become of him.

The party was nearly over by the time she managed to catch Captain Flynn off by himself. While some of the guests were still eating and others preparing to leave, the harbour-master stood in one corner of the veranda sipping a cup of punch while he gazed out towards the sea.

"Keeping watch over your harbour, Captain?" Bethan grasped for an opening that might lead into her question without sounding suspiciously abrupt. "Master attendant of such a busy port must be a very important post."

"It *was* at one time." With a fierce scowl, Captain Flynn bolted the last of his punch. "Before our current Resident saw fit to strip away the prerogatives of my office."

"What a shame." It was clear the man nursed a deep grievance of some sort, but Bethan did not have the time to hear all the particulars. "I was hoping you might be able to answer a question for me, about a ship that passed through Singapore three years ago."

The captain gave a derisive chuckle. "My dear young woman, have you any idea how many ships have come through this harbour in that time?"

Before she could hazard a guess, he provided the discouraging answer. "Almost a thousand square-rigged vessels and perhaps ten times that many native craft."

She should have known it was hopeless, that far too much time had passed to discover anything useful. Stubborn resolve made her clutch at straws. "It wasn't a native ship. It would have come from England."

"That's different," the captain replied, much to her

surprise. "We've had less than two-score ships from Europe since this place was founded. That number is expected to rise dramatically now that a treaty has been signed and Singapore is an official British possession. What ship did you want to know about?"

"The *Dauntless*." A tantalising flicker of hope almost made Bethan forget the excuse she'd invented to explain her interest. "A man from my village was among the crew and he hadn't been heard from since his ship left Singapore."

It was not an outright lie, she told herself in an effort to ease her conscience. She'd only failed to mention that the man was her brother.

"The *Dauntless*…hmm?" Captain Flynn stared off towards one of the ships at anchor as if picturing another that had been there three years ago. "Didn't she go up in flames during a mutiny off the Coromandel Coast?"

"Oh, dear." In spite of the heat, an icy chill swept through Bethan. This was the first she'd heard about a fire. "Did all hands perish?"

The captain shrugged. "I don't recall much about it, though I do know there was at least one survivor. Doctor Ellison took passage from Singapore aboard the *Dauntless* on his way to an assignment in Madras. He's back here now, staying just up the road with his friend Dr Moncrieff."

"Fancy that." It took every scrap of self-control Bethan could summon to keep from betraying her excitement. "I must think to ask him about it if we happen to meet."

She chatted for a few more minutes with Captain Flynn, then excused herself. For the rest of the party, she went about in a hopeful daze. To think that all these weeks she'd tried in vain to glean any scrap of news about her missing brother, when someone with reliable information about Hugh was so nearby.

The first chance she got, she would be off to question this Dr Ellison to find out what he knew about the *Dauntless* mutiny.

Chapter Fifteen

"The party was a great success, thanks to you." Simon lifted his cup of punch in a toast to Bethan.

Their guests had long since departed, not wanting to be caught away from home after dark. With some difficulty, Bethan and Simon had managed to put his overtired, overexcited little daughter to bed. Now they sat together on the veranda, watching the stars come out above the eastern horizon.

Bethan did not reply to his praise. She seemed lost in thought. Now that he came to think of it, she'd been preoccupied ever since the party got over.

"How many of the ladies tried to hire you away to work for them?" Though he strove to make it sound like a jest, Simon was very much in earnest. Had she realised how great a demand there might be for her services? And did it make her regret the impulsive decision to place herself in his keeping? What if she discovered there were men in Singapore willing to offer her not only comfort and security but respectability as well?

His question seemed to jar Bethan out of her musing.

Or perhaps it was the anxious edge he hadn't been able to keep out of his voice. "Only one, though another did ask me to let her know if I'm ever looking for a new position."

"Do you intend to?" he asked. "Is that what's been on your mind this evening?"

"No!" Bethan batted the air with her hand as if to dismiss such an absurdity. "I told them I'm quite contented where I am."

"I'm glad to hear that." Thank God he was in no immediate danger of losing her. A pressing weigh seemed to lift off Simon's chest, allowing him to breathe properly again. "Mrs Bertram asked if Rosalia might like to come to their house next week to visit and stay the night."

"Will you let her go?" asked Bethan, her attention fully engaged.

"I wanted to talk it over with you first. Do you think it's a good idea? Mrs Bertram assured me their place is as well guarded."

"Of course!" Bethan cried almost before he'd finished. "You saw how much Rosalia enjoyed playing with the other children today. I know you want to keep her safe, but there are other things just as important. If you let her go, I'll guard her with my life."

"I'm sure you would." Her devotion to his daughter stirred something deep within him. "But I thought we might let Rosalia stay on her own. It would allow her a taste of independence and give us some time alone. What do you say?"

For a moment he thought Bethan might object, but something seemed to change her mind. "It might do her good. And she won't be far away."

Simon set down his empty glass and went to kneel beside Bethan's chair. "It might do us good to have more than stolen moments together when Rosalia is sleeping."

She reached up to brush a lock of hair back from his forehead. "I think it might."

He caught her hand and brought it to his lips, where he dusted kisses over each of her fingertips. Those clever, supple fingers of hers were becoming deliciously adept at rousing him. Her natural curiosity and playfulness made each encounter a sort of fresh adventure that even a cautious man like he could relish.

"I know what I will enjoy most," he whispered.

"Are you going to tell me?" She rested the tip of her little finger in the shallow cleft of his chin. "Or do I have to guess?"

Simon chuckled, enjoying this intimate banter more than he'd ever imagined he could. "I am going to enjoy waking up next to you, knowing you will not have to rush away to tend my daughter."

"It will be a treat to sleep in." Her eyes sparkled with innocent mischief.

"You could pretend to be asleep…" Simon leaned closer to nuzzle her neck "…while I find inventive, pleasurable ways to wake you."

"I like the sound of that," Bethan murmured, her voice husky with desire.

"It's settled then." He got to his feet, scarcely noticing the familiar pang in his leg. "Tomorrow I'll send word to Mrs Bertram, accepting her very kind invitation." Seizing Bethan's hand, he hoisted her up from her seat and into his arms. "But for now, I have a very amusing game I'd like to play with you."

"Good day, sir," Wilson greeted Simon when he strode into the office a few days later. "There was a man came by last night after you'd gone and left a parcel for you. He said it was from Mr Hong, with his compliments."

The clerk held out a small box.

For a moment Simon could not imagine what it might be. Then he recalled asking the Chinese trader to make enquiries about Bethan's stolen property. Prying open the box, he lifted out a silver locket.

"Is that Bethan's?" Wilson broke into a broad grin. "The one that was stolen?"

"So it would appear." Simon unfastened the delicate catch and opened the locket, relieved to find the miniature portrait of her father still intact.

The handsome Welshman stared back at him with grey-green eyes as merry and curious as Bethan's. His hair had been the same rich shade of auburn too. And his chin had the same intrepid tilt as his daughter's. Mr Conway had been a fine-looking fellow in his youth. No wonder he'd attracted the desire of a woman other than his wife. What if a penchant for inconstancy ran in the family?

"She'll be glad to get that back." Wilson's voice broke in upon Simon's doubtful brooding. "I never saw her without it the whole time we were sailing from home."

Snapping the locket shut, Simon chided himself for his unjust suspicions. Here was proof Bethan had been telling him the truth from the first day she'd set foot in Singapore.

If anything, she was *too* honest. Informing him with brutal candour that he was neglecting his daughter, admitting the desire she felt for him even when he might have exploited it, challenging his stubborn reluctance to talk about painful events from his past. Uncomfortable as her frankness could be at times, he found it refreshing and admirable. She was one woman he would never have to fear deceiving or betraying him.

"When you've got a minute, sir," said Wilson, returning to his ledger, "George had a question about the different grades of indigo. And the captain of an American ship wanted to buy some coffee, tea, sugar and spices. I told him to come back today."

"Good." Simon headed towards the warehouse. "By treaty we're not permitted to sell trade goods to Americans, only enough to provision their ships. I'll talk to George about the indigo. All the different grades can be confusing."

He tucked Bethan's locket into the breast pocket of his coat for safekeeping. Throughout that day it rested against his heart, a constant reminder of her many sterling qualities and how great a temptation she might pose to some other man. He could not run the risk of having such a precious treasure stolen from him.

This visit of Rosalia's could not have come at a better time, Bethan reflected as she and Simon drove back up Beach Road after delivering his daughter to visit her little friends. Besides allowing them more time alone, it would give her a chance to seek out the doctor who might have information about her brother.

"You're quiet." Simon's voice called her back from her thoughts and plans. "That isn't like you. Nothing wrong is there."

"Not at all." Realising she needed an excuse to explain her silence, Bethan offered one that was more than half-true. "Though I am a bit worried about Rosalia. I know she'll be safe enough, but I hope she'll have a good time and not be lonely."

Simon's features relaxed. "I don't suppose there's

much chance of that with four other children for company. Did you see how taken she was with the baby?"

Bethan chuckled. "I think she'll be pestering you for one the minute she gets home." Realising how that might sound, she blushed furiously. "I didn't mean… that is… she'll likely want a doll or some such."

The sight of the Bertram's youngest, with its thatch of dark downy hair, plump wee cheeks and sweet milky scent had called forth a tender, brooding yearning in *her* as well. But it had also raised questions she'd been foolishly trying to ignore about the possibility of Simon getting her with child.

Her mother had told her little enough about how babies were bred, except for a few furtive words when she first got her monthly flux. The mysterious jests and whispers of her fellow servants had done little to cure her ignorance. She was certain Simon would explain it all to her if she asked, but it was such an thorny subject to raise. She didn't want him to think she would use a child of theirs to get things from him, the way his late wife had. Neither did she want to sort out all her confused feelings about motherhood and what it would mean for her. A joy, quite likely, given how much she loved children, but a burden and worry too. A child would tie her to Simon as tightly as wedding vows, even if he could not love her.

"Don't worry." He gave her knee a reassuring pat. "I know what you meant."

Did he really? Somehow Bethan doubted it.

"Rosalia isn't that far away if she wants to come home," he continued. "See, we're back already. Now, I want you to change into your prettiest gown—that green one, perhaps. I've only seen you wear it once and you looked lovely in it."

"You mean my wedding dress?" The words popped out before Bethan could stop them. "I mean, the dress I bought to wear for…when I thought we were… Good heavens, I'm all tongue-tied today!"

A glance into the garden as they drove to the stable provided the perfect change of subject. "What's that table doing out in the middle of the grass? And what are those coloured balls hanging from the trees?"

"Chinese lanterns." Simon's voice had a jaunty ring to it. "Part of a little surprise I planned for this evening. I hope you'll enjoy dining out in the garden. I asked Cook to prepare us a banquet of his most interesting and toothsome dishes."

"What's the occasion for all this fuss?" Bethan asked as he helped her out of the gharry.

"You'll see," he replied with a mysterious half-smile.

Curious to find out, she changed quickly into her green gown. But on her way to join Simon for dinner, she happened to glance out the window that looked down Beach Road. Only four plots up the street, in a house she'd passed several times since coming to Singapore, was the man who could tell her what she'd come so far to find out.

Eager as she was to speak to him, she also felt a qualm of dread. What Dr Ellison had to tell her might threaten the life she hoped to make with Simon and Rosalia. It was no use getting ahead of herself, though. This evening promised delights she did not want to spoil by borrowing trouble.

"You've never looked more beautiful." Simon swept an admiring glance over her when she appeared in the sitting room a few moments later. "May I escort you to dinner? *Al fresco* as the Italians would call it, if we had any of them in Singapore. They are one of the few nationalities not represented here."

He led her out to the garden, where darkness was beginning to fall. The brightly coloured paper lanterns cast a warm glow over the whole area. The lush fragrance of jasmine perfumed the air. Beneath the spreading canopy of a tall saga tree, a compact table was set for two with a white cloth, gleaming china, crystal and silverware. The middle of the table held an array of flowers in the most vivid and varied hues Bethan had ever seen—coral pink, golden yellow, rich purple.

"What are these?" she asked as Simon held out her chair. "They're so perfect, they don't look quite real."

"Orchids. They grow wild around here, clinging to the trees like weeds."

"Prettiest weeds I've ever seen." Bethan smiled up at him. "I can't believe you've gone to all this trouble for me. I feel like a princess in a story."

Simon might not be the perfect hero-protector she'd once dreamed of. His armour was dented in places and he'd needed *her* help to slay a few of his dragons. Yet somehow that made him all the more appealing.

A few moments later, Ah-Ming appeared bearing bowls of bird's-nest soup. The broth wasn't full of little twigs like Bethan expected from the name. Instead it was thick like unset jelly and rather sweet.

"It's not to everyone's taste," murmured Simon when Ah-Ming was out of earshot. "But the Chinese regard it as a great delicacy. They say it keeps a person healthy and young."

"I like it well enough." Bethan made sure to clean every drop from her bowl so Cook would not be insulted.

She liked the dish of prawns that followed much

more, and the Chinese capon was so moist and tender she savoured it to the last morsel. While they ate, Simon entertained her with stories of Singapore's earlier days and the time he'd spent in India and Penang with his partners. Now that he was not so anxious to suppress unpleasant memories, he seemed free to recall happier times.

As they lingered over a final course of tropical fruit and sweet little cakes called *kueh*, Simon removed something from his pocket. "Now for the surprise I promised you."

"I thought all this *was* the surprise."

"Part of it." His lips remained solemn, but his blue eyes shimmered with an expectant smile. "The introduction."

He hesitated for a moment, as if searching for the right words to continue. "I have something to give you. I hope you'll pardon my delay in doing so. I wanted to present it under the proper circumstances."

Reaching across the table, over the vibrant mass of orchids, he opened his hand to reveal her silver locket.

"You found it!" Bethan seized the locket and pressed it to her lips. "Where? How? Oh, thank you, Simon!"

He explained about seeking help from one of the Chinese merchants.

Bethan's eyes misted with tears when she opened the locket to find the tiny image of her father undamaged. He smiled up at her as if happy to be reunited after so many weeks.

She scarcely noticed what Simon was saying as he continued. "I realise a ring is the customary medium for such requests. And the locket already belongs to you, so of course you must keep it no matter what your answer."

"Answer?" She wrenched her gaze away from her father's face to stare at Simon. "I don't understand. What's the question?"

"I should think that was obvious." He cleared his throat. "Will you marry me?"

Those words took her breath away. A surge of love for him swept through her so powerfully that it made her want to laugh and weep and dance all at once. She knew what it must have cost Simon to set aside his stubborn vow never to wed again. And for him to trust that she would not betray him.

She wanted so desperately to accept and she would as soon as she recovered her voice.

Struggling to rally her composure, she glanced down at the locket. She was touched that Simon had gone to such lengths to recover it and that he'd chosen to use this most precious of objects to honour her with his proposal.

But as she stared at her father's likeness, his expression appeared changed from what it had been only a moment before. It seemed to warn her that marriage was no guarantee of love. His resemblance to Hugh reminded her of her family duty—an obligation so vastly at odds with her desire to be Simon's wife.

It was a duty she could not abandon when she was so close to finding out what had become of her beloved brother.

Why didn't Bethan answer?

As Simon awaited her reply, his belly twisted in tight knots as if he'd just taken the most reckless risk of his life.

She had been about to accept—he'd seen the answer

sparkling in her eyes. Or was that only the reflection of the paper lanterns?

When she looked up from the locket, her fresh, vibrant beauty was shadowed with distress. "You swore you'd never marry again."

"I know I did." Pride and caution warned him not to beg. Her hesitation hurt him enough. He did not need a bitter dose of humiliation on top of that.

Still he could not keep from trying to persuade her. "But I've changed my mind. *You* helped me make that change, along with a great many others. Rosalia has become very attached to you and I see now that she needs a mother. I know you are nothing like Carlotta or my stepmother. I can trust you."

Words that should have caused her to smile or look tender made her flinch instead. Why was that? In spite of what he'd just said about trust, dark suspicion reared its ugly heads. It was like a hydra—whenever he lopped one off, two more grew in its place. Did Bethan sense that? Did it explain her reluctance to marry him?

"You don't know how much it means to hear you say that." Her gaze met his for an instant, then fell. "But why can't we just go on the way we are?"

"Why are you balking now?" Simon's anger rose, as it always did to protect his wounds. "You came to Singapore to wed me. You only went to bed with me the first time because you thought we were going to be married. What has changed since then? I was a stranger, but now you know me better than anyone. Did you not like what you discovered? Would you rather have a *perfect* stranger than a familiar man with flaws?"

"No!" she cried with a ring of sincerity Simon yearned to believe. "You're a fine man and everything I've found out about you has only made me care for you more."

"Why don't you say 'yes' then? I know my first proposal was a great deal less than civil, but I thought... all this..." Simon caught her stealing a glance at the locket. He was beginning to wish he'd never recovered the cursed thing. "Is it your father? Are you afraid being married will lead me to stray and abandon you like he did?"

Again she flinched.

Simon dropped his voice to a whisper in case any of his servants or neighbours might be listening. "If that is the problem, you need to realise I am no more like him than you are like Carlotta. I honour my obligations. I always have. I took her back even after she'd betrayed me. I raised Rosalia even when I thought she might not be my child."

He had meant to reassure her, but his words seemed to have the opposite effect.

"I don't want to be an *obligation* to you, Simon!" Bethan stumbled up from her chair. "Kept around on sufferance no matter what your feelings for me, because your child needs a mother or you're worried what people will think of you keeping a mistress. Is that why you proposed to me? You thought you wanted a mistress, but once you got one, it made you feel like those vile mutineers who took the women away on that ship. Well, you can put that notion to rest. You didn't force me to become your mistress. It was my choice."

How could he answer that? Simon could not deny guilt had played a part in his decision—guilt and possessiveness and fear of losing her to another man if she were free. But there was more to it than those mean motives, wasn't there?

Bethan seemed to take his silence for a confession.

"I thought so." She backed away from the table.

"Thank you for returning my locket. It puts me even more in your debt. But I can't go into bondage for it, just to ease a load of guilt you needn't feel."

"That isn't…" Simon sputtered. "I didn't…"

"I know what an honour it is for a man like you to offer the respectability of your name to a girl like me. But I wouldn't have any respect for myself if I became your wife on those terms."

As she spun around and marched away, fear gripped Simon. He wanted to go after her and make her listen, the way he had that night in the experimental garden. But he could not risk driving her out into the night again. This time he might not find her.

Besides, he could not escape the poisonous suspicion that there was something more behind her rejection of his proposal. Something she was hiding from him.

Chapter Sixteen

Bethan spent a miserable night in the little room off the nursery. Again and again she reached for Simon in her dreams, only to find her arms full of orchids—beautiful to look at, but cool and waxy to the touch, with none of the sweet fragrance of humbler blossoms.

Last night had been so close to what she'd hoped for when she agreed to become Simon's mistress. She'd imagined him slowly letting down his guard enough to fall in love with her, *then* asking her to marry him. By that time she might have discovered what had happened to her brother and found a way to tell Simon about Hugh. Then nothing would have stood in the way of their happiness.

She'd never expected Simon to propose so soon, and now she wished with all her heart he'd waited. She didn't want him to marry her out of obligation or to provide Rosalia with a mother. Those might be worthier reasons that the ones that had prompted his first proposal, but they were still not enough. Had her father wed her mother for reasons like those, only to find that marriage without love was a trap from which he'd had to escape, no matter who else got hurt?

But perhaps she'd been too hasty in refusing Simon. This time he would have no reason to feel she'd forced his hand nor any cause to suspect she'd tricked him into marriage. If he did not feel pressured or deceived, perhaps he could still learn to love her as wife rather than a mistress. At least he *might*, as long as that whole business with her brother did not scuttle her plans.

The moment that thought passed through her mind, Bethan regretted her selfish disloyalty. She was still committed to finding her brother, wasn't she, even if it meant leaving Singapore to continue her search?

But what if Hugh was not alive to be found? What if he had died in the fire aboard the *Dauntless*, or drowned trying to escape it? What if he'd survived only to be captured and hanged for his part in the mutiny? If she knew for certain he was beyond her help, she could find comfort with Simon and Rosalia.

"There's no use thinking of all that, now," Bethan muttered under her breath as she crawled out of bed and prepared to face the day. "First you have to find out what's become of poor Hugh."

She must call on Dr Ellison and hope he could provide her with answers that would light her way forwards.

Once she was dressed and groomed, with her locket fastened around her neck where it belonged, she tiptoed out into the hallway, her senses alert for any sign of Simon. After their quarrel last night, she could not bear to face him until she was certain what her future held.

She managed to steal out of the house unseen by anyone, only to find the *jagga* man guarding the door. Since the outlaw attacks, Simon had taken the precaution of having the place guarded night and day.

"Good morning, Jodh." She opened her parasol to protect her from the sun and the chance of sudden showers that often fell before noon. "I'm off for a little walk. I should be back soon."

The big man looked troubled. "Mamhud took master to work. I go with you, missy?"

"Thank you, but that won't be necessary. I'm not going far." Bethan tried not to let it bother her that Simon had gone to his office as usual after what had happened between them last night. After all, the business had always his refuge from the turbulent events in his personal life.

As Bethan headed up North Bridge Road, she found the street busier than she'd ever seen it. A party of Malay men carried a *palanquin* toward the square while several servants scurried past in the opposite direction, carrying baskets of produce from the market. Bethan shrank to the edge of the street when she saw a line of convict labourers marching toward her, their chains making an ominous clatter.

"Senhorita Conway?"

She gave a violent start when someone called her name, but relaxed at once when she recognised Mr Quintéra in his gharry.

"Can I offer you a drive?" He cast a pointed glance at the convicts as they trudged past. "I'm surprised Mr Grimshaw would permit you to go out alone these days. Did you hear the outlaws made away with the East India Company cannon last night? Impudent devils!"

The news sent a shiver through Bethan that defied the tropical heat of the morning. She'd seen the gun Mr Quintéra spoke of, near the shore only a stone's throw from where she now stood, guarded by *sepoys* night and day. The outlaws were growing bold indeed.

"Thank you for your kind offer…" she bobbed the merchant a curtsy "…but I don't want to delay you. I'm not going far and I plan to head straight home after. I doubt the outlaws are foolish enough to strike in broad daylight."

"I hope not." Mr Quintéra consulted his pocket watch. "If you're certain you do not want a drive, I should be on my way."

"Quite sure, thank you."

Once he pulled away, Bethan hurried the last few steps to Dr Moncrieff's house.

"Doctor *sahib* is out," announced the Indian manservant who answered her knock. "Come back tomorrow, please."

"It's Dr Ellison I've come to see," she explained. "Is he away as well?"

"He is here." The servant beckoned her inside.

She gave him her name and waited while he went off to enquire if the doctor would see her. A few moments later, the servant returned and led her upstairs to a deep veranda, like the one around Simon's villa. A short, dark-haired man put down a book and rose from his chair when she appeared.

"Doctor Ellison?" She curtsied. "Thank you for seeing me."

"My pleasure, miss." He motioned her toward a cane-backed chair opposite his. "I must confess I'm not accustomed to being sought out by young ladies. How may I be of service?"

Now that she was so close to the answers she'd sought for the past two years, Bethan could scarcely master her nerves to ask the question. "I—I was told you were a passenger aboard the *Dauntless* on her final voyage. Is that true?"

The doctor nodded.

"Could I trouble you to tell me what happened to the ship and her crew? I heard there was a mutiny and a fire. Were you the only survivor?"

"May I ask the reason for your interest in such a gruesome subject, Miss Conway?" As he said her name, a flicker of recognition crossed the doctor's face. "I say, you aren't any relation to the Conway who was second mate aboard the *Dauntless*?"

His question made Bethan's pulse pound so loud she wondered if he could hear it. She hadn't reckoned on him remembering Hugh by name. That made it all the more likely he would know for certain what had become of her brother.

"Please, Doctor," she cried, "there is something I must confess. But you have to promise me you will not tell anyone else!"

"You have my word I will keep it in the strictest confidence."

There was no use trying to keep her secret now that Dr Ellison had guessed most of it. So she took a deep breath and blurted out the truth she wished she had dared tell Simon. "Hugh Conway was…*is* my brother. I came to Singapore to find out what happened to him. Can you tell me, please?"

The way the doctor's brow furrowed, she knew the news would not be good. She braced to hear it with the thought that at least it would end her uncertainty and let her get on with her life.

The doctor stared off into the distance just as a sudden rain shower began to fall. "There was trouble between the captain and crew of the *Dauntless* long before we sailed from Singapore. I don't know how it all started, but I could feel the mutual hostility from our first day out. It built and built like a great storm brewing—a storm that finally broke off the coast of India."

Bethan leaned closer, straining to catch every word above the sound of rain that had started and was cascading off the tile roof.

"The captain ordered the ship brought closer to shore than the helmsman deemed safe," Dr Ellison continued. "The next thing we knew, he was set upon by some of his crew while the officers and passengers were herded below decks at gunpoint and locked in the hold."

"And Hugh took part in that?" The thought horrified Bethan far more after hearing Simon's account of the *Sabine* mutiny.

"Your brother seemed like a decent fellow, Miss Conway. He was good humoured and obliging and had a far more civil tongue than the rest of the crew. That is why I recall him so clearly. I never saw him take an active role in the mutiny, but I cannot swear he was out of it altogether."

"Can you at least tell me whether he lived or died?"

The doctor shook his head. "I wish I could. I never saw his body, but then so many were lost in the fire or drowned. I feel certain he must have been among them, for I never saw him after that day."

So Hugh *was* dead. How many times during the past two years had Bethan thought he might be? Still, Dr Ellison's words struck her like a spring mudslide thundering down a Welsh hillside. She clutched her chest and let out a strangled whimper. How could she have been so wicked as to half-hope for this, so she would not be forced to make the difficult choice between Hugh and Simon?

The doctor pulled out a handkerchief and offered it to her. "I am grieved to be the bearer of such distressing news, Miss Conway. You have my deepest sympathy."

Bethan refused his handkerchief. She was too dazed for tears yet, though she knew they would come. She did not want to let them fall in front of a stranger, no matter how kind.

"Thank you, Doctor." She lurched to her feet. "At least now I know. It's better than wondering."

That was a lie. In time it might get better. But for now, she would have given anything *not* to know.

The doctor rose from his chair. "If it is any consolation, your brother was probably more fortunate than those crewmen who did survive. They were all hanged."

It was no consolation, but Bethan did not say so. Instead she mumbled a few more words of thanks and fled from the house while her trembling knees would carry her.

It was still raining out, though not as hard. Opening her parasol, she stumbled back down the street toward Simon's house, muffled in a fog of misery so heavy she could not imagine anything making her feel worse.

Then, behind her, she heard the clop and splash of hoofbeats and Simon's voice. "Bethan, what were you doing at Dr Moncrieff's?"

On top of her grief for her brother, the prospect of explaining the situation to Simon was more than she could bear. How could she bring herself to tell him that, like so many other women he'd known, she had used and deceived him?

What *had* Bethan doing at the doctor's house? The possibilities that rushed through Simon's mind included a few he was ashamed of thinking, but he could not help himself.

Motioning for his driver to stop the gharry, he climbed out from beneath the carriage's bonnet into the rain. Then he waved Mahmud to drive on while he walked Bethan back to the house.

With none of the pleasures he'd anticipated to keep him in bed this morning, he had risen early and gone in to work. Business was a good deal less complicated than what he was dealing with at home, yet, lately, he had a nagging suspicion it was a good deal less important as well.

In any case, he didn't intend to bury himself in his work, as he had for the past several years, to hide from his personal problems. He would find no escape from his feelings for Bethan there. Nor any insights into their future. He only stayed long enough to leave orders about what work needed to be done. Then he hurried home, hoping a good night's sleep might have made Bethan readier to listen to reason.

He didn't know what to think when he spied her emerging from Dr Moncrieff's house. He only knew he wanted answers.

She didn't turn when he called out to her, but kept on walking.

"Bethan, did you hear me?" He caught her by the elbow. "I asked you a question."

Her steps slowed and she glanced toward him. There was a look in her eyes like nothing he'd seen in them before—a heartrending compound of pain and sorrow that did not belong there.

"Are you ill?" A garrotte of fear tightened around his throat. "Is that why you went to see the doctor? What is it? If Moncrieff can't help you, I'll take you to Penang or Calcutta. I'll—"

"It's nothing like that. Oh, Simon, I'm so sorry for

the things I said last night! I should have known better. Can you ever forgive me?" Her lower lip trembled and her eyes flooded with tears, as swiftly as the Singapore sky with rain showers.

Overcome with relief to hear she was not ill, Simon gathered her into his arms. The easing rain pattered down upon them while she wept as if her heart would break. Their public embrace drew some curious stares from passers-by but Simon did not care.

Ever since she'd arrived in Singapore, Bethan had offered him advice and comfort. It felt good to be able to return the favour at last, striking a vital balance between them that had been missing until now.

"There's nothing to forgive." He rested his chin against the brim of her hat. "You aren't the only one who said things you wish you could take back. It seems marriage isn't an easy subject for either of us to talk about. I shouldn't have sprung my proposal on you out of the blue like that."

Another reason occurred to him why she might have paid a call on the doctor. Was she carrying his child? Her tearful outburst made him suspect so. Perhaps that explained her emotional reaction to his proposal. She hadn't wanted him to think she would use a child of theirs the way Carlotta had, to manipulate him.

It was not a subject he wanted to quiz her about on a public street.

"Come along," he murmured as her weeping eased. "Let's get back to the house. We can talk better there."

He fished out his handkerchief and press it upon her without breaking their embrace altogether. While Bethan wiped her eyes, he wrapped his arm around her waist and steered her towards the house. By the time they reached it, the sun had come out again and vapour was rising off the wet garden. Bethan had wiped her face and regained her composure.

Ah-Ming appeared when they entered, but withdrew discreetly when Simon shot her a warning glance. Leading Bethan out to the veranda, he eased her down on to the wicker settee beside him.

"It's not your fault." She toyed with the damp handkerchief in her lap. "Your proposal did come as a surprise, but it was lovely. I should never have taken on the way I did. It was good of you to want to do right by me, whatever your reasons."

Did she truly believe that's all there was to it? Thinking back over his clumsy, unromantic proposal, Simon decided he could hardly blame her.

"I don't think I explained my reasons very well. Or perhaps I could not bring myself to recognise them for what they are." Even talking about it like this, glimpsing the truth, sent his heart into a fast, shallow beat, as if he were about to take the deadliest risk of his life.

"I should not have spoken that way about your father." He offered the apology as he tried to work up the nerve to say something he had not been able to admit to himself, let alone her. "I suppose I needed to find some other reason you would refuse me. Besides the most obvious one, I mean—that you don't…care for me."

Was it cowardly of him, hoping to solicit a declaration of her feelings before making one of his own? Perhaps, but the terrible power of love frightened him more than any physical threat.

Bethan did not leave him twisting in doubt. "I *do* care about you, Simon! You're the finest man I've ever met."

Her words had the pure, sweet ring of sincerity. And

when she lifted her face to meet his gaze, he could not deny the glow of admiration and affection that shone in her eyes. At the same time, he sensed a lurking secret shame that troubled him.

Fearing his suspicion made him unworthy of her praise, Simon tried to make light of it. "You haven't met many men, have you?"

"Enough to know I'd have to go a long way to find one better. You weren't so far off the mark in what you said about my father. I think part of me still doesn't believe I'm good enough for any man to want to spend his whole life with. The more I care for you, the harder it is for me to believe I'm half worthy to be your wife."

Was that the secret shame he'd glimpsed, the one she hid behind blunt-spoken bravado? Yet again Simon reproached himself for suspecting something worse. He must stop making her pay for the betrayal of those other women.

"Good enough—of course you are!" Suddenly it was more important for him to defend her from the spectre of self-doubt than to protect himself from rejection or betrayal. "You're honest and loyal and kind. You swept into my life like an Indian monsoon after the parched season, with warm rains that brought everything inside me back to life."

As he spoke, her shoulders heaved and she lifted his handkerchief to her eyes again. Simon hoped they were happy tears. He never wanted to be the cause of her shedding any other kind.

"It means so much to me, to hear I've helped you." She fumbled for his hand and gave it a fierce squeeze. "You've helped me, too, though I didn't know how much until just now. You make me feel as if I'm worth pro-tecting and giving pleasure."

"But I made you doubt your worth in other ways, didn't I?" Simon pulled her close until her head rested against his chest. "By wanting you as my mistress instead of my wife. By pretending I felt only desire for you when it was so much more than that."

He heaved a sigh from the murkiest depths of his soul. "You must believe none of that was any reflection on you. I was only trying to protect myself from being betrayed again. If you must measure your value by my actions, consider how you won my trust. After the life I've had, you must see what a special woman it took to make me risk my heart again."

"I don't know what to say," Bethan whispered. She sounded as frightened of the risk as he was.

"Why don't you say 'yes' to my proposal? I promise you I am making it for the only reason that truly matters." He strove to keep even the slightest hint of hesitation from his voice. "Because I love you."

In the silence that followed, his words hung naked and vulnerable.

"I *want* to say yes," Bethan murmured at last. "You have no idea how much. But there's something I need to work out for myself first."

What did she need to work out? Was it something he already knew about or something she'd kept secret? Whatever it was, Simon hoped she would confide in him.

Did Simon realise she hadn't told him what she was doing at Dr Moncrieff's house? Perhaps he'd forgotten about it or thought he knew. Perhaps he didn't care.

Over the next several days, Bethan tried to sort out her feelings and decide what to do next. One of the hardest parts to wrestle with was her grief and guilt over Hugh's death. She knew his fate had been decided many months ago, before she'd ever dreamed of coming to Singapore. Yet she could not escape the haunting sense that her brother was dead because her faith had wavered, because she had stopped wanting so desperately for him to be alive.

It helped her understand Simon's guilt about the fate of those female passengers on the *Sabine*. Such feelings might defy reason, but that did not lessen the heavy burden they placed upon the heart. The last thing she wanted was to add to the burden Simon already carried.

The only thing that made her hesitate to accept his proposal was the fear she might do something to turn him against her and lose his love. He'd placed her on such a high pedestal it would be far too easy to fall, damaging their marriage beyond repair. The only worse thing she could imagine than being abandoned by a husband was continuing to remain in a marriage after love and respect had gone. Was that why Carlotta had fled into the night to meet her death?

How would Simon react if he discovered she had already fallen off his dangerously high pedestal? If he found out that the woman he'd praised for her *honesty* and *loyalty* had been deceiving him from the moment they met, could he ever forgive her betrayal of his hard-won trust? Especially when her deception had all been to protect a mutineer, the kind of man he hated above all others.

Her anxious heart argued that Simon need never know what she'd done. The *Dauntless* mutiny was long past and forgotten by most people. Doctor Ellison had promised to keep her secret. Finding out how she'd lied to him would only hurt Simon, who had been hurt too much already.

Against all those sound, self-serving reasons stood the troublesome conviction that if she continued to keep her secret from him, their marriage would be built upon a lie. How could anything with such a flawed foundation hope to stand the test of time? She must find the courage to tell him and hope he could find the compassion to forgive her.

Then, one evening, she overheard Simon telling Rosalia a bedtime story. "This ivory fan belonged to your mama. She brought it from Macau when she came to Penang. That is where we met and got married. It's where you were born. The fan was given to your mama when she was a little girl by *her* grandmother, Rosalia Alvares."

"Rosalia—just like me!"

"That's right. You were named after her. I think your mama would want you to have this."

Bethan could scarcely believe her ears. Simon was talking about his late wife, a subject he'd spent the past few years trying to avoid at all costs. For Rosalia's sake she was delighted, aware how much the child longed for any connection to the mother she'd never known.

"Thank you, Papa. But why did Mama go to Penang? And how did we come to Singapore?"

From where she was listening, Bethan sensed Simon's hesitation. Somehow, he managed to overcome it. "That is a rather long story, but if you would like to hear it, I suppose we could begin it tonight…"

"Oh, yes, please, Papa! You tell even better stories that Bethan and Ah-Sam."

"High praise, indeed." Simon gave a warm chuckle. "Very well, then. Your mama left Macau with her uncle, who was her guardian. He was taking her back to Lisbon to marry a man she had never met. Your mama was afraid she would not like this man and she did not want to leave the Orient, where she had lived all her life…"

Bethan marvelled at the way Simon told the story to his daughter, leeched of the poisonous bitterness she'd heard when he confided in her. This version sounded as if it might have happened long ago to someone he barely knew. For Rosalia's sake and perhaps his own, Simon was trying to make peace with the painful events of his past.

Seizing upon that fragile wisp of hope, Bethan crept back down the hallway and wandered out into the garden, which was shrouded in the long shadows of nightfall. If Simon could begin to break free of the blight cast upon him by past betrayals, perhaps there was a chance he could understand and forgive her deception. Unlike Carlotta, she had never meant to hurt him—she'd only been trying to protect her beloved brother.

Pacing up and down the garden path, Bethan muttered under her breath, practising the words she would use to tell Simon the truth at last. Now and then she glanced towards the veranda, hoping he would appear soon, before her nerve failed her.

As she passed the rhododendron bush, Bethan thought she heard footsteps behind her. Thinking it must be Simon, she turned to greet him.

But before she could, rough hands seized her and pulled her behind the bush, out of sight of the house.

One strong, calloused hand clamped tightly over her mouth while her captor ordered in a harsh whisper, "Not a peep or you'll regret it!"

Chapter Seventeen

It hadn't been easy at first, talking to Rosalia about her mother, dredging up so many painful memories. But once he'd begun, Simon did not regret it.

The rapt expression on his daughter's small face was well worth the effort. Recalling how much he'd missed and mourned his mother at that age, he wished he had not kept Rosalia in the dark about hers for so long. He'd tried to justify his actions by pretending he was protecting her from the sordid truth about Carlotta. Bethan had made him see he'd been trying to spare his own feelings more than the child's.

He had so much to make up to Rosalia and he would do it, no matter what it cost him. He was making a start tonight. Though the exquisitely carved ivory fan was a priceless heirloom, Simon sensed that the story about her mother was far more precious to Rosalia. For that reason, he forced himself to step back from his bitter feelings about his late wife and relate the account of their meeting and marriage as though he'd been a disinterested observer.

To his surprise, the effort rewarded him with some unexpected insights. For one thing, he recalled how young Carlotta had been when they first met. Afflicted with the wilful selfishness of youth, she'd also fallen victim to the destructive indulgence often accorded beauty. She had made mistakes. But then again, so had he.

The worst of those was that he'd never truly loved her. He'd been captivated by her fiery beauty and compelled to rescue her. Perhaps it had eased his lingering guilt over the *Sabine* mutiny. Or perhaps he'd needed to see himself through her eyes as the heroic knight, so he could feel worthy of a woman's love.

Reluctant to tarnish that shiny mantle, he'd never confided in her the hurts and regrets that made him only human. Without trust and honesty, the desire and protectiveness he felt for her had never ripened into anything deeper. When she'd betrayed him, it was his pride that had suffered, not his heart.

Could he blame Carlotta for turning to another man when she lacked a true connection with her husband? The perfect hero might make a fine subject for romantic fancies, but such a man could not be easy to live with day in and day out. When she'd repented her mistake and tried to correct it by coming to Singapore with his child, begging another chance, he'd done the honourable thing without an ounce of true forgiveness in his heart. How long had he expected her to stay when it was clear he despised her and would never relent?

"Tell me what she looked like, Papa?" Rosalia clutched the fan in one hand and Simon's fingers in the other—two precious links to the mother she'd never known.

"Like you, *querido*." For the first time ever, Simon

used the Portuguese endearment with his daughter. "Beautiful as a midnight garden full of red roses. She had wide brown eyes and long lashes. One look from them made men want to scale mountains and swim oceans for the favour of her smile."

He wasn't certain he could praise Carlotta's character so lavishly. But if their daughter asked, he would try to recall every single good thing he could about his late wife. He braced himself for more questions, but none came. When he glanced down at the child, her wide brown eyes were closed.

Simon sat for a while, stroking her hair, while the love he'd denied them both for too long washed over him. When he was certain she would not wake, he slipped his fingers from her slack grip and grazed her forehead with a kiss. Then he extinguished the lamp and backed out of the nursery with soft steps.

Eager to talk to Bethan, he looked for her in the sitting room, then the dining room. He wanted to tell her how much more clearly he saw his past, thanks to her. He wanted to make certain she knew how much he loved and needed her. Perhaps if he admitted all the mistakes he'd made with Carlotta, it would help her overcome the foolish notion that she was somehow less than worthy of him.

Next he checked the veranda, but she was not there either. Could she be waiting in his bed, perhaps? The possibility brought a smile to Simon's face as a briny breeze wafted from the sea to caress his cheek.

Then something else rose from the garden below that made his body tense—the sound of furtive whispers. Could a party of outlaws be hiding among the bushes, their faces blackened with soot, waiting for his household to retire for the night so they could launch an attack?

Keeping a tight rein on his mounting alarm, Simon retreated into the house. He rushed to his dressing room and loaded a pistol with swift, practised movements.

Heading down the stairs a few moments later, he met Ah-Ming. Her eyes widened when she spotted the weapon in his hand.

"It's only a precaution," he assured her. "Please go sit with Rosalia until I get back. Have you seen Bethan?"

The housekeeper replied with a tight little nod. "Just before dark, she went out to the garden."

Perhaps the voice he'd heard was only Bethan talking to herself. Simon tried to calm his fears with that thought, but it did not work. Without another word, he stole out the front entrance. When Jodh started to speak, Simon pressed a finger to his lips.

"I thought I heard someone in the garden," he whispered. "But it may only be Miss Conway. If I need your help, I'll call."

Continuing on his way, he circled the stables and slipped into the back garden. He could hear the voices more clearly now. One belonged to Bethan.

The other was a man's.

Had the outlaws captured her? Simon's blood boiled with the desperate urge to rush to her rescue, pistol blazing. But he could not risk her safety.

Instead, scarcely daring to breath, he edged toward the voices, alert for every whispered word. Bethan didn't sound frightened, but then again she always underestimated risks. Perhaps she hoped to charm her way out of trouble again.

"Can you...hands...some money?" the masculine voice demanded. It didn't sound like a native English speaker, but not Chinese, Malay or Indian either.

"Isn't there some other way?" asked Bethan.

"We won't get far without money, *cariad*," replied the man. "This gentleman can spare it by the look of his fine house."

"He can, but I hate to—"

"You want to get away, don't you and start a new life? That's why you came out here, wasn't it, so we could do that? There's an American ship at anchor out in the roads and there's no love lost between them and the English. If we can reach that ship with passage money, they're bound to take us. Then we can make a fresh start in America—I hear it's a grand place."

Simon clenched his lips together to keep a groan from escaping. He felt as if he'd stumbled into the middle of a nightmare, reliving the wretched events of four years ago. Though he hadn't actually heard Carlotta plotting to run away with her lover, he knew it must have sounded just like this.

"It's too dangerous for you here." Bethan's voice fairly ached with loving concern, which made Simon writhe because it was for another man. "You must go now! Head down to the beach and wait for me there. Once everyone's asleep, I'll come find you and we can decide what to do."

Every word out of her mouth struck Simon a vicious blow. For, unlike his late wife who had only trampled his pride, Bethan Conway had the power to tear his heart to pieces and leave it bleeding in the sand. Like a fool, he had given her that power.

Even now she had such a hold on him that he wanted to deny what he was hearing, find some innocent explanation for it, no matter how far fetched. The sense of caution he had muzzled for far too long finally threw off its gag. It reminded him in the harshest possible terms of all the warning signs he'd refused to heed, all the petty suspicions that taken together would have pointed to something like this.

How Bethan must have laughed at him behind his back for all the secrets he'd confided in her, the trust he'd placed in her and his daft belief that she was honest and true. Still Simon taxed his imagination to make excuses for her.

"All right, then," whispered the man Simon longed to throttle with his bare hands—if only he wasn't afraid to make an even bigger fool of himself by breaking down and begging Bethan to stay. "But think about what I said, will you? If you can lay hands on enough money, we can be off this very night. The longer we wait, the greater chance there is that something will go wrong."

Footsteps moved towards the garden gate and the sound of their voices faded until Simon could not make out a word of their parting. Peering out from behind the hibiscus bush, he spied their shadows locked in a tender embrace. He could not ignore the evidence of both his eyes and ears, no matter how much he wanted to.

Bethan was just like all the others. Worse, in fact, for she had pried into his secret weaknesses and preyed upon them. And she had made him a willing accomplice in his own deception.

As her brother slipped off into the night, Bethan bolted the garden gate and slumped against it, gasping for breath as if she'd run a mile. In the past few days, her heart had been pulled so hard in so many different directions she wondered that it had not been torn to pieces.

First grief and guilt over Hugh's 'death' had blighted her hope for a new life with Simon and his daughter. Then her shame over deceiving Simon and her fear that he might never forgive her had clashed with her conviction that he deserved the truth, even if she did not deserve his trust. Just when she'd begun to see her way clear through that tangle, the events of the past half-hour had made her heart a battleground again.

Terror had ripped through her when she'd been seized in the darkened garden. But her assailant's next words, after ordering her to keep quiet, had made her want to shout for joy.

"It's me, Bethan—Hughie. What in the name of heaven are you doing in Singapore?"

For an instant she wondered if her mind had conjured up a vision of her brother because she could not bear to have her long search for him end in failure. Then the hand covering her mouth slipped down to give her chin an affectionate tweak. It was a fond gesture she recalled so well from her childhood.

"Dearest brother!" she whispered in Welsh, tugging her arms free to throw around him. "Is it really you? After Ma passed on, I came here looking for you, but I was told you were dead."

"I came close enough." He returned her embrace. "And I'd just as soon the rest of the world believes Hugh Conway is gone for good. As far as anybody else in Singapore knows, I'm a convict labourer serving a sentence for thievery."

"Convict?" Bethan drew back from him a little.

"I walked right past you the other day on the street. You've grown up so much since I left Llanaled, I might not have recognised you if that man hadn't called out your name. Once I found out where you were staying, I've come here every evening, hoping to catch you alone."

"What about the *Dauntless*?" Bethan wasn't certain she could bear to hear, but she had to know. "How did you get away? You didn't harm anyone, did you? I've heard terrible stories of what goes on in mutinies."

"So have I," Hugh muttered. "And I didn't want any part of that, I swear. The mutiny wasn't planned. It just… happened, like a pot on the hob that boils over. I can't say I'm sorry about the captain—a proper tyrant he was. But the officers and passengers didn't deserve to be harmed."

A sickening lump in the pit of her stomach eased for the first time since Simon had told her about the *Sabine* mutiny.

Simon! She couldn't let him find her brother here.

"I tried to give the others a chance," Hugh went on in a desperate rush, as if he'd been waiting three long years to tell someone the truth of what had happened. "I unlocked the hold where they were being kept, then I slipped overboard. I knew I'd be a dead man no matter which side won, so I took my chances with the sea instead. She almost had her way with me, but not quite. I don't know how the fire started on the *Dauntless*, but when I heard about it afterwards, I was afraid it might be my fault. Perhaps if I'd left things alone, or if I'd stayed aboard instead of thinking only of my own skin…"

"Hugh, please," Bethan managed to get a word in when his voice trailed off, "I'm glad you saved yourself, but you can tell me the rest later. Right now you need to get away from here before someone sees you."

"We *both* need to get away," Hugh replied. "Can you get your hands on some money?"

Perhaps she could, but it would mean stealing from Simon. "Isn't there some other way?"

"We won't get far without money, *cariad*." Hugh seemed to sense her misgivings. "This gentleman can spare it by the look of his fine house."

"He can, but I hate to—" She'd been deceiving Simon for weeks, her conscience sneered, why did she balk at thievery?

"You want to get away, don't you, and start a new life?" her brother pleaded. "That's why you came out here, wasn't it, so we could do that? There's an American ship at anchor out in the roads and there's no love lost between them and the English. If we can reach that ship with passage money, they're bound to take us. Then we can make a fresh start in America—I hear it's a grand place."

"It's too dangerous for you here. You must go now!" It wasn't only fear for her brother's safety that made her beg. She needed time to think. "Head down to the beach and wait for me there. Once everyone's asleep, I'll come find you and we can decide what to do."

"All right, then," whispered Hugh. "But think about what I said, will you? If you can lay hands on enough money, we can be off this very night. The longer we wait, the greater chance there is that something will go wrong."

Bethan knew her brother was right about that, yet she couldn't bring herself to promise what he asked. Instead she tugged him towards the gate, telling him how happy she was to have found him at last. That was partly true.

"Be careful out there." She hugged her brother tightly, wishing she did not have to be parted from him again so soon.

"I'll be waiting for you," he murmured. "I'm anxious to hear *your* story about how you got from Llanaled all the way to Singapore."

Once Hugh had slipped away, Bethan began to feel as if she could breathe properly again. But her heart laboured under the crushing weight that had settled on it.

She turned her gaze toward Simon's villa, the golden lamplight spilling out of its large open windows. It was as different as could be from the snug Welsh cottage where she'd grown up. Yet in the past weeks it had become a home to her.

She wondered if Simon had finished telling Rosalia her bedtime story. Was he looking for her now, wondering where she'd gone, worried for her safety? If his house had become a home to her, it was because he and his daughter had become like family. How could she think of abandoning them?

On the other hand, Hugh needed her help and he was the reason she'd come to Singapore. He was her only living blood kin, the last remnant of the broken family she'd spent years longing to mend. Having suffered the grief of believing him dead made her more desperate than ever to secure his safety.

But when she thought of leaving Simon and Rosalia, slipping away in the night like Carlotta had, her heart quailed. Not only for herself, but for them. The child was bound to feel she'd done something wrong to make Bethan go away. For Simon, this might well be one betrayal too many. She could hardly blame him if he refused to trust any woman ever again.

Was it possible she could test his trust without breaking it? A faint hope tantalised her as she headed back into the house. Perhaps she would ask Simon for a loan and use the money to send her brother to safety. Once Hugh was out of harm's way, she'd confess the truth and hope for Simon's forgiveness, though she was far from certain she deserved it.

As she crept back inside, she smelled the mouthwatering aromas of dinner cooking. After a good meal and a glass of wine, Simon might be inclined to hear her out and grant her an enormous favour…on trust.

She checked the dining room where the table was set for their meal, but she saw no sign of Simon. Could he still be with Rosalia, telling the child more stories about her mother?

On her way to the nursery, Bethan glanced into the sitting room and saw Simon in one of the armchairs, holding a half-empty glass.

"There you are!" She tried to sound as if nothing had changed in the past half-hour when, in fact, *everything* had. "I hope I haven't kept you waiting for dinner."

"Come in." Simon did not shout the words, or snap in a sharp tone. Yet something about them made Bethan quail just the same.

She hoped it was only her guilty conscience imagining trouble.

"Is everything all right?" She forced herself to enter the room.

Simon nodded toward the low table in front of him. A small mound of gold and silver coins lay on top of it.

"That's all I had in the house." He bolted the last of whatever was in his glass—arrack, most likely. When he looked up at Bethan, his icy blue gaze pierced her like a freshly whetted blade. "Go ahead, take the money. I thought I would save you the trouble of stealing it."

Chapter Eighteen

Though Simon considered his remark quite civilised under the circumstances, it seemed to take the legs out from under Bethan.

She staggered to the nearest chair and sank on to it. "You heard."

Struggling to maintain control of his raging feelings, he gave a curt nod. "More than I wanted to. But I am curious about one thing. Who is this fine fellow you plan to run off to America with?"

"You don't know?" The depth of relief in her voice enraged Simon.

Clearly she wanted to protect this blackguard the way he'd once wanted to protect her. It unnerved him to discover that, in spite of everything he'd just seen and heard, part of him still longed to save her from the folly she was about to commit.

Keeping a firm grip on his wits against the tug of such mutinous urges, he feigned indifference with a shrug. "I must have missed something of interest after all. I hope you will indulge my curiosity."

To his surprise and vexation, Bethan shook her head. "That is the one thing I cannot tell you. I'm sorry, Simon. I know I have no right to expect you to believe me, but I swear that whatever you overheard in the garden does not mean what you think. I was coming to find you, to tell you as much as I could in the hope that you might understand."

A grunt of bitter laughter burst from his tightly clenched lips. "You expect me to believe that? After weeks of lying and sneaking around behind my back, you were just about to tell me the truth, if only I hadn't stumbled upon it myself. How very inconvenient! What kind of fool do you take me for?"

He wanted to stride around the room, venting some of the force of his blazing wrath while putting more distance between them. But that would have exposed the weakness of his lame leg and he was already feeling far too vulnerable.

She flinched from his scornful outburst as if it had been a vicious blow. Hard as Simon tried to remain unmoved, a qualm of shame seethed through his belly. He had spent his whole life defending those in distress. It went against his nature to inflict misery, no matter how richly deserved.

Bethan Conway would know that, of course, because she had made it her business to delve into all his deepest secrets. Now she would use that knowledge to manipulate him with her plausible-sounding explanations and her look of injured innocence. If all else failed, she might stage a most affecting show of tears. He had better mend his defences in short order if he hoped to withstand such tactics.

"I don't think you're a fool, Simon." She hunched forwards in her seat, meeting his hard, accusing stare with a helpless gaze that was no doubt calculated to draw him in. "I think you're a fine man who's been hurt too many times by the people you've tried to help. I can't blame you for thinking I'm no better than the rest, because I'm not. I didn't expect you to believe me because I don't deserve to be believed."

She sounded so sincere, so sweetly contrite, that part of him longed to surrender to her touching appeal. Simon clung to the memory of the captain's unfaithful wife begging him not to tell her husband that he'd caught her in the arms of the first officer. And Carlotta, pleading with him to take her back for the sake of their infant daughter. They'd appeared repentant, too, when all the while they were playing him for a fool.

"I wanted to tell you the truth," Bethan claimed. "You can't imagine how much. At first I wasn't certain I could trust you because you seemed so cold and severe. Later, when I found out the kind of man you truly are, I tried to tell you. That's when I found out…there was too much at stake. The longer I went on lying, the harder it became to admit the truth because I was afraid it would make you hate me. I couldn't bear the thought of that because I'd come to love you so much."

His whole wasted heart ached to believe her, but it was a risk he could not afford to take. Not daring to speak in case his lips betrayed him, he struggled to maintain his wintery glare before her imploring gaze.

Bethan must have glimpsed some sign of thawing that encouraged her, for she continued. "That was why I balked at your marriage proposal—because I was terrified I would do something wrong and lose your love. I told you I didn't feel good enough for you. That was the truth, I swear. When you praised me for my honesty, all the while I knew it wasn't true, I never felt so low."

Her eyes brimmed with tears as soft and warm as spring rain. They might have melted Simon's icy resolve if he had not been so well prepared to withstand them. "This is all very touching, I'm sure. But I insist on knowing the identity of your mystery lover, the man you came all the way to Singapore to find. I think you owe me that much at least. Tell me, have you been trysting with him behind my back the whole time I've been fretting about your safety?"

"He's *not* my lover—you are!" Bethan dashed away her tears with the back of her hand as if angry with herself for that betrayal of weakness. "Tonight is the first time I've met with him. I did come to Singapore looking for him, but I didn't expect to find him here. At best I hoped I'd get word of where he'd gone so I could trace him. Lately, I thought he was dead. I know I owe you more than I can ever repay, but I *cannot* tell you anything more about him."

Why was he dragging this out? Simon asked himself in disgust. Did he take some twisted pleasure in tormenting himself? Was that why he sought out women he sensed would betray him? Or was he prolonging this painful interview and giving Bethan the opportunity to employ all her wiles on him because he secretly hoped she would succeed? Did he want her to breach his defences so his rebellious heart could overthrow cautious reason? Whatever his motives, they were clearly destructive ones. The time had come to put an end to this.

"You are not in my debt. Anything you received from me has been well earned, I will say that for you." He pushed the pile of coins across the table toward her— silver Spanish dollars and sikka rupees, gold British guineas. "Now take the money and go to this mystery man of yours. It's worth every farthing to be rid of you."

Bethan's hand trembled. She looked torn between wanting to seize the money and disgust at the prospect of touching it. "No matter what you think, I couldn't have brought myself to steal from you, Simon. Not even for his sake."

"Easily said now that there is no need. Go ahead—take it. As your *friend* so rightly pointed out, I'm rich enough not to miss it."

Was that why she was trying so hard to worm her way back into his good graces—because of his fortune? Had this other man shown up after she'd set her sights on a richer prize, threatening to spoil her plans? Perhaps it was the other fellow she'd intended to betray—sending him off to America while she slipped back to Singapore and the fine marriage that awaited her. Could that be her reason for protecting her paramour's identity, so Simon would not question him and discover the truth?

That possibility did not redeem her in Simon's eyes. Quite the contrary, in fact.

Forced by his relentless glare, she reached for the coins gingerly as if she feared the purity of those precious metals might burn her sinful fingers. "What if I told you I don't want to go with him, that I'd rather stay here as your wife or mistress or however you'll have me?"

Just as he'd suspected, reason crowed over his hapless heart. And where Bethan Conway was concerned, he dared not risk ignoring his suspicions.

Still his lips turned stubborn when he ordered them to heap scorn on her offer. Perhaps they recalled the taste of her kisses too well and it made them weak. "I don't believe that would be a very good idea, do you?"

An unintended note of regret slipped into his voice,

which he hoped Bethan would not recognise and exploit.

With a sigh, she continued to pick up the coins. "After all this, I suppose not. I admit I deceived you, Simon, but I didn't betray you. I had good reasons—at least they seemed good to me at the time. If I could tell you them now, I think you'd agree. Then you might be able to forgive me, the way you're beginning to forgive your wife."

Had she overheard him talking about Carlotta? So much had changed since that conversation with Rosalia, it felt like ages ago. What had he been thinking afterwards about mistakes and forgiveness?

Bethan must have sensed his troublesome second thoughts, for she hazarded one final appeal. "If you only trust me for one week, then I can answer all your questions."

Part of him longed to agree, yearned to believe that the happiness he'd found with her these past weeks was not an illusion. But the nature of his feelings for her made that impossible. He'd never truly loved Carlotta, never let her close enough to discover his secrets, yet she had devastated his life. He'd only survived because that's what he was—a survivor. If he was foolhardy enough to risk trusting Bethan despite the overwhelming evidence of her betrayal, he would give her the power to destroy him once and for all.

Still he could not keep from offering her one final chance. "Trust is a two-way street, you know. Hard as it has been for me, I've trusted you more than any other woman I've known. It is you who have not trusted me with the truth. If you will tell it to me now, perhaps we do have a chance for a future together. The choice is yours."

* * *

Bethan had never seen so much money all in one place—not even when Hadrian Northmore had given her gold for her passage to Singapore. But these coins felt like blood money. She'd vowed to find and rescue her brother, no matter what the cost, but she had never dreamed how high a price she might have to pay.

If it had only been her own happiness at stake, she would have paid Fate's toll willingly. But when the happiness of Simon and Rosalia were added to the scale, it became a much heavier cost—one that threatened to ruin her.

She'd tried every way she could think of to haggle and bargain, to keep from paying the full, crippling price. But when Simon offered her that agonizing choice—her brother's secret in exchange for a chance to repair what she had damaged between them—she knew it must be all or nothing.

Was it a question of trust, as he claimed? Could she trust him with her brother's life, knowing the bitter hatred he felt toward mutineers? Would he be willing to believe Hugh's claims that he hadn't plotted treachery against his captain, but tried to help the ship's officers and passengers? After a lifetime of knowing her brother, she did not question the truth of his account. But how could Simon, based on his sorely abused trust in her?

Even if he did, could he risk his hard-won success, perhaps even his liberty, to aid a fugitive? If she acted without his knowledge, it would spare him any consequences if Hugh's escape went wrong.

"I'm sorry, Simon." She channelled all her remorse into a heartfelt look, hoping some part of him might believe it, even if he could not trust her words. "When you know what this is all about, I hope you'll understand why I can't tell you. It's not only for *his* sake—but yours and Rosalia's, as well. You know what it's like, needing to protect the people you love."

With the burden of heavy, dirty money in her hands, she rose from her chair.

A flicker of emotion crossed Simon's face, one she felt sure he had tried to suppress. Was it longing to ignore the hard lessons of his past and take one rash gamble on her? Or was it only the hurt she'd done him that he was too proud to let her see?

"So you admit you love this man?" he demanded, rising from his chair.

There she went again! Bethan wanted to bite her tongue out of frustration. Once more she'd managed to say the worst possible thing. Might Simon have relented at the last moment if she had not mentioned her feelings for Hugh? He could not understand they posed no threat to him, because she'd refused to explain. All he could do was assume the worst, as a lifetime of betrayal had taught him to do.

"I love him very much, but not in any way that takes away from what I feel for you, Simon—even now. Please be extra-kind to Rosalia when I'm gone and make sure she doesn't think my leaving is her fault."

"You needn't worry." It was impossible to tell whether Simon was being defensive or trying to reassure her. "I will take care of my daughter."

Bethan turned to go.

She had only taken a few steps when he called after her. The words sounded as if they'd escaped against his will. "The other day when I saw you coming out of Dr Moncrieff's…you aren't by any chance…with child?"

So that's what he'd assumed. That was why he hadn't

questioned her more closely. Could it be the true reason he'd pressed his proposal?

"No." She didn't turn around—she could not bear to glimpse either the disappointment or the relief her answer gave him. "I'm quite certain, so don't fret that I'll turn up next year with a babe in my arms. I called on the doctor looking for…information."

She didn't dare say any more in case Simon puzzled out her secret. She'd probably told him too much already, if he cared to investigate.

"Goodbye and thank you for your kindness. I only wish I'd repaid it better." Bethan turned down the hallway toward the stairs.

"Wait a minute." Simon's uneven footsteps fell behind her. "Aren't you going to pack?"

She shook her head. "I don't fancy trying to drag a trunk behind me, and I don't want to disturb Rosalia. I'll make do. And some day I'll find a way to repay you this money, I promise."

"To hell with the money!" Simon snapped. "I hope you don't think I plan to let you walk out of here on your own at this hour. I'll have Mahmud drive you down to the beach…then you can spend the night at my old house. I'm sure your friends from Durham will make you welcome there. You can catch a boat from the quay at first light. I'd rather you didn't try to board one in the dark…you understand."

Fresh tears stung Bethan's eyes. Even after all she'd done to abuse his trust, Simon still felt compelled to protect her. "That is very kind of you."

"I don't want any more accidents on my conscience, that's all. I'll have your trunk sent over before morning."

"Of course." Bethan's head bowed under the weight of his final rebuke. How could she have thought his offer meant anything more than that? Whatever Simon once felt for her had been killed by his suspicion and her lies. Both had good reasons for being, but that did not make it any easier to live with the damage they'd done. "I'm grateful just the same."

Would he believe *that*? Would he believe anything she ever said again? Putting an ocean between them might be the kindest thing she could do for them both now.

Simon followed her outside and gave instructions to his driver. While Mahmud harnessed the gharry, they waited around in tense, awkward silence. When the vehicle was ready, Simon helped her in with a stiff but surprisingly gentle touch. Bethan soaked it in, wishing she could make that brief instant last for ever, but it passed almost before she realised it.

Not expecting such a civil parting, she had already bid him goodbye once. Now her throat was too tight to repeat the word.

Simon did not say it either. It seemed as if he might not say anything at all. Then at the last moment, he spoke with hoarse intensity. "Take care, will you?"

As the gharry pulled away, Bethan held back her tears. There would be time enough in the weeks and months ahead to let them fall. For now she must put her heartbreak aside and direct all her energy towards the thing she'd come here to do, the thing she'd sacrificed so much for.

On her instructions, Mahmud drove her around to Beach Road. There she got out and walked up and down the shore calling softly for her brother.

But no answer came.

Simon had passed quite a number of sleepless nights since Bethan Conway arrived in Singapore and this was no exception.

Not that all those nights had been unpleasant by any means. Memories flooded back to bedevil him—the fragrant softness of her hair, the smooth warmth of her skin, the taste of her lips, sweeter and more succulent than any tropical fruit.

He rolled over and pounded his pillow, but that did little to relieve his frustration or his emptiness. Now that Bethan was no longer present to challenge his control, he found it impossible to silence his nagging doubts. What if there *was* some innocent explanation to answer all his questions? And what if she did have some compelling reason for keeping it from him?

After all she'd done for him, did he not owe it to her to find out if there was any evidence to support her claim? If her need for secrecy was as urgent as she made it sound, perhaps she was in some danger.

That thought drove Simon from his bed to question his driver. "I'm sorry to wake you, Mahmud. But I need to know everything you can tell me about the man you collected from the shore last night."

The driver shook his head. "I took missy down Beach Road. She got out and called, but no one came. After a while she said she would not keep me up any later. I drove her to the old house on the river then came back to fetch her trunk. Did I do wrong, master? Should I have brought missy back home too?"

"You did well," Simon reassured his driver, though he could not say the same for himself. "Could I trouble you to saddle my horse before you go back to bed?"

A few minutes later, he rode towards the square, puzzling over what Mahmud had told him. Why had Bethan's paramour failed to keep their planned meeting? Had something happened to him? Or had he betrayed her? Simon wondered if this might change her mind about confiding in him. Before he sought her out with more questions, there was someone else who might shed a little light on this disturbing mystery.

When he appeared on Dr Moncrieff's veranda at such an early hour, the surgeon cast Simon a puzzled glance over the rim of his coffee cup. "Good morning, Mr Grimshaw. You're not ill, I hope. That old leg wound giving you trouble?"

Simon shook his head. "I haven't come on my own account. It's about Miss Conway…the young woman who's been looking after my daughter. A few days ago, she paid a call on you. I was hoping you might tell me why."

"I would if I had the vaguest idea what you're talking about." The doctor motioned him toward a chair, but Simon remained on his feet. "I haven't been home much lately between visiting patients and rounds at the hospital. Perhaps the lady spoke to my friend Ellison. Unfortunately he's out at the moment. A call came in the night—an escaped convict injured while being recaptured. Where did the poor fool imagine he could hide in a place this size, I ask you? After the long day I'd had, Ellison was kind enough to go in my place. I'm surprised he isn't back yet."

A convict—could that be Bethan's mystery man? It would explain why he'd been sneaking around at night and his desire to flee to America. Perhaps it explained her reluctance to confide in Simon as well. She must have known he would never let her go off in the company of a convicted criminal.

"I'm sorry to trouble you, Doctor." Simon bowed and prepared to hurry away to the gaol. "Good day."

He was on his way out when another man arrived.

"Doctor Ellison?" Simon offered his hand and introduced himself. "I hear you have been out to treating an escaped convict."

"A most extraordinary thing." The doctor seemed in a daze. "I didn't recognise the man at first. Then it came to me where I'd seen him before. I thought he must be dead—that's what I told his sister, poor girl."

"His...*sister*?" The word scoured Simon's throat like shards of glass.

"Damn my hide!" Doctor Ellison clenched his lips together, too late to recall the words he'd spoken. "I told her I would keep her confidence—not that it matters much now, I suppose."

To Simon's bewildered look, the doctor replied, "The convict they captured was a crewman involved in the *Dauntless* mutiny a few years ago. When he stands trial for that, a lifetime of convict labour will seem merciful compared to the sentence he's in for."

Chapter Nineteen

"Are you certain of that?" Simon nearly choked on the words. "The fellow's identity, I mean."

Why did he even ask when he knew it must be true? It explained all his tiny suspicions about Bethan from the very beginning. What's more, it made sense of everything she had tried to tell him last night. She'd admitted loving the man very much, yet she'd been outraged at Simon's accusation that they were lovers. She said she'd been on the point of confiding in him when she had learned something that made it impossible.

He recalled their quarrel about whether mutineers deserved sympathy or the gallows. At the time, he'd been too infuriated and too haunted by returning memories to question what made her raise such an improbable subject. In hindsight, her motive was clear.

"Quite certain, I'm afraid," replied the doctor. "I reckon Hugh Conway has been living under a false name ever since the *Dauntless* mutiny. The unfortunate irony is that I might never have known him if I had not been speaking about him so recently with his sister. I pity the poor devil. He doesn't deserve to swing."

"You mean he didn't take part in what happened aboard the *Dauntless*?" Why did it matter? Ever since the *Sabine*, he'd believed one member of a mutinous crew was as guilty as the next and every one of them deserved the noose.

The doctor shook his head. "I never saw Conway raise a hand against anyone on that ship. He claims it was he who opened the hold allowing the officers and passenger to break free and attempt to regain control of the ship. I don't know if that is true, but I do know *someone* opened that hold and I doubt anyone would have known of it except the man responsible."

"Surely that will mitigate his sentence." His pity for Bethan weighted heavily against his hatred of mutiny. To think that all her well-intentioned efforts might have brought about her brother's capture and execution would devastate her vital, caring spirit.

"In another case it might." Doctor Ellison looked beset with regrets. "But the late captain of the *Dauntless* came from a very powerful family. They were determined to have vengeance upon the crew, but few survived to stand trial. I doubt their thirst for blood was satisfied. I've promised Conway I will testify on his behalf, but I doubt it will help. I wish I'd held my tongue when I first recognised him. But it came as such a shock, I said far too much without considering the consequences."

"Do not fret, sir." Simon knew all too well the guilt that would gnaw at Dr Ellison if the man who might have saved his life was hanged because of his actions. "None of this is your fault. Now, I have detained you long enough. Thank you for answering my questions."

What would he do now? Simon wondered a few moments later as he untethered and mounted his horse. Scarcely aware of what he was doing, he pointed the beast in the direction of Government Hill and jogged the reins.

He'd uncovered Bethan's secret at last, but it was too late. If only he'd put aside his poisonous suspicions and really listened to what she was trying to tell him last night, he might have recognised what should have been glaringly obvious. It might not have changed Hugh Conway's present situation, but at least Simon would have had the right to comfort Bethan and assist her in any way she might have asked. Instead he had failed her, as he'd failed the women of the *Sabine*, and Carlotta and even as his daughter for too many years.

A stray breeze carried the aroma of spices from the experimental garden, raising memories of the night he'd followed Bethan there. He'd begged her to heed his explanation. Generous creature that she was, she had listened, understood and forgiven.

But when she'd pleaded with him for understanding last night, he had refused, placing the responsibility on her shoulders by setting an impossible challenge. Perhaps if he'd been less harsh, less quick to condemn, less consumed with his past at the expense of their future, Bethan might have been able to confide in him. How could he blame her for being cautious in matters of love?

When he reached the top of Government Hill, Simon halted his horse beside the lofty signal flag pole and stared down at the settlement. The gaol that held Hugh Conway was so near the house where Bethan had spent the night. Had she heard yet of her brother's capture? Or was she waiting and worrying, wondering what to do next?

More than anything, Simon wished she knew she could count on his help. But after last night, he was probably the *last* person in Singapore to whom she would turn. In that case, he would have to provide his assistance unasked.

Unfortunately, he could think of only one thing Bethan would want. And that was beyond his power to grant unless he wanted to risk his business, his fortune and his reputation. Everything he'd worked so hard to establish. Everything that proved his worth.

But in the end what did any of that matter if he could not use it in the service of the woman he loved? Was that something Ford and Hadrian had discovered when they returned to England? Somehow he knew his partners would approve his decision.

He must act quickly, though. The sun was rising steadily above the eastern horizon. If he waited too long, the news would be all over town and security at the gaol would be tighter.

He was not doing this to win back Bethan's heart. After the way he'd treated her last night, Simon knew he did not deserve it. He'd been fortunate to have her in his life even for a little while—long enough to work her magic. All he wanted now was the privilege of helping fulfil the dream that had led her to him.

Sipping from a cup of rich, faintly bitter Java coffee, Bethan sat on the veranda of Simon's old house and watched the Chulia boatmen manoeuvre their *tongkangs* around the crowded mouth of the river. Grief and worries jostled about in her heart, with no outlet.

Where was Hugh? Why had he not met her on the beach as they'd planned? How would he find her again, now that she had left Simon's villa? Or should she go looking for him?

Wilson, Ralph and the other lads had been surprised by her sudden arrival last night, but they'd made her welcome and not asked too many questions, though their eyes blazed with curiosity. Now they were all off to work.

Bethan wondered if Simon had come to work yet. Would he ask the lads about her or would he just assume she'd left Singapore and good riddance?

She knew better than anyone how much she had hurt him. After he'd spent years guarding his heart, she had challenged him to trust and love again, even though she was keeping secrets from him that might force her to leave at a moment's notice. Simon had claimed he wanted a mistress and a straightforward relationship based on simple desire. Yet everything he'd told her about his past pointed to a longing for true, lasting love that had been thwarted by his dread of betrayal.

With all her heart Bethan wished she could explain to him why she'd acted as she had. Though she was not tied to him by law or vow, her heart recognised a bond between them that she could never betray. But much as Simon's happiness mattered to her, she could not put it ahead of her brother's life.

Once they were safely away from Singapore, she would write to Simon and explain everything. For his sake and Rosalia's, she would beg him not to let her mistakes blight his future happiness. She would urge him to take the risk of loving a better, wiser woman— one without so many hurts and secrets to spoil their life together. As for her, she doubted the world held many men as good as the one who'd almost been hers.

Approaching footsteps made her heart leap, only

to fall again when she realised it was not Simon's uneven gait.

"Pardon me, Bethan." Wilson strode on to the veranda. "There's a bit of news going round that I thought you might want to hear."

His flushed face and anxious look told her the news was not good. Her fallen heart sank deeper. Had some harm come to Simon or Rosalia?

"The *sepoys* caught a convict on the loose last night."

Hugh! Bethan cringed with shame that she had not thought of her brother first. But why would Wilson assume this was something she needed to know?

He did not keep her guessing. "They say the convict is not the man he claimed to be. They say he's a Welshman named Conway who is wanted for taking part in a mutiny a few years ago. No relation of yours, is he?"

It took Bethan a moment to summon her voice. "Not that I know of. Conway is a very common name where I come from."

Much as she hated to tell yet another lie, she needed to protect her friends. What they didn't know could not incriminate them.

"I see." It was clear Wilson didn't believe her. He seemed puzzled and a trifle hurt that she would tell him such a blatant falsehood. "Sorry to bother you then. I just thought after you showed up last night out of the blue, it might have something to do with this. Anyway, I'd better head back to the office before Mr Grimshaw gets in."

He turned and walked away, leaving Bethan shaken to the core. What could she do to help her brother now? After coming all this way to find him, it was her fault he'd been found out. She was certain nothing else could have made him risk slipping out of custody at night. But how had his true identity have been discovered? Had the doctor betrayed her confidence or had Captain Flynn become suspicious of her questions about the *Dauntless*?

What a terrible mess she'd made of everything! If ever she'd needed a white knight to ride to her rescue, now was the time. But she'd learned such characters were only the stuff of legend. True heroes had battle scars and armour that had grown too thick for them to remove without a great deal of help. True heroes were sometimes held hostage by their own demons.

Squaring her shoulders, Bethan hurried to don her best gown and fetch the reticule she'd filled with Simon's money. She'd forfeited the right to seek his help. He had already done more for her than she deserved. Even if his code of honour would force him to assist her, she did not want to embroil him in this mess.

She would go to the gaol and demand to visit Hugh. He might have an escape plan that would require her help. If not, perhaps she could use a combination of charm and bribery on her brother's guards.

As she dashed along Hill Street toward the gaol, she spied Simon riding towards her. Had he heard the news about Hugh? Did he now despise her as the deceitful sister of a mutineer? She only hoped he did not think she'd shared his bed as part of some devious plan. Unable to bear the loathing she feared she would see in his eyes, she kept her gaze downcast. She could not decide which would distress her more—if Simon denounced her in the street, or if he refused to speak to her at all.

A moment later, a man's voice issued from atop Simon's horse…but it was not his. "Bethan, thank God I didn't miss you."

"Hugh?" Bewildered, she stared up at her brother, sitting in Simon's saddle, wearing Simon's clothes. "I thought you were—"

"I haven't time to explain." He leaned down and extended his hand. "We have to go *now!*"

The urgency in his voice prompted her to grab her brother's hand and let him hoist her up in front of him.

"Where did you get Simon's horse and his clothes? You haven't hurt him, have you?" A fierce protective impulse flared within her, strong and hot. If Hugh had harmed a hair on Simon's head, she would turn him in herself!

And what about Rosalia? If any harm had come to Simon, who would look after that sensitive child?

"I didn't want to, I swear." Hugh urged Simon's horse forwards. "He told me I must to make it look as if I'd overpowered him."

"He what?" It was all Bethan could do not to hurl herself to the ground and fly to Simon that instant.

"It happened so fast," said Hugh. "He came to the gaol and blustered his way past the guards. The moment we were alone, he started stripping off his clothes. I didn't know what he meant to do to me. But he told me to put them on and pretend I was him to get back out past the guards. He said I must find you and get the hell out of Singapore. Then he told me to strike him on the head and lay him on the pallet facing the wall so the guards would think he was me. When the switch is discovered he'll claim I attacked him and stole his clothes."

Recalling the ruse Simon had used to rescue her from that angry mob on her first hour in Singapore, Bethan glowed with pride at his resourcefulness and audacity. In spite of his cautious nature, he could take a risk and carry it off with the best of them. No wonder he'd been able to make such a success of his business.

By now they had reached the *godown*. Hugh slipped from the saddle and lifted Bethan down. "He said you had money to pay for our passage."

"That's right." She shook her bulging reticule, making the heavy coins clink.

"Let's hail a boat then." Hugh hauled her down a narrow alley toward the quay.

A few minutes later they were aboard a *tongkang*, being rowed out to a ship that flew the American flag.

The excitement of his escape made Hugh talkative. "I've had enough of the sea to last me a lifetime and enough of being bossed by folks above me. I hear there's plenty of free, fertile land in America for anyone willing to settle it. How good it will feel to work for myself and not be looking over my shoulder every minute."

The eager zest of his words conjured images of challenge and adventure that would have enthralled Bethan not so long ago. Now they washed over her as she gazed toward the shore and picked out Simon's white villa from those of his neighbours, nestled among the Indian laurel and saga trees.

Her earlier fears for Simon had eased, but not gone away altogether. She longed to see for herself that he was all right. What if the authorities did not believe his story of Hugh's escape? What might they do to him, and what would become of Rosalia?

Overwhelmed by her desire to protect them both, she suddenly understood the way Simon had felt about her. It was far deeper and stronger than he had been able to put into words or even to show with the tender thrill of his lovemaking. It was the kind of devotion that could weather mistakes and hurts, even the worst of them, and emerge stronger for it.

The *tongkang* came alongside the hull of the American ship. Hugh called up a request for passage and was given a price.

"You got here in the nick of time," the crewman informed them in a cheerful bellow. "We're just about to set sail."

"Do we have enough money?" Hugh glanced anxiously towards his sister's reticule.

Wistful sadness welled up in Bethan. What she was about to do felt like abandonment, something that came very hard to her. Tempering those feelings was a sense of sweet certainty.

She nodded to her brother with a fond smile. "More than enough, *cariad*."

"Papa, you're hurt!" Rosalia ran toward Simon when he arrived home. "Where is Bethan? All her things are gone. What happened?"

"Don't fret, *querido*." As Simon opened his arms to his daughter, it occurred to him how much the Portuguese endearment was like the Welsh one Bethan used. He'd thought the international language was money, now he wondered if it might be love. "Everything will be all right. I'll tell you all about it, but first I have to step out to the veranda."

He wished he could have given Bethan's brother more time to get safely away. But the Resident had heard about the capture of one of the *Dauntless* mutineers and come to investigate for himself. Simon prayed Bethan and her brother had wasted no time making their escape. He wasn't certain the Resident had believed his story about being knocked out and having his clothes stolen. If there was hell to pay, he would pay it willingly for Bethan's sake, but he was too practical a businessman to abide seeing his efforts wasted.

"Very well." Rosalia spoke in a determined tone, unlike anything he'd heard from her before. "But you must sit down when you get out there. I'll fetch some water to wash your head. It's bleeding a little."

In spite of his worry and his heavy heart, Simon could not help but smile at his daughter's motherly air. "As you wish, my dear."

He limped out to the veranda, his gaze searching the waters offshore for the American vessel. There it was with a *tongkang* alongside. Simon's legs felt suddenly weak with relief. He staggered back to the nearest chair and sank on to it as he had promised his daughter.

Rosalia appeared a few minutes later with a basin of water. Ah-Ming came too, carrying the medicine chest. As the pair of them fussed over him, Simon tried to placate their worries with a story of bumping his head on a low doorway.

His housekeeper's disbelief showed plainly on her face, but for Rosalia's sake she did not voice her doubts.

"What about Bethan, Papa?" Rosalia looked pleased with the gauze bandage she'd insisted on wrapping around his head.

Simon thought it might prove useful to disguise the suspiciously minor nature of his injury. "She had to go away very suddenly, I'm afraid. She didn't want to leave us, but something very important came up."

He knew that, regardless of her feelings about him, Bethan must be sorry to leave his daughter.

"It's all right, Papa." Rosalia patted his arm with reassuring sympathy. "I'll take care of you."

A lump rose in his throat and a strange sense of peace stole over him. This didn't feel like either of the times Carlotta had left him. There was sadness and regret, but no rancour, no bitterness.

"I know you will." He pulled the child on to his sound knee and wrapped his arms around her. "We'll look after each other."

They sat like that for a while as Ah-Ming packed up the medicine chest and bore it away.

"Would you like to play a game, Papa?" Rosalia asked. "I could fetch the cards and board for *Dou Shou Qi*."

Was she trying to provide him with an amusing distraction from his sadness? A fresh surge of love for his daughter provided balm to his aching heart. "An excellent idea. Only try not to beat your old father too badly, will you?"

Rosalia did not scamper off to the nursery at once in search of the game. Instead she moved to the veranda railing, staring out toward the sea. "That's very odd."

"What is it, *querido*?"

"That *tongkang* is not going back to the river as it should. It's coming this way."

That couldn't be right. Simon rose and joined his daughter at the railing.

"See." She pointed to a boat that was now only a few yards away from shore.

If the lightermen weren't careful, their *tongkang* would end up beached.

Then someone jumped overboard into the waves, landing waist deep in the water. Simon blinked his eyes. Was that knock on the head making him see things?

"It looks like Bethan." Rosalia confirmed the amazing impossibility. "You didn't tell me she would be back so soon."

In the distance the American ship was hoisting sail. Bethan could not possibly reach it again before it weighed anchor.

"Let's go meet her!" Rosalia caught Simon's hand. "If you think you can manage," she added in a solicitous tone.

He tweaked her nose. "I'm not quite an invalid yet."

Together they hurried downstairs, through the garden and across Beach Road. Bethan was just staggering ashore when they reached her. Her hat had blown off, sending her auburn curls in a mad tumble around her shoulders. Her sodden skirts clung to her slender legs in the most fetching manner. More than ever, she reminded Simon of Venus emerging from the sea.

"Bethan!" Rosalia pelted toward her, flinging her arms around Bethan's waist. "What made you come back so soon? Did you forget something?"

"No, *cariad.*" Bethan caught Simon's eye over his daughter's head. Her sparkling gaze told him the endearment was meant for him as well. "I came back because I *remembered* something."

"What was it?" Rosalia asked the question that was foremost in her father's thoughts.

Bethan bent and pressed a kiss to the crown of the child's dark head. "How much I care about you both."

"We care about you, too." Rosalia glanced back at Simon. "Don't we, Papa?"

Too overcome to do more than nod, Simon hoped his eyes were more eloquent. He could almost feel them sparkling with delight as he drank in the sight of her.

The child gave Bethan a fierce squeeze, then danced away. "I'm going to find seashells for you and Papa."

She raced off down the beach.

Without his daughter's immediate presence, an uneasy silence fell between them. Simon was reluctant to break it for fear he might shatter the spell that had summoned Bethan back to him.

"Are you all right?" she asked.

"This?" He reached up to touch the bandage. "A little excessive attention from my young physician." He nodded toward Rosalia.

"I see," she murmured in her clear lilting voice. "Well…I want to…thank you for what you did for my brother. I know how hard it must have been for you. I can never begin to re—"

Simon's heart sank. "That isn't why you came back, is it, to repay a debt you feel you owe me? I don't want you as a slave out of gratitude. I want you free to love me as I love you. I know I've given you plenty of cause to doubt my feelings—"

"And I've given you plenty of cause not to trust me. Still, you must believe me when I say it wasn't gratitude that brought me back."

"What then?" He could guess, but until he heard it from her own sweet lips, he did not dare build his hopes too high.

"For the reason I told Rosalia." She unclasped the locket from around her neck, opened it and handed it to him. "Also because I realised my father was wrong and I didn't want to repeat his mistake. He shouldn't have left my mother when things started to go wrong in their marriage. He should have stayed and tried everything he could to make it work."

She drew closer to him, until she was near enough to embrace, if only he raised his arms. But she wasn't finished and he wanted to hear her out.

Bethan waved her hand toward the American ship, its sails catching the breeze. "I believe true love isn't meant to be all smooth sailing any more than the rest of life is. There will be squalls and pirates and mutinies. But if we keep sailing and don't abandon the ship, we'll share plenty of adventures and we'll always have a safe harbour."

What could he add to that? It summed up everything he hoped they would have together in the years ahead. Words were not adequate to convey what he wanted to tell her. So, instead, Simon let his gaze, his embrace and his kisses speak for him.

Joy washed over them in powerful, warm waves as they stood on the beach, wrapped in each other.

They did not draw back until Rosalia ran toward them. "Look! I found two limpet shells just alike—aren't they pretty?"

"They're lovely, *querido.*" Keeping one arm around Bethan, Simon drew his daughter into their embrace. "One for each of us."

"Look what happens when I put them together?" Rosalia held up the shells to show them. "They make a heart!"

Like the sun emerging after a sudden shower, Bethan's eyes beamed with love for them both. "Then I think we'll have to keep them together, won't we, Simon?"

Lavishing his daughter and wife-to-be with the warmest, most enduring smile his lips had ever given, Simon nodded. "Always."

Epilogue

February 1844

"So this is what Singapore looks like twenty-five years on." Ford Barrett, Lord Kingsfold shook his head in disbelief.

Having just returned from a ride around town, the three Vindicara partners sat in the grand saloon of the elegant London Hotel enjoying a drink. Ford, his wife Laura and their four children had come to Singapore to help celebrate the twenty-fifth anniversary of its founding.

"Wouldn't recognise the place, would you?" said Hadrian Northmore, who had returned here with his family a few years ago. "You won't see many of the old *attap* houses outside the Malay *kampongs*. We've got a racecourse and a proper theatre. There's even talk of starting a cricket club."

"Some things haven't changed, though." Simon lifted his glass. "Trade is as brisk as ever and the arrack is still first rate."

Simon was delighted to have his partners and their families all together for this celebration. In the early days of their partnership, he had often felt on a lower footing than Ford with his aristocratic blood and Hadrian with his forceful personality. Today he knew himself to be every bit their equal, for he was the luckiest and happiest man in the world.

"I'll drink to that." Hadrian bolted a tot of the potent drink that would have made most men's eyes water. Then he leaned back in his chair with an appreciative sigh. "I must say, I had no idea when I started Vindicara how the firm would grow. My nephew Lee tells me he's not interested in going into politics the way I planned for him. He wants to start up a branch of the company in Hongkong."

"Speaking of politics," said Ford, "you'll be pleased to hear that shortly before we left England my brother-in-law, Lord Ashbury, introduced a mining reform bill in Parliament that will keep women and children out of the collieries. I sincerely hope it is law by now."

"That news is long overdue—" Hadrian's voice grew husky with emotion "—but it could not be more welcome."

For years a fierce opponent of employing children in underground mines, he now looked like a man who'd realised the dream of a lifetime. Some of the boys he'd sent from County Durham to work in Singapore now held positions of authority within Vindicara and other firms. A few had started their own businesses with great success. One such ambitious young man was married to Simon's daughter, Rosalia, with a baby on the way.

"There they are." A woman's clear lilting voice rang out as Bethan marched into the room with Lady Kingsfold and Mrs Northmore. "Didn't I tell you we'd find them here, Artemis? Drinking to old times over a bottle of arrack."

"Have you forgotten, my love?" Artemis Northmore snatched the glass out of her husband's hand, a feat the bravest of men might hesitate to dare. "We have an appointment to get our picture made."

The new art of photography had recently taken Singapore by storm. The hotel's proprietor had a lucrative side business creating daguerreotype portraits.

"Forgive me, pet." Hadrian rose from his chair and offered his wife an apologetic kiss that was not altogether chaste. "We forgot the time. Ford was just telling us that young Ashby has gotten a mining reform bill before Parliament at last."

"What marvellous news!" Artemis Northmore gazed into her husband's eyes in a moment of sweet intimacy.

Lady Kingsfold needed only to cast a significant glance and her husband put down his glass. "Monsiuer Duplessis says he has never attempted a picture of such a large group."

Simon did a quick count in his head. There would be twenty of them altogether. Could everyone manage to stay still during the exposure time? He wasn't certain his fourteen-year-old sons, Hugh and Hadrian, had *ever* stayed still that long.

Bethan must have been thinking the same thing, for she caught his eye and grinned. "You'd better come at once. The children are already getting restless."

"Very well, *cariad*." Simon rose and offered her his arm. She looked positively radiant today with her hair done in two cascades of ringlets, wearing a gold-coloured gown with a full skirt and lace bertha that showed off her bare shoulders.

Leaning closer, he whispered, "I heartily approve of these new fashions from Europe."

To demonstrate, he grazed his lips down her neck.

"Enough now," she chided him. But he could hear a breathless tremor in her voice that never failed to rouse him. "If the twins catch you at that again, they'll fall about pretending to retch and get grass stains all over their new trousers."

"Besides," she whispered, "we'll soon be grandparents. We shouldn't be carrying on that way."

"In a pig's eye!" Simon was tempted to kiss her into a puddle of molten desire then and there. "You look far too young and beautiful to be a grandmother. And I intend to carry on like this for as long as I can tempt you to join me."

"In that case…" Eyes twinkling with mischief, she reached up under the tails of his coat to run her hand over his backside. "I reckon we'll be at it for a very long time indeed!"

* * * * *

COMING NEXT MONTH FROM

HARLEQUIN®
HISTORICAL

Available April 26, 2011

- **HAPPILY EVER AFTER IN THE WEST**
  by **Debra Cowan, Lynna Banning, Judith Stacy**
  (Western)

- **HOW TO MARRY A RAKE**
  by **Deb Marlowe**
  (Regency)

- **THE GAMEKEEPER'S LADY**
  by **Ann Lethbridge**
  (Regency)
  First in duet: *Rakes in Disgrace*

- **CLAIMED BY THE HIGHLAND WARRIOR**
  by **Michelle Willingham**
  (Medieval)
  The MacKinloch Clan

REQUEST YOUR FREE BOOKS!

 HARLEQUIN® HISTORICAL:
Where love is timeless

2 FREE NOVELS PLUS 2 FREE GIFTS!

YES! Please send me 2 FREE Harlequin® Historical novels and my 2 FREE gifts (gifts are worth about $10). After receiving them, if I don't wish to receive any more books, I can return the shipping statement marked "cancel." If I don't cancel, I will receive 6 brand-new novels every month and be billed just $4.94 per book in the U.S. or $5.49 per book in Canada. That's a savings of at least 18% off the cover price! It's quite a bargain! Shipping and handling is just 50¢ per book in the U.S. and 75¢ per book in Canada.* I understand that accepting the 2 free books and gifts places me under no obligation to buy anything. I can always return a shipment and cancel at any time. Even if I never buy another book from the Reader Service, the two free books and gifts are mine to keep forever.

246/349 HDN FC45

Name _____ (PLEASE PRINT)

Address _____ Apt. #

City _____ State/Prov. _____ Zip/Postal Code

Signature (if under 18, a parent or guardian must sign)

Mail to the **Reader Service**:
IN U.S.A.: P.O. Box 1867, Buffalo, NY 14240-1867
IN CANADA: P.O. Box 609, Fort Erie, Ontario L2A 5X3

Not valid for current subscribers to Harlequin Historical books.

Want to try two free books from another line?
Call 1-800-873-8635 or visit www.ReaderService.com.

* Terms and prices subject to change without notice. Prices do not include applicable taxes. N.Y. residents add applicable sales tax. Canadian residents will be charged applicable taxes. Offer not valid in Quebec. This offer is limited to one order per household. All orders subject to credit approval. Credit or debit balances in a customer's account(s) may be offset by any other outstanding balance owed by or to the customer. Please allow 4 to 6 weeks for delivery. Offer available while quantities last.

Your Privacy—The Reader Service is committed to protecting your privacy. Our Privacy Policy is available online at www.ReaderService.com or upon request from the Reader Service.

We make a portion of our mailing list available to reputable third parties that offer products we believe may interest you. If you prefer that we not exchange your name with third parties, or if you wish to clarify or modify your communication preferences, please visit us at www.ReaderService.com/consumerchoice or write to us at Reader Service Preference Service, P.O. Box 9062, Buffalo, NY 14269. Include your complete name and address.

HHII

*With an evil force hell-bent on destruction,
two enemies must unite to find a truth that turns
all-too-personal when passions collide.*

*Enjoy a sneak peek in Jenna Kernan's next installment
in her original* TRACKER *series, GHOST STALKER,
available in May, only from Harlequin Nocturne.*

"**W**ho are you?" he snarled.

Jessie lifted her chin. "Your better."

His smile was cold. "Such arrogance could only come from a Niyanoka."

She nodded. "Why are you here?"

"I don't know." He glanced about her room. "I asked the birds to take me to a healer."

"And they have done so. Is that *all* you asked?"

"No. To lead them away from my friends." His eyes fluttered and she saw them roll over white.

Jessie straightened, preparing to flee, but he roused himself and mastered the momentary weakness. His eyes snapped open, locking on her.

Her heart hammered as she inched back.

"Lead who away?" she whispered, suddenly afraid of the answer.

"The ghosts. Nagi sent them to attack me so I would bring them to her."

The wolf must be deranged because Nagi did not send ghosts to attack living creatures. He captured the evil ones after their death if they refused to walk the Way of Souls, forcing them to face judgment.

"Her? The healer you seek is also female?"

"Michaela. She's Niyanoka, like you. The last Seer of Souls and Nagi wants her dead."

Jessie fell back to her seat on the carpet as the possibility of this ricocheted in her brain. Could it be true?

"Why should I believe you?" But she knew why. His black aura, the part that said he had been touched by death. Only a ghost could do that. But it made no sense.

Why would Nagi hunt one of her people and why would a Skinwalker want to protect her? She had been trained from birth to hate the Skinwalkers, to consider them a threat.

His intent blue eyes pinned her. Jessie felt her mouth go dry as she considered the impossible. Could the trickster be speaking the truth? Great Mystery, what evil was this?

She stared in astonishment. There was only one way to find her answers. But she had never even met a Skinwalker before and so did not even know if they dreamed.

But if he dreamed, she would have her chance to learn the truth.

Look for GHOST STALKER by Jenna Kernan, available May only from Harlequin Nocturne, wherever books and ebooks are sold.

HNEXP0511